THIRTEEN MILES *from* SUNCREST

THIRTEEN MILES from MILES SUNCREST

DONALD DAVIS

August House Publishers, Inc.
LITTLE ROCK

Published 1994 by August House, Inc.,
P.O. Box 3223, Little Rock, Arkansas 72203,
501-372-5450.

Printed in the United States of America

10 9 8 7 6 5 4 3 2 1

LIBRARY OF CONGRESS CATALOGING-IN-PUBLICATION DATA

Davis, Donald D., 1944-
Thirteen miles from Suncrest: a novel / Donald Davis.
p. cm.
ISBN 0-87483-379-5 (hardback): 19.95
1. Title.
PS3554. A93347T48   1994
813'.54—dc20   94-12998

Executive editor: Liz Parkhurst
Project editor: Rufus Griscom
Design director: Ted Parkhurst
Cover design: Harvill-Ross Studios, Inc.

The paper used in this publication meets the minimum requirements of
the American National Standard for Information Sciences—Permanence of Paper for
Printed Library Materials, ANSI Z39.48-1984.

AUGUST HOUSE, INC.   PUBLISHERS   LITTLE ROCK

to Merle

This book is a work of fiction. The characters and the local setting are fictitious; any resemblance to actual people or events is coincidental.

However, the historical events referred to in this work and the way of life reflected in the day to day events of the account are described with as much accuracy as possible.

Donald Davis

Prologue

My name is Medford Henry McGee, and for the first time in more than fifty years, I have been up most of the night.

Yesterday was my ninety-third birthday. Yes, I was born January 1, 1900, the first day of the new century, in Close Creek, North Carolina.

Yesterday was a great day for me as the entire assemblage of my interested earthly relatives gathered for the celebration of what they surely believe to be one of my last birthdays.

It is difficult to give gifts to a ninety-three-year-old man who certainly needs nothing. The event itself is much more meaningful and important at this age than a trinket, and yesterday was certainly an event to be appreciated.

There was, however, one great gift that was unexpected and which has kept me up throughout the night. It has been a gift of memory and contemplation.

From age ten to age thirteen I kept a journal of my own weekly life. It was a bit of childhood writing which I never re-read either during or after its writing. I thought that it had been destroyed when our family home burned in 1923. Yesterday, however, I discovered that it had not been burned up at all.

The manuscript had been in the possession of my youngest sister for a number of years and yesterday my niece, Laurie Anne, who is herself a female attorney of fifty-four, presented to me my own childhood diary. Now bound in a modern cover, it was handed to me and for the first time in eighty years I looked upon these pages.

Throughout this night I have read, and thought, and read again. I have rediscovered myself and the world of my formation. I have realized why I wrote to begin with, and more importantly, why I stopped writing when I did. I have touched people and places long dead and forgotten, and at last I can remember both the whats and the whys of a long-ago written down life.

1910

Sunday, January 2, 1910

My name is Medford Henry McGee. I am ten years old and I have been ten years old since my birthday which was on yesterday.

Yesterday was Fathers birthday also. But he was sixty years old. He is a old man and I have besides my Mama three brothers and four sisters that are all older than me. They call me Baby.

I do not want to rite about this but I have to do it. On my birthday yesterday Father said that it was time for me to start riting out my life. He said that I could think about it and that I could start on today. It is not as hard to think about it as it is to do it.

The reason that today is the day to start riting is that today is Sunday. On Sunday afternoon after we eat dinner we dont do nothing. We cant work any on Sunday and we cant play fast or loud either one. We can set and we can read and rite.

Father rites a lot on Sunday afternoon. He rites a lot of letters to our relations. He also rites to the Govenor and sometimes to the President of the U S A but I dont think that he knows either one of them real well. He also rites farm records.

I told Father that I just dont have nothing to rite about but he says that ever Sunday afternoon I will have to do it until I just learn. He says that I could pretend like I am riting to somebody who dont know us but would like to. It seems foolish to me because anybody who dont know us dont know that they would like to know us. But I guess that I will have to do it just the same.

So on yesterday I got to be ten years old. I live in North Carolina but close to Tennessee. Our house has mountains around it. And now Father has told me I can stop riting until next Sunday.

Sunday, January 9, 1910

It is one week after my first riting and I am still ten years old. It is real cold and ever where that there is any mud puddles they are froze over hard with ice clean to the bottom. And there is a lot of mush ice sticking up like needles out of the mud along the road.

My Aunt Louise is Fathers sister. She lives in Nashville Tennessee. Ever Saturday she buys a news paper in Nashville Tennessee. It is called the Nashville Banner news paper. She sends it through the Post Office to Father. It gets here on up in the week after she sends it. It comes with some white paper rapped around it and sometimes the ends that stick out get all tore up and hard to read.

Father does not open this news paper when it comes. He keeps it on the mantle until Sunday after noon and then after we finish dinner he reads some of what he wants to read out loud to all of us. This is at the start of the time when we set and do not play on Sunday.

Now I have got a good idea. Since I have to rite out my life right after that sometimes I can get a idea about something to rite by thinking of what Father has just read to us in that Nashville Banner news paper.

He always starts by telling us on what day Aunt Louise bought the news paper so we will know that what he reads to us happened over a week ago. So today he read the paper that was bought at January the first.

It made me feel funny to hear him read about things that had happened on the day when I was ten years old that I dont even know to start to think about on that very day.

Father lately reads to us about a war that is going on in a country named Nicaragua. I copied how to spell that out of the news paper after he laid it down. They are having what is called a revolution. A general called Estrada is trying to win the country and claims that he can make it peaceful.

It sounds to me like the U S A is going to help him but that the U S A wont really do nothing until he wins anyway. The Red Cross is helping too. Mama dont like Father to read about wars. She says that there was a Spanish American war that I dont remember and that people that they knew got killed in it and not even from fighting in our own country like they did in the war between the states.

The funniest thing that Father read today was about a woman in Pencilvannia who got scared to death. She must of been a old woman because her daughter had already got married. Then the daughter had run off from her husband and had come back home to live with the mother and the daddy. The husband that the daughter had run off from came looking for her. The mother went to the door and wouldnt let him come in. He pulled out a pistol and shot in the air three times. The shooting didnt shoot the woman but she dropped dead in the floor from being scared to death. I never heard tell of that. And the husband then run off and is still hid out.

Father read to us a lot of other things. But now he says that I can stop and so I will.

Sunday, January 16, 1910

I have been thinking some of this week about what I will rite about today. I think that I should rite some about whos in my family where I live. If I dont rite about this then anybody who reads this will think that there is just me here by myself.

First I will tell about my sisters because one of them is sometimes called Baby like Me. But she is called Baby Sister. Baby Sister is also named Annie Laurie McGee. She is just one year older than me which is eleven years old. She is called Annie Laurie because that was the name of one of our forebears away back in time in Scotland. Mama says that she always wanted a baby named Annie Laurie but Father thought it was foolish since the real one lived so long ago and we sometimes still sing a old song about her. But now she does have a baby named Annie Laurie foolish or not.

My next sisters are called the Twins. They are fifteen years old both of them at the same time but they do not actually look much alike at all. Margaret Angeline is a lot taller than Mary Adeline and her hair is also redder. They spend a lot of time off with thereselfs and just with one another.

Lucee Ella is my oldest sister. She is twenty years old now and a man called Harlan Chambers Junior comes here on Sunday after noon and goes courting in the parlor with her. They are in there right now at this very minute courting. Which is why I am riting this on the kitchen table. If they would get married then I could go in the parlor and rite where it is a nicer place. That is all of my sisters.

I also got brothers to tell about. First there is Zeb and Merry. Zeb and Merry are not twins but sometimes they sure do act like it as bad as Margaret Angeline and Mary Adeline do. They are eighteen and seventeen years old each and they think that they know something about ever thing there is in the world. They call me Baby a lot of times but sometimes they are also nice. Their whole names are called Zebulon Vance and Meriwether Lewis.

My oldest brother is Champ Ferguson McGee. He is married and has a wife and a baby boy. Champ is twenty four years old and he lives up past the Pine Chapel Church on land that came from his wifes people. She was a Medford herself and her own name is Sallie Jane. Her Daddy is Fathers cousin. The baby is just called Junior but we do not get him mixed up with Harlan Chambers Junior.

That is all of my family except for Father and Mama. Father is named Cato Jefferson McGee and Mama calls him Cate. He calls her Mama but he knows that her real name is Martha Elizabeth. Before she got married to him she was a MacDonald and was a cousin to Champs wifes mama.

Now that is ever living soul that lives here except for the animals and also for Grandpa. Grandpa does not live here all of the time but he does come in the summer of the year and sometimes stays about half through the fall. Then we take him to Suncrest and he rides the train back to Nashville Tennessee to live with Aunt Louise through the cold time of the winter. He says that he cant take what he calls the Tennessee tobacco tanning heat waves that come through there in the summertime.

Now Harlan Junior has gone home and I can stop riting because Mama wants me to carry some firewood in the house for her since it is real cold.

Today I am sick. On Wednesday I got real sick at the school house. I had been coffing in the night some. But on the walk to school I got to coffing real bad. Up in the morning at school Mister Robinson told Annie Laurie to take me back home because he was afraid that I was getting the whooping coff.

It is about two miles to walk to the school house and the same to get back home from it. It mostly takes less than a hour of time to get either way. But that day it took a lot longer.

I got to coffing so hard that I got dizzy and would haf to set down for a while and get my breath back again. I never did get to where I had to vomit though.

When we was finally onto our own farm land Annie Laurie told me to set and wait and she would go and get some help to come. She put me under a hemlock tree and got me to set behind a log out of the wind and then she ran for the house. I must of went to sleep because the next thing I knew Father was picking me up.

He got me up close to him and got me on old King with him. He rapped his big coat around me and then he took me home like that. There was not even a saddle on King because he did not take the time to put on the saddle.

When we were at home Mama was crying. Its happening again Cate. That is what she kept crying over and over and over. She put me in the bed where she and Father sleep. She made me drink some whisky and put a hot poltice on my chest. Then she kept crying by herself because Father was gone up toward Sandy Bottom to get Doc Graham.

After I had got over choking on that whisky I did not keep on coffing but I did go to sleep. I had not had nothing to eat but still I was not hungry one bit. Mama kept waking me up crying and checking on me and I just wanted to sleep and get left alone.

After a while Father and Doc Graham got here. Doc Graham listened to my chest and my back. He used a listening pipe that looked like a horn you could blow through. But he put his ear on the blowing end and put the big end on to my chest. He knocked on me like knocking on a door.

Finally he said to Mama who was crying that I did not have the whooping coff but had new monia and that it was not the same but was still real bad but that I was not like to die with it because I was strong and was not a baby or a old person either one. I had not even thought about dieing and when I heard of this I was glad that I had not thought about it especially at the time when Annie Laurie left me by myself on the way home from school.

Doc Graham told Mama to stop giving me the whisky because it was good for me to coff stuff up. Then he got Father and Mama to hold me while he stuck a big long needle between my ribs and pulled out a lot of bloody water from my right side. He did not do it on the other side which is a good thing because I think I would have run off before that happened to me. I did not see what he was about to do until it was all over with or I would have just died right there from being scared just like that old woman did in Pencilvannia.

Doc Graham told Mama to keep putting the poltices on me and to be sure that I turned from one side to the other pretty offen. He also told Father to make me set up and to beat me on the back ever morning and night. He did not give me any kind of medicine and he said that I was strong but not to go to school or to even get out of the bed until he told me to.

Mama cried a lot after that but finally she stopped. When I asked Annie Laurie why Mama was crying she had to go ask Lucee to find out. Lucee came and told me that Mama was afraid I was going to die with the new monia like her two babies had died with the whooping coff in eighteen and ninety eight except that they were older than babies when they died.

I did not tell about them when I told about our family because they are dead but I know about them because we neaten up their graves and put flowers on them on decoration day. They were dead before I was born but I heard the story of it again and again.

Flora Dare was seven years old and Arthur Moody was three years old when the whooping coff came through. She got sick first but then

Arthur got sick and died in under two weeks. Then Flora Dare just coffed herself right to death in another six days. Mama calls them her Dead Babies and I can tell this all real well because I have heard it so much but it does still not seem real to me.

Anyway I do not have the whooping coff and so I will not be dead like they are. I am still in the bed riting this but I do feel as well now as I can. Maybe Doc Graham will come back soon and I can get up but he will not come today because it is Sunday and I am not sick enough for that.

Sunday, January 30, 1910

I am still at home in the bed with new monia and have not been to school or out of the house in ten days. I dont feel that bad but Father is letting me off from having to rite on my life until I am all better and so I rite only this much today to explain that.

Sunday, February 6, 1910

Doc Graham came yesterday for the fourth time since I am sick. He listened to me and knocked on my back and when Mama told him that I had not been coffing any since the last time he was here which was nearly a week he told me that unless it was real cold and windy that I could start on back to school tomorrow.

Mama told him that Father would like to take me to school on King or in the buggy. He told her that was not really necessary but she said that it was necessary to her and so I guess that I will get to school but not haf to walk. I do not know about getting home.

Anyway I am well I guess and back to riting my life again which is not really so bad once you do it some. I have even missed going to school since I have been at home with nobody but Mama so long and the ones who go to school have been going ever single day of the week in all of that time. I am like to have to drop back to the fifth reader for a while which is where I was anyway until Mister Robinson put me all the way up to the sixth grade in ever thing back in the fall. But I will probably get put back up into the sixth grade again when I am back for a little while.

Merry and the Twin girls and Annie Laurie and I all go to school. Champ and Lucee and Zeb are finished with school. Merry could of stopped after last year but Mister Robinson told Father that he would get a lot out of going for another year and Father agreed for him to go. Father is a kind of a politishun and he told Merry that if he wanted to be a politishun or even a paid lawyer that he ought to go to school as long as he can even if it is just at our school house. This is a good idea because Mister Robinson has him to help all of the younger children out a lot.

We have twenty six pupils who go to school at the school house. Most people call it the Sandy Bottom School house but some people just call it Frog Level because that is the area of Sandy Bottom where it is located. Close Creek is the name of the whole community where we live and Sandy Bottom is the lower part of it. I dont care what they call the school house. It is all the same to me.

Mister Robinson teaches all of us. He is this years new teacher. He went to a college called Washington College over in Tennessee and has just started teaching with us. He is just a little bit older than Sister Lucee and he tried to come courting her on one Sunday afternoon but then Harlan Chambers Junior came along and they nearly had a fight.

Now March will be a interesting month because Mister Robinson lives with a different family in Close Creek ever month and in March he comes to stay with us. Maybe I will get to either see some real courting or a real fight one or the other. After that first time Father told Mama that it was a good thing that Mister Robinson didnt have to spend a month at Harlan Juniors house. He said we might not have a teacher if that happened.

Anyway the school house is Mister Robinsons. We set on benches with the littlest ones in front and the eleventh graders in the back. It is real noisy because when Mister Robinson is teaching one grade or one certain subject ever body else has to read or cipher or recite out loud to show that we are working and not just day dreaming. Father says that this is what is called a Blab School where that is done that way.

I set at about the middle since I am in the sixth reader and that decides our grade. I will be glad to get back to that blab school on tomorrow.

Our entire family got very excited listening to the reading of the news paper today. Father read to us about aeroplanes flying in the country of France and also in Losangeles Californya.

At the school house we already heard a long time ago about Wilbur and Orvil Wright making the first aeroplane that would fly in the air and then flying it down on the coast here in North Carolina seven years ago.

It is hard to believe now that they are building aeroplanes after just those seven years have past. I cannot even imagine what these aeroplanes look like because I have not yet seen a automobile either but we have read about both of them.

It sounds to me like they will have two kinds of aeroplanes to fly out in Losangeles. One kind the news paper calls lighter than air. This kind has some kind of big bag which they fill up with something named hydrogen. The hydrogen is lighter than the air around us and the bag full of it pulls the aeroplane up in the air. It must be like a big blowed up hogs bladder I guess. After it is up in the air there is some kind of engine that makes some of them go where they want them to go. Others are called a balloon but the ones with a engine are called Zepalines.

I have seen a train and also a steam sawmill and from that I do not see how they could lift what is called a engine up in the air for anything.

The biggest mystery of all to me is what they call heavier than air aeroplanes. They have some kind of wings but they do not flop like birds wings do. They have a engine that makes them fly. But if they go off of the ground then how can a engine keep them moving if their wheels are not even touching the ground.

Even women will ride in these machines in Califronya. Father says that in my own lifetime I will probably someday take a ride in one of these machines but I do not pay any attention to that at all. I believe that he is just trying to fool me or to get me to read about more things if I am curious.

I would be happy to see a automobile and think that I will get to do that in my lifetime. I have heard that there is one in Erwin Tennessee and we have seen advertisements of them which have pictures in the Nashville Banner news paper.

The other story I liked today was about a man in New York who tried to dig a tunnel under the road from his house to get into a bank and a jewelers store. He got the tunnel dug way out under the road and then it fell in on him and smothered him to death. It said that it took thirty six hours to dig his body out. His wife told the police that he was not digging to rob but that he just went down into the basement and fell into a hole.

I think that I could stay awake thinking about aeroplanes all night and could still not be able to get a picture in my head of what they look like. That is a great puzzle to me.

Sunday, February 20, 1910

We have had a very great and terrible snow storm this week. It started snowing last Sunday after supper and snowed for two days without stopping. Out on the flat ground the snow is over knee deep on Father and since the wind has been blowing it is piled up to the windows on the west side of the house. Father says that in places where it snows a lot up North that is called Snow Drifts but it does not snow enough down here for it to get a name from us. It is just what we call deep snow.

The hardest part about the snow is several things. One is getting to the barn to feed the stock. When it started to snow so hard Father and Rounder who is our dog went out and got the cows and the sheep and put them in the barn. King and Outlaw and the mules were already in there. There is not really room for all of them so the sheep are in the open runway between the stalls where the cows and the horses and the mules are put. They would not like to be there in normal weather but Father says they seem to know that they would rather be in there now than outside and so they are all very quiet and still and behave good.

Ever morning and evening Merry and Zeb and Lucee and Father put on all the clothes they have and go to the barn to feed and check on ever thing there. The snow is froze now so much they can walk on top of it. I am not allowed to go out in the snow by Mama because of the new monia so I have to watch them out of the window. When it was still snowing I could not see the barn and they would all disappear into the falling snow and just go out of sight into another world before they were very far from the house. Now that the snow is over it is real clear and I can see them breathing big clouds of steam all the way to the barn even though they have scarfs rapped over their mouths and noses.

Father is not very scared of running out of hay and fodder. Mama says that he would put up more food for the animals than for the family if he had his choice about it. He says that people can think and take care of thereselfs but that animals can not do that and we have to think for them and that is why we have to have enough food for them no matter what.

It takes a long time to feed and then to milk the cows. Somebody has to climb up in the barn loft and throw down hay and fodder for the stock in the barn. Lucee likes to do that and so she does that while Merry and Zeb start milking. We are milking three cows at the present time though we have six in all and some of them are not for milking. Also Teddy Roosevelt our bull is not for milking. Nobody likes to have to mess with Teddy Roosevelt.

Father carries the bucket of slop from the house to the pigs and then he goes to the corn crib and takes them some corn besides that.

The pigs just stay in the pig pen and keep thereselfs warm. I never did hear tell of a pig freezing to death. I guess they just pile up or snuggle down in the mud if they are real cold. Sometimes Father gives the pigs some of the fresh milk from milking if there is a lot because we can only use so much of the milk unless in this weather Father thinks to walk and take some to one of the neighbors who dont have any cow.

It seems to me like it is awful cold in the house. Snow blows in the bedrooms upstairs under the edge of the roof. It also blows under the doors and around some of the windows. But it is a lot warmer than a log house with loose chinks between the logs. And besides that when Father and the others come back from the barn they think that the house is the warmest place they have ever been.

A lot of the snow is melted off by now on Sunday but it is amazing to me to see how I can still see it in my head when I stop to rite about it in my riting out of my life. Maybe Father did not have such a bad idea to make me to do this.

We are all hoping for a little warm spell. Father is ready to burn off the garden and to hope that he can plow it early and get some greens started before too long.

Also Mama sends the twins to feed the chickens and gather the eggs because that is not far from the house. They also stop by the springhouse and bring two buckets of water to the house. One is for drinking and cooking and one is for washing.

Sunday, February 27, 1910

Today I am very happy to be riting out my life because a thing has happened this week which is the most interesting thing which I think has ever happened here in my life.

On Wednesday night we had all just finished our supper when we heard a awful screaming and screeching racket coming from out toward the barn. Father and the older ones had just finished feeding and milking before we had our supper and they did not see anything strange out there. There was still snow ever where on the ground and the warm day had soffend it up so it was pretty slushy and wet. We could not imagine what such a noise was.

Somebody is in the pig pen Father said.

How do you know that it is somebody Mama asked him. It could be a animal of some kind.

Father would not let anybody go with him to see what it was. He rapped all up and loaded his rifle and lit a lantern so he could see in the dark. Mama told him not to shoot anything unless he was sure of what it was because she said that some of the neighbors might of starved down to where they got to steal a pig and she wouldnt want to shoot a neighbor. He promised to be careful.

We all tried to see out of the window. It was pitch dark now and the squalling was worse than anything. We saw his lantern light all the way to the barn but then he went out of sight going around the other side to where the pig pen is. Then the squalling trailed off and it sounded like just one pig a hollering and then nothing at all.

It seemed like Father was gone forever before we finally saw the lantern light coming back toward the house. We never had heard him shoot at anything in the meantime though.

He came in the door and Mama was shaking and asking What was it Cate. He didnt give a answer but told all of us and even that included me to put on our clothes because that he wanted us to see something right now in case the snow melted in the night. He told Mama that he would carry me so that my feet wouldnt get cold but that I just had to see this and we would remember it all of our lives.

We got rapped up and Father rapped me under his big coat and he led us with the lantern light out to the pig pen. We could hear the pigs sounding excited and upset before we even got there.

Once we got close we could see a lot of blood on the snow in the light of the lantern and then we saw what he had come to show us.

Right there in the snow we saw big bear tracks. They were all over the place but when we followed them away from the pig pen they had all been made by one bear.

Mama said she thought bears slept in the wintertime. Father said that this one must of woken up. He said that he had heard of bears coming out in the wintertime and looking for something to eat but not very offen. Anyway this one had got one of our pigs and had carried it off with him to eat somewhere off in the woods.

We did not try to follow the tracks in the dark because Father said that a bear that hungry would not be safe to get up close to. He had fixed the pig pen back where the bear broke into it so that other pigs wouldnt get out. Ever since when I see that broken place in the pig pen I will remember that bear.

We talked real late after that about that bear and at school the next day we told all of the other children and even Mister Robinson about it all. I am not sure he wants to come to live at our house for the month of March after hearing about that bear.

On the next day Father followed the tracks way up in the cove. He said he came to the place where the bear ate the pig but that he couldnt follow it any farther because after it got in the woods most of the snow was gone and besides he didnt really want to find it anyway.

I have never heard of a bear getting up in the winter and as long as I live I will never forget the sound of that pig screaming or the sight of that blood and those bear tracks. It would have been nice for us to be the ones to get to eat that pig this late in the winter because the rations are getting low and mostly we have fat back. But that is not the way it worked out. Father says he would trade the pig just to have the story of the bear to tell. He says that the story will feed us a lot longer than the pig would have anyway but I do not understand that.

Sunday, March 6, 1910

The month of March has begun and a lot is starting to happen. First of all Mister Robinson is living with us and now I realize that I have not rote out anything about the actual house where we live. When Mister Robinson first got here Mama said to show him around the house. I thought What would I show him. There wasnt nothing interesting here to show. Then I realized that all the things we see ever day still have to get shown to somebody who has never seen them. I showed Mister Robinson and so now I know how to rite about it.

Our house is wooden and it is two stories tall. It sets on a little rise of land above the creek which runs from the springhouse down and between the house and the barn. It is not a big creek as it actually only comes from out of the spring that the spring house is built over.

The house faces to the south. The mountainside slopes up behind it and the barn is down below. There is a big porch across the front where we like to set on Sunday afternoons when it is summer. Sometimes even late in the fall of the year it is warm on that porch because it catches all of the sun.

Downstairs there is the parlor inside the front door. It runs from the front door to the left and right. Maybe now it should be called the Court Room because that Lucee and Harlan Junior are courting in there. To the right is the dining room where we eat. The dining room also has a door onto the porch and I do not know why that is except that it makes it faster to get to the table when dinner is called.

While Lucee and Harlan Junior are in the courting room Mister Robinson is out on the porch thinking. I cannot imagine what he is thinking about.

Behind the parlor is the bedroom where Father and Mama sleep. I remember sleeping in there too when I really was a actual baby but that was a long time ago to me.

The kitchen is the big room behind the dining room and it is where we live. That is probably because it is warm in there in the winter because of the woodstove and then I guess that being in there in the winter just hangs around as a habit for the rest of the year.

On the back there is a porch which is all screened in with screen wire. It is where Mama churns in the warm weather and where we hang things to dry when we get them from the garden. I mean like onions and peppers and beans. The porch has a wall around it about half way up and then a screen wire on top of that.

Upstairs is just like a upstairs. The stair steps goes up out of the kitchen but there is a door at the bottom to keep the heat in the kitchen in the winter. Up there are two bedrooms. There is one with Zeb and Merry and me where Mister Robinson is staying. He sleeps in the bed with me since I am the smallest of the three of us and that gives him more room.

Then there is the room where Lucee and the twins sleep. Lucee has really stayed right in that room nearly the whole time since Mister Robinson got here. She has said that she has a lot of knitting to do but when Harlan Chambers Junior comes around then she does not have any knitting at all to do. I know that she just does not want to take any chances of getting to like Mister Robinson because that would make her courting with Harlan Junior too confusing.

The only other thing that is upstairs is a attic which actually goes from our bedroom out over the kitchen and out over that downstairs bedroom since our bedrooms are over the front part of the house. If we had a hole in the floor we could watch Lucee and Harlan Junior a courting down below us. Maybe I will tell that to Mister Robinson and he can help me cut a hole and both of us can watch.

The house is painted white all over and it has a tin roof. It was built in the same year when I was born and so it is also ten years old. And there are four big maple trees out in the yard which are very fine shade trees.

Sunday, March 13, 1910

Mister Taft has been the President of the U S A for one year right now since he got inaugurated in March a year ago but it is a funny thing that President Roosevelt is still written about in the news paper more than President Taft is. About ever week Father reads us something about President Roosevelt and his travels around the world and about the only thing I can remember hearing about President Taft is that he is the fattest President in our history and that he has a great big bath tub in the White House so he can fit himself into it to take a bath.

At this present time President Roosevelt is in Africa but since it takes a few weeks for the news about where he is to catch up to us he may actually not still be in Africa at this very moment. But in my mind that is where he still is because that is what we are reading about in the news paper.

Today we read about President Roosevelt going on a elephant hunt in the country of Yougonda in Africa. They have a lot of big elephants there and he shot one and killed it and it had tusks which weighed a hunderd and sixteen pounds. It must of been a big elephant for Mister Roosevelt to hit it because Father showed us his picture in the news paper and he wears real little glasses pinched onto his nose. If the elephant were not big then he would not be able to sight at it through those little bitty glasses.

Father says that President Roosevelt was a President interested in saving what is called our natural resources. But if that includes elephants I do not know why he saves ours and then goes off to Africa and shoots theirs. I think that it would be a whole lot better if they captured some elephants and let them loose out in the west in one of the parks Mister Roosevelt made and then we would have elephants in the U S A too. I would like very much to see a elephant. I have seen a picture.

Father says that Mister Roosevelt wants to be the President again like Grover Cleveland was. He thinks that Mister Roosevelt will finish going around the world and then come back to California so he can go all the way across the country telling about his trip and showing all the things like elephants tusks that he collected and that after that he will get nominated in nineteen and twelve to run again instead of President Taft.

Mister Roosevelt is only fifty one years old Father says and he has not had his fill of being the President. I think that he better stay traveling around the world until nearly 1912 or people will forget about him. He ought to come back just before the time comes to vote and that would be smart.

If the President is going to be a Republican then I would rather have Mister Roosevelt than Mister Taft because that Teddy Roosevelt does a lot more interesting things to read about than just put overgrown bathtubs in the White House. I wonder how big President Tafts bed has got to be. Maybe I will rite to him a letter and ask him because Father has got his address and knows how. I dont want to be the President if people are even going to know about how you take a bath. I will just leave that job to somebody else.

Sunday, March 20, 1910

Father says that this is the hardest month of the winter. It is not because it is cold because it is not. It is hard as far as food goes. We are completely out of apples now. The pork in the smokehouse is down to just some fatback. We have some potatoes which are kept in our bedroom so that they will not freeze and we have some dried beans. We get plenty of eggs and milk and we have plenty of cornmeal so we know that we will not starve. But we do not have any cabbages left or carrots and the turnips are just froze into the ground. We can not even get a little mess of turnip greens right now but they will come out pretty soon.

We did have a little dry spell a week ago and Father burned off the garden to kill the weed seeds and then hitched up the mules to plow with. The mules are U S Grant and Robert E Lee. Father named them that because he says that they are both real strong but that it is all but impossible to get them to co operate and to pull together. Anyway he finally did get the garden plowed and harrowed.

He always plants peas on Saint Patricks day which was on last Thursday. But he planted a patch of turnips on yesterday because it was in the dark of the moon. He says that things that grow under the ground grow better if you plant them in the dark of the moon and things that grow on top of the ground do better in the light of the moon. I like the turnip greens better than the turnips so I wish he had just waited and planted them when the moon gets light again.

What I want to know is what is best to do when Saint Patricks day comes in the dark of the moon like it just did. Should you still plant the peas then or wait until the moon changes its phase. We always plant potatoes on Good Friday because Father says that you plant potatoes when Jesus was in the grave. What if it is the light of the moon then. Maybe it doesnt work out that way though since Easter slides around on the calendar according to the moon anyway. I dont understand planting by the moon.

If we can make it on cornbread and beans around here until about the first of May we will start to have some turnip greens to go with them. It just about hurts my jaws to even think about that but I am riting about it because I know that the time is coming just like it does ever year. I hope the peas come up.

Sunday, March 27, 1910

It is now really getting close to the time to start putting in the main garden. The turnips and the greens and even the dark moon peas have already come up. And even though the plowing and this early planting has been done by Father when the real main garden time comes Mama is in charge.

In Fathers farm records he has figgered out that the last big frost of each year comes on the average date of April the seventeenth. So after that day it is fine for those things that get killed by the frost to come up. It is important not to get things killed and also important to plant them as early as we can because we do run out of food and we have to have ever day of growing that we can get to grow enough for the next winter. We keep planting a lot of things ever few weeks to be safe and also to keep it coming in all through the season.

Since Mister Robinson is here I have realized how much I know about farming. He asks so many questions that by hearing about all the stuff he doesnt know I am learning how much I do know. It is a funny thing for a school teacher to be so ignorant about simple things.

Yesterday Mama spent a lot of time getting out all of the seeds she has saved from last year and planning on her garden for this year. She has pole beans and halfrunner beans and some speckled beans which we also dry for the wintertime. Beans are easy to put up for the winter because you can dry them whole or shelled either one and they are good at anytime. We call the speckled beans the McCracken beans because Mama says that the first seeds she ever got came from the France McCracken family.

After she checked on her bean seeds Mama checked out her seed corn. She keeps the seed corn in a tin can with a lid on it because if you dont it is the easiest thing in the world for mice to get to and eat in the wintertime. It would be a awful thing to get out your seed corn in the springtime just to find out that the mice had ate it all up in the winter. If that happened I guess that we could just eat horse corn instead of having any good sweet corn at all.

Mama also laid out squash and cucumber and punkin and okary seeds. She did not get any onions gone to seed last fall so she is going to swap some halfrunner beans with Mizz Chambers who is Harlan Juniors mama for some onion seeds because she knows that they have some. We have some multiplier onions also though.

After that Mama unfolded some little papers where she had rapped up her tomato and her pepper seeds. Then she spent a lot of the afternoon getting ready to grow tomato and pepper plants in the house so they would be ready to set in the garden about the first of May. Even though Father has figgered that it will not frost on the average after the seventeenth of April since you only get one chance with the tomatoes and the peppers she does not set the plants out until it is warm for good which is at least the first of May and sometimes even later than that. She says that starting them in the house is better and safer in ever way.

She starts about fifty plants for tomatoes and then both green peppers and red hot peppers. The peppers are the easiest to keep in the winter because you can just string the red ones up. Most of the tomatoes we just eat up as they come in and then try to keep the green ones as long as we can after it turns cold in the fall. Mama also makes green tomato pickles with a lot of the little green ones when they start slowing down in the fall of the year.

Last fall after the first big frost had come Father spread a big wagon load of manure from the barn over the whole garden. It laid there and rotted over the winter and then that is partly why he burned the garden off this spring because that manure has a lot of hay seed in it. Besides that he piled up a big pile of manure at the end of the garden so it could rot in the winter and be ready for Mama to put under the hills of things as she plants them. That manure pile just steamed and steamed in the cold weather. Father says that shows that it is rotting and that if it really steams enough that will kill those weed seeds and the manure will look just like black dirt in the spring. Father surely does hate weeds.

Besides all that we also plant watermelons. There is a awful lot to do to keep from starving to death around here.

This week is Mister Robinsons last week with us. On Friday he goes to stay at the Taylors house. I do hope that the Taylors dont try to get him to help out in their garden.

Sunday afternoon, April 3, 1910

Today is a beautiful day. It is warm outside and the sun is shining like it does in the best of summertime. We walked to church this morning instead of rapping up and taking the wagon the way we have had to do all through the winter. I think that we have made it through the cold and soon we will even have the first greens to eat from the garden. Also the potatoes are up and looking real fine.

Also this is the twins birthday. Margaret Angeline and Mary Adeline are both sixteen years old today. Father says that back in the old days that would mean that they were old enough to get married and start helping their husbands take care of thereselfs. But he will not even let them have a beau to come to see them on Sunday afternoon yet so I guess that they wont be getting married very soon. Besides that I think that Lucee and Harlan Junior should get married and then the parlor should get aired out a little bit from all of that courting before those twins start up in there all over again. But I just dont know anybody who could take both of them on and since they are never apart in this world it would take either one real good man or better yet two pretty good ones who would have to be real good friends with one another.

On Friday Father woke us all up and told us that the bear had come back. When we set up in bed he said that the bear had come back with money in his paws and wanted to buy another pig cause the one he ate was so good. Then he said April Fool and laughed real big. I never can remember to get a April Fool joke on anybody so I will just not try.

Sunday, April 10, 1910

When Father was reading the news to us today we all thought he was trying to April Fool us again when he read about the top exploding off a Mount Etney in a place called Sissily. Then he went on to tell us that it was called a volcano and that there used to be a lot of them in the world back in the old days and that there could even have been one right here on this mountain where we are living.

He read that melted rocks came up out of the hole that blew out of the top of that mountain and that ashes and smoke were everywhere. I cannot imagine anything being hot enough to melt a rock but if it is that hot I know that it can for a fact blow the top off of a mountain. I do not know where Sissily is though but he says it is a part of Italy. When he read about the people who live near there running for their lives I could really just see that and imagine that if something like that happened around here that we would run for our lives too.

Up in the afternoon the twins got in a fuss over who of them had got to be sixteen years old first. Mama told them that Margaret Angeline had been born first but that it had been a pretty even race ever since then. Father said that it was fittin that that volcano should blow off around the time of their sixteenth birthday because it was just like them. I think so too.

Sunday afternoon, April 17, 1910

I do not understand why all of the peculiar stories in the Banner news paper happen to people who live in New York or in Pencilvannia but today we heard Father read another one in that news paper which did happen also in Penncilvannia.

There was a old woman who was not married. Ever body thought that she was poor and she must of lived like a poor woman or they would not have thought that way. Anyway she must have disappeared for a while until some of the neighbors and other people who knew her got to looking for her. She did not have any family or friends.

Her door was locked shut but there must of been a awful smell because when the police was called they broke the door down and got into where she lived. I bet that was hard to do because it said that when they got in the door there was five locks on it and ever one of them was locked.

Well they found the old woman dead. She must of been dead for a long time because they said that rats had eat up half of her dead body. That is a awful thing just to hear of and a worse thing to think about.

Anyway they found a lot of stuff with her dead body. There was a lot of deeds to show that she had bought land all the way from Pencilvannia to Nevada and Californya and there was a lot of checks and notes she had rote. She had over a hunderd thousand dollars of money and she didnt have any people to leave it to so it went to charity.

But the funniest thing was some of the notes. She was scared that she would get thought to be dead and buried alive before she was all the way dead. Father said that George Washington was scared of that too and he wanted to get buried in a coffin with a bell on the top and a string he could pull to ring if he was not really dead.

Anyway she wanted to be kept for ten days after she was dead so that the doctors would be sure. Then she wanted a doctor to stab her through the heart three times to be sure that she was dead. She left twenty dollars to the doctor if he would do that. After all of that she wanted her body to be burned up and just the ashes buried. She really must of been awful scared of being buried alive. Judging from the shape they found her in with the rats having already eat up half of her I dont think there was any more questions about where or not she was dead.

What I wonder is if that doctor stabbed through what was left of her heart and got his twenty dollars. Anyway it is a awful thing to die all locked up by yourself with not even anybody to know that you are dead except a lot of rats.

I thought the twins were going to throw up during this story. I think Father sometimes picks a story like this to read just when the twins get to giggling and it sure does quiet them down in a hurry.

Sunday, April 24, 1910

Today is another beautiful spring day but the most interesting thing that has happened today came when Father showed to us the front page of the news paper which had on it a story about President Taft and President Roosevelt side by side on the page.

The story about Mister Taft was just about some very dull speech he made about the wonder of the broad and tolerant Republican party but it didnt sound like much of a party at all to me.

Beside that was the story of Mister and Missus Roosevelt arriving in a town in Italy which was called the Port of Marizzio which is where Missus Roosevelts sister spends her summer vacations. It didnt tell if it was close to where that volcano blew off.

The paper did say that ever single living person in the entire town was standing along the street to get to see Mister Roosevelt and his wife and that there were many people from other little towns all around there who had also come to see him. The mayor of that Italian town called Mister Roosevelt a great man and then they named a new street which was to be the finest street in the town as Roosevelt Boulevard.

I would still bet you that man is going to try to get to be the

President of the U S A again. It has been a long time since Father has read anything to us about the revolution in Nicaragua and what I wonder is why doesnt Mister Roosevelt go to Nicaragua and use his influence to get peace there. After all that country is not really too far from where he went up Sanwan hill in the Spanish American war that Mama was talking about.

Now I think that I do feel sorry for Mister Taft because as big as he is it is just not fair to have ever body cheering Mister Roosevelt when he doesnt have anything to do but travel around and get entertained and Mister Taft has to try to hold the country together. But I am beginning to think that is the way the world is.

May Day, the first of May, 1910

Today it is May Day and is the only Sunday of the year when we can have some fun because May Day has come on a actual Sunday itself. I am riting at bedtime because we only just got home and there is some good things to tell about.

We got up real early to help Mama finish fixing food for dinner on the ground at church. She had already fried chicken and packed it up with biscuits and then we made some potatoes baked in the oven of the stove. We wanted her to make some devil eggs because we like them for picnics but she said that they might spoil since it was going to be after church before we ever even spread out the food let alone get to eat.

Father hitched King and Outlaw to the wagon and we loaded up our food and also oursels and started off for the church. The church that we go to is the Pine Chapel Methodist Church but on today we were meeting together with the Pine Chapel Babtists to share in the dinner.

We had our own Sunday school classes and the Babtists had theirs too at there own church before they came on over to our church for the preaching.

Even Mama didnt know that it would be so long until time to eat as it was because both of the preachers preached before we got out to eat. It was like a preaching contest I thought.

The Methodist preacher preached against sin and evil in general and it was fairly calm but when the Babtist preacher got to preaching right down against particular by name sinners it got right hot in there.

Finally we got out and that food sure did get spread out in a big hurry. All of the children had to wait and go through the line last but Mama had hid one of the pulley bones from the fried chicken under a rag in the biscuit basket for me and it was still there when my turn came.

We ate like hogs in the trough to get on to the next part. As soon as the eating was over we went over to the school house to where Mister Robinson had already used lime to mark off a start and finish line on the play yard.

Then we had the May Day races. I fell down in the sack race and couldnt get back up again until it was all over. But me and Annie Laurie teamed up for the brother and sister three legged race and we won that thing flat out. We was all the way back to the finish line before some of the others even turned around at the other end. Then on top of that me and Merry and Zeb and Champ won the family Relay for four. I ran first and got pretty far behind but by the time that Champ grabbed the stick for the last round we beat the Mayfield family by about ten yards.

After all of the May Day races was run then we had pie and cake and milk which we had waited from dinnertime to have now. By now also it was time to go home so that Father and Zeb and Merry could milk and feed before they had to just do it in the dark.

We had only cornbread and milk for supper but after all that we had ate and done through the day it sure was just enough. At the supper table Annie Laurie asked Father where we got May Day from. He said it had just come down from our forbears from along ago in the old country. He said that they were super stisious and thought that they had to have May Day to make the crops come up. But he said that they danced around a pole and did a lot of other dances to make things grow. I guess that all of that dancing shook the ground and woke the seeds and plants up and let them know to come on up.

He said that we might of even had a square dance ourselves at the School House tonight if May Day had not come on Sunday. He said that it was hard enough to get to run the races with the preachers around there all day and that next Sunday there might be preaching against three legged racing at the Babtist Church. I dont understand that and I dont think that Mama does either because when he said that she told him to hush.

If I could go back to the old days I sure would like to see grown up people dancing around a pole to make crops come up. I never did hear of nothing at all like that in this world.

Sunday, May 8, 1910

Missus Elisabeth Chambers who is Harlan Juniors Grandmother has died. She was ninety seven and was a real old woman besides that.

The sad thing is not that she is dead because at the age of ninety seven years old somebody could expect to be dead at almost any time. The sad thing is thinking of how she died.

It seems that something that was brought to the May Day covered dish dinner had the food poisoning in it and a lot of people got sick. Mama had said that nobody should ought to bring any devil eggs but there was some there. We sure knew better than to eat them. But Father said that it might not have been the devil eggs at all but it might of been somebody that canned some beans because sometimes he heard that they get the food poisoning in them which is why we always dry most of our beans. He says that the modern practice of canning beans is just not as perfected as it ought to be for it to be safe for ever body to do it.

Anyway a lot of people got sick after the May Day picnic though most of them was young and got off with a lot of throwing up and loosened bowels. But it was too much for Missus Elisabeth being ninety seven years to get that sick and get over it. So she died on Wednesday of the week and she was buried at the graveyard of the

Methodist Church on Friday Afternoon.

She was a little tiny woman with skin that looked like the inside of a muskrats hide after it has been curing on a board for about six weeks. But she was a real nice old woman and I did like the way that her house always smelled whenever we went there to visit. Her kitchen was always real warm and she set on a little bench that was built into the corner behind the stove like she couldnt get close enough to the stove to get all the way as warm as she wanted to get.

She almost all of the time would have big soft molasses cookies that she would give to all of us to eat when we was there. A lot of times we would carry milk up to her because she always lived by herself instead of living at Harlans house with his Mama and Daddy. She liked it by herself I guess. I would not like that myself very much but she did.

I think that she is part of the reason that Harlan Junior is a pretty nice man because he has stayed a lot with her and she is a nice old woman or she was before she was dead.

I guess that ever one of us is going to end up in that graveyard sooner or later but it would be nice if it is later. Besides that it would be nice not to have to die of something like the whooping coff or the food poisoning. I dont know if you can die though without having to die of something.

As long as we have those May Day picnics I will remember Missus Elisabeth. And I will be careful not to eat anybodys food except my own Mamas.

Sunday, May 15, 1910

Yesterday we planted some corn and some beans real early in the morning and then we spent the rest of the day helping Mama clean the house for the spring. It was a pretty and warm day with clear sun shine and so was a good day for cleaning out the house and washing clothes.

Mama has a big iron pot which stays leaned up against the house to keep the rain out when we do not use it. We have not done any washing since the fall of the year so ever thing in the house was dirty.

While the beans and the corn was being planted by the others me and Annie Laurie helped Lucee get the washing ready. We pulled the wash pot out into the road and got it on a good level place. Then while Annie Laurie and I carried buckets of water from the watering trough to fill up the pot Lucee laid a fire around the bottom of the black pot. She did not light it though until we got the pot full enough cause we couldnt put the rest of the water in it if the fire was already coming up the sides.

It takes a pretty long time it seems like to get the water hot but once it is hot that pot sure does stay hot. Once in the news paper in a story called McCutcheon in Africa there was a picture of some missionaries getting cooked in a pot just like our own wash pot. But it was a drawing and not a actual photograph so I dont know if it was true or not.

Mama had gathered up all of the longhandles and clothes that we wash. She also got the bedsheets off the beds and even the aperns. She brought out some of the lye soap that we make and also her big wooden washing paddle.

She put all of the clothes in the pot but first she put in some soft globs of that lye soap. While the water is too hot to put your hands in it she stirs and jabs at the clothes all around in that soapy lye water with that wooden washing paddle. It is about plumb white on that end from being washed so much its own self.

As soon as she can put her hands in the water which is a lot hotter than I could stand to touch it she takes her scrub board and gives the clothes a real working over.

Then we line up and she hands each one of us as many wet clothes as we can carry in our hands and then we are careful not to drop our load while we take it and rinse all of the soap out in the watering trough. Then we ring out the water and hang ever thing over the fence so it can dry in the sun.

Father does not let any livestock drink out of the watering trough for the rest of this day because he does not want them to drink any lye soap water. They just have to drink out of the creek until the next day comes.

While the clothes were drying we just about took the house apart. We put the feather mattresses in the attic until next winter. At that time we will pick the geese and add more feathers. For the summer we sleep on straw ticks. Father gets the ticks out of the attic. They are like big flat empty sacks. We fill them up with clean wheat straw and Mama stitches the ends shut. They are a lot cooler in the hot weather but they sure are rough to sleep on until you get them mashed down and push all of the hard straw nubs out of the way. I think that it is awful early in the spring of the year to get geared up for hot weather like this but Mama says that if we dont do it now that there just wont be time when the real crop work comes and Father has to have ever bodys full time help with the crops.

We finished off the day with a big breakfast meal for supper. Mama used about the last of the wheat flour to make biscuits and she came up with some ham she had saved and hid in the smokehouse. We had scrambled eggs and hominy and red eyed gravy. That sure was a real fine supper after all of that cleaning work. We even scrubbed all of the floors in the house with lye soap before it was all over.

But last night I hardly slept a bit trying to get fixed so I could stand it on that new straw tick. And besides that since I sleep by myself I have to do all the breaking in on my own. If this had been Mister Robinsons month with us he would of had to help me break the bed in.

I sure am glad that warm weather has come though.

Sunday, May 22, 1910

We have had a thing to happen here at Close Creek which I cannot stop thinking about even though it happened on last Monday night nearly a week ago. On that night Mister Glenn Taylors big barn burned to the ground and also burned up his best team of draft horses.

Harlan Junior told that they could see the sky lit up all the way over from his mama and daddys house. It was at about midnight when Mister Taylor heard a big roaring noise and when he opened his eyes he could see the firelight already shining from the barn right into his house. They said that Missus Taylor fainted dead away when she looked out of that window and saw the barn burning. If Mister Robinson hadnt already gone to the Woodys house he would of passed out too I am sure. There was no way to get the horses out.

The barn loft was real full of hay and some of that hay was still giving off smoke until it rained hard rain on Wednesday.

Nobody knows what started the fire. Some people have even said that it could have been set on purpose but I cant think that any person would really do that. Mister Taylor cant figger it out.

Anyway that fire has taken all of my thought up for this entire week and I cannot even think about anything else at all. We also talked about it a lot at school.

Sunday, May 29, 1910

Father has read to us that Governor Charles Evans Hughes of the state of New York has been made into a judge on the Supreme Court of the U S A by President Taft. I do not understand what the Supreme Court exactly does since Father says that all of them set up there at once and that they are the ones who decide who is guilty or innocent instead of having a jury at all. I guess that the stuff they have got to decide about is a lot more important or at least a lot more complicated than what a normal jury of people can handle.

Anyway Father says that Governor Hughes wanted to be the President of the U S A and that it is a shame that he didnt get to be the Republicans President instead of just having to set and set and set up there with the other old judges of the Supreme court. He also said that being on that Supreme Court is actually what President Taft wanted to be instead of having to be the President of the U S A. I guess that nobody cares how a judge on the Supreme Court takes a bath and so it is a more private job all in all.

I wish it could have been that they could have just swapped jobs and they both would have been happy. Father says that would have made some other people happy too.

I do not understand how it is that politicks works. It sounds like the first rule is that you never say what you really want and that you play like you dont wont to be the governor or the President and if you do that good enough you might get to be it. It would be a whole lot simpler if you could just tell the truth. I told that to Mister Robinson at school and he thought it to be a good idea and said that I ought to rite to the people who make the laws and get that in as a law. Then I told Father and he said that politicks didnt have nothing to do with the law and that if ever body started telling the truth there wouldnt be no such thing as politicks anymore anyhow.

Maybe we dont even need no politishuns anyhow. We could all just divide up the money that the goverment has got and then do good with it. That would work real well I think because there would be so many more ideas about how to do good than there is now with just one big President. I think it would work.

The only other person who might have got to go into the Supreme Court Father says is Mister William Jennings Bryan. The trouble is that he said that he would like to be on it and that is not what you do when you are in politicks. So I guess that telling the truth ruined him and that he will just have to keep on trying to be a lawyer.

Sunday, June 5, 1910

Father has been reading to us some terrible news about bad forest fires up north in Minnysota. I do not understand why the newspapers call Minnysota the midwest since any place that is that cold in the wintertime is clearly in the North to me. I would think that the news paper people thereselfs would even know more than that.

Anyway Father has read in the Nashville Banner news paper that more than five thousand people have had their houses burn down in the big forest fires in the North in Minnysota. I think this is especially scary to me since Mister Glenn Taylors barn burned down. That barn could of set the woods on fire and then even our own house might of got burned down.

Father says that the fires in Minnysota came from lightening and that the woods are dry in the fall. He said that the news is that three hunderd people have actually been killed not to count the cattle and wild bears and mooses and all that kind of animals that have burnt up or got smoked to death.

Fire may be useful to us but it is sure a terrible thing to get on the loose. I do hope that it comes a big rain soon in Minnysota. It is so far up North there that maybe it will just come a big snow and that will surely put out the fire.

Sunday, June 12, 1910

Well now School is let out for the summertime. Mister Robinson is not going to be our teacher again for the next year. He told all the parents and the students at the commencement last week that he had already got a offer to teach school in the city of Richmond Virginia for the next year. He said that it was in a school where they had different teachers for each grade and that he was going to be teaching in the fourth grade part. I am sorry that it is this way and that he will not be back with us next year. I did not even mind for him to sleep in the same bed with me when he stayed at our house for the month of March as he was a lot better to sleep with than Grandpa is when he is here with us. Sometimes Grandpa turns toward me and his breath smells just awful and he always snores real loud.

But it is done and Mister Robinson is already gone back to Tennessee to spend the summer with his own Mama and Daddy before he goes up to Richmond Virginia where he says he will even have a room of his own to live in all of the whole year.

After he told this to all of the parents and students Father stood up and made a speech to thank him for teaching us this year. Then he rote on the blackboard the name of Governor William Walton

Kitchin and the address of the State Capitol in Raleigh North Carolina and asked all of the parents and the older pupils to rite to the Governor and ask him to get the law makers to get more money for the schools. He said that he thought there should not be as many schools as there are now so that each one would be bigger and have different teachers for the older and younger students. He told all of the people there that blab schools with a different teacher almost ever year would not help us to get ready to be a part of the future of the U S A.

A lot of the people said that they would rite a letter to Governor Kitchin. Father said that he would pay for the postage and if people would just rite the letters and give them to him he would see that they got sent to Raleigh. I was proud of him.

All in all I guess that I do think that school is a good thing. Some of the pupils fuss about it and act up and do not want to come to school but I think that if we did not have to go that we wouldnt know nothing at all and that we have to do it. Besides I will miss Mister Robinson and hope that we get another teacher who was as good to try to help us learn things as he was. But I sure dont want to be a schoolteacher. I dont think I could whup nobody and that is a essential part of the job.

Sunday, June 19, 1910

It has happened again. Another barn has got burned down and now ever one is just certain that a person is the cause of it.

This time Mister Stanley Woody was the one whose barn it was. It happened last night. Mister Woody and his wife heard their dog barking real mad and when they looked out they thought that they saw something running away from their barn in the dark.

Mister Woody got his clothes on and his gun and went out there to see what it was and when he got toward the barn he could hear the fire inside before he saw it. The good thing is that he got the barn door open and got the horses out in time to save them. They had already broke out of their stalls and were just inside the big doors trying to break out of them. The fire was set in the cutting room but by the time the horses were out it was way too far gone to stop anything. Mister Woody did manage to get some tools out from the tool room before it was too late for that. It all burned up. The funny thing is that Mister Robinson just missed it again because the Woodys was the last place he was staying at before he left.

Right now at this time Father is gone to a meeting of a lot of the men in Close Creek which is being held at the Woodys house. They spent a lot of the afternoon poking through what was left of the barn and out in the woods from it there was found a empty tin can that had kerosine in it. Ever body is just sure now that we have a firestarter on the loose.

I do not know what they can do about it but I sure do hope that they come up with a idea because I am scared to death that sooner or later that fire starter will try to burn down somebodys actual house where they live. That would be more awful.

Sunday, June 26, 1910

Today Father has read to us that the King of England who is called Edward the seventh has died. He has actually been dead since May but his being dead did not get in the Nashville Banner News Paper right away and the paper where it did get told about on the next Saturday did not get on to our house until the middle of this week.

It does seem strange to me to think about it. I have just heard of the King Edward being dead and so to me it has just happened. But by now it seems like Missus Elisabeth Chambers has been dead for a long time even if she has just been dead a few weeks longer than the King. I am wondering if people from different countries meet on the way into heaven when they are dead and if two people as different in life as King Edward and Missus Elisabeth would get to meet up there. They both could understand the English language so that would be a help to them getting acquainted. I bet that both of them could each teach the other one a lot if they was to get to meet in heaven. I asked

Father but he says he does not know about things like that and that nobody does even if the preachers say that they do.

When Father was reading to us about this and Lucee asked him what the King died of he looked at her real hard like he didnt wont to read that part. But then he read it. It like to of scared me to death to hear him read that the King died of the new monia. It said that he had been on a trip just ten days before that and that when he got home he was in good health but he died of bronchitis and new monia.

I asked Father what bronchitis was and Lucee said Its what you had Med and that just made me shake all over. If new monia could kill a King in good health then it could of killed me. I thought about that for a long time.

Anyway Father said that King Edward had only been the King for nine years which seems like a pretty long time to me because it is nearly all of my life but it is not a long time at all for Kings and Queens because his Mama was the Queen Victoria for over sixty years.

The Prince of Wales is going to get to be the new king. His name is George and he will be called King George the Fifth. He is really already the King but they will have a big crowning party and crown him again anyway after a year goes by and the people in England get over his Daddys dying.

He is not called the King of England but is called the King of Great Britain and Ireland and the Emperor of India and the Defender of the Faith. When I asked Father what all of that meant he said that if he told us we would understand why our forbears came from Scotland and Wales into this country instead of staying there in their home lands which they did not really have anymore.

He said that as long as Scotland and Wales were countries of their own with their own Kings our forbears were glad to live there. But when the old King of England took over Scotland in the year of 1707 our ancient ancestors left and went to part of Ireland and then came to this country. He said that was when Annie Laurie which our Annie Laurie is named for was living in Scotland and ran away and got married for love. I think it could not have been so awful long ago if he can still tell us about it.

Father said that we have never had anyone in our family to have a Kings name because of that. Nobody has ever been named John or George or Edward or James or anything like that because that those English Kings took over the countries where our ancestors lived and that we got as far away from them as we could. I said that my middle name was Henry and wasnt that a old Kings name. He said it was but that I was named Henry after the last name of one of our forbears who was Patrick Henrys daddy and I could be proud of that.

Anyway that was then and this is now. And I am kind of sorry for George the Fifth. I do not know how old he is but it must be hard to have to lose his father and then to start having to be the King hisself at exactly the same time. But that is the way it works with Kings and Queens.

Sunday, July 3, 1910

The firestarter is caught and now we know the truth.

On last night somebody tried to set fire to Mister Johnny Campbells barn. The only thing was that Mister Campbell and his son Jackie had been spending the night in the tool shed beside the barn on a lookout since the last fires. They took turns sleeping and sitting up and watching.

Way up in the night Jackie heard a noise and woke up his Daddy. They eased around the barn and heard somebody inside the feed cutting room of the barn. When they looked through a crack in the wall they could barely see somebody sloshing kerosine all over the place. Mister Campbell hollered out for whoever it was to stop right there but whoever it was started to strike a match anyway and when that match flared up Mister Campbell shot him clean dead. It was Duck Mayfield.

As soon as ever body saw who it was who was the firestarter they figgered it out. Duck is the biggest of all of the Mayfield boys at about the age of twenty five. They are the very ones we beat at the family relay race at May Day. For the last five years Duck has been on the chain gang for breaking into Missus Elizabeth Chambers house when he was nineteen years old and she was still alive.

About three months ago he got paroled from the chain gang. Now ever body has it figgered out because Mister Taylor and Mister Woody and Mister Campbell were all on the jury that sent Duck to the chain gang to start with. What I wonder is if they suspected this was the story at that meeting that Father went to and that maybe this is why Mister Campbell knew his barn might get burned.

Anyway Duck is dead and Sheriff Black says it is just as well because if he had of got caught he would have got tried and then hanged anyway because fire starting is a hanging crime in this state.

So the fires are over. I do sometimes feel sorry for that whole Mayfield family and especially for the Mama. But I am glad that Father was not on that jury.

Sunday, July 10, 1910

This week was a week of good weather and we got all of the last of the planting done that could get done before dinnertime in the middle of the day on Friday. At the dinner table Father said that he thought that all of us should go to town on Saturday to get Grandpa because he was riding the train from Nashville to Erwin Tennessee and then he would ride the Narrow Gauge on up to Suncrest. Suncrest is the closest town to Close Creek and it is where we go to town when we need to.

Ever body was excited to hear this because we had not been to town since before cold weather started last fall and besides that we all wanted to help to get Grandpa. I think that father also wanted to take all of us to town to help us get the Duck Mayfield business off our minds. I have not stopped thinking about that and all of us have talked about these things ever day. It turned out to be a good thing to go to town because what happened got all of us cheered up a lot.

It is thirteen miles to Suncrest and we took the wagon with King and Outlaw so all of us could ride and so we could get Grandpa and whatever he might of brought with him. We got up real early because we wanted to get to have enough time to go all over town during the day.

On the way there Father let each one of us take turns driving the team and the wagon and that is even the girls. He wants us all to know how to do things as soon as we can because he says he is getting old but I think he was old already when I was born.

Anyway we got to Suncrest about ten oclock in the morning and just as we were coming into town we started hearing a noise. It didnt sound like a locomotive but it did have a kind of clicking sound to it. Father said Oh No it is that automobile that Doc Graham has got and it will scare the horses to death.

He jumped down from the wagon and unhitched King and Outlaw and led them way up above the road in the woods while we saw the automobile come around the curve and toward us. It was a terrible scary thing to see.

At first it looked like it had eyes but they turned out to be lamps. It had rubber wheels and the front end of it looked like a little house seen from the end. It had a top that folded up and down like a buggy but there was a window glass in front of the driver because it goes so fast that you just cant breathe without that.

It was Doc Graham all right and when he got to us he stopped and said to Mama Morning Missus McGee. She just looked at him. He made the noise it was making stop and got out and told us not to be scared of it that he would show it to us.

King and Outlaw didnt seem to be scared of it and so Father brought them back down to where we were and hitched them back up. We got down out of the wagon and looked that automobile over from one end to the other.

The very front looked like a honeycomb and Doc told us you put water in a spout on the top to keep the engine cool. It had two seats and a extra wheel on one side of it. It also had a red lantern on the back so that people could see you just in case they was deaf. And you guided it with a big wheel that turned the front wheels to the right and to the left.

Then the most unbelievable thing of all happened. Doc Graham told Father that he would take us for a ride if we would make up two loads and Father said that we might as well learn about automobiles right now and so we did.

Father the twins and I got to go first. I got to set right beside Doc Graham in the front seat. He set some handles and then got down in front of the car and cranked a crank. It like to of scared me to death because the automobile engine started up and was running before Doc Graham even got back into the drivers place in the car.

Doc started moving levers and pushing pedals and the automobile started moving. He rode us all the way into Suncrest and back and then took the rest of us on the same ride.

Father and those of us who took the first ride was standing there watching smoke come out of a pipe in the back of the automobile and Father said It is called a Ford Model T and it was built by Mister Henry Ford.

Then he said that they would soon be ever where and that I would even have one someday.

After that ride the whole day seemed like magic. We walked all over town and bought a bucket of peanut butter and ate it on the biscuits we had brought for our dinner. Finally the Narrow Gauge whistled into town and Grandpa got off. We loaded his trunk in the wagon and got home just as it was getting dark. Father and us had to milk and feed with a lantern and I wondered if some day we could get lamps in the barn like that Ford Model Tee had on the front of it.

I do not know what exactly to think about what I have been through this day. I do not even know if King Edward the Seventh even ever got to ride in a automobile before he died. Maybe I have now done something that even one of the Kings of England had not done. This is a modern world.

Sunday, July 17, 1910

I always do like it when Grandpa is living with us even if his breath does smell bad when he sleeps turned towards me. He has false teeth and he does not take them out at night the way Father takes his teeth out and puts them into a cup of water. Sleeping with his teeth still in his mouth makes that snoring worse than ever because those teeth rattle when he snores. But still I am glad that he is here.

One time last year a funny thing happened when he was sleeping with me. When we got up in the morning his teeth were not in his mouth. He looked at me and said Med What did you do with my teeth.

I said that I did not do anything and that he must of lost them in the night. Mama came in and he told her that he had his teeth stole in the night. She said that they were not stolen but that they must have just fallen out and that we just all had to look for them.

We looked all under the bed and then all over the room. Finally Mama pulled all the cover back on the bed and there were those teeth right down under the cover at the bottom of the bed. We all laughed but Grandpa just put them right back in his mouth.

When Father came back from milking the cows we told him what had happened. He looked at me and said Med you are surely one of the luckiest people in the world.

I asked him why was that and he told me that the way that Grandpa runs his McGee mouth all of the time that I was lucky that those teeth didnt eat my toes off down there in the bed cause they were so used to moving that they coudnt stop.

We all laughed and even Grandpa laughed this time the hardest one of all. Then he did the funniest thing that I have about ever seen. He took those false teeth out and held them between his thumb and fingers and made them click like they were biting something all on their own. He chased me with them and then he talked out of the corner of his mouth without moving it while he moved those teeth just like they were talking all on their own. They said Im goin to get your toes Medford McGee.

Boy did we ever laugh at Grandpa. He is eighty years old and my Grandma is dead. I am glad that he is here for the summertime at last.

Sunday, July 24, 1910

Well it is finally happened between Lucee and Harlan Junior. Lucee had already asked Mama if she could invite Harlan Junior to come home with us after church and eat dinner with us today and Mama said that it was just fine. Then while we were eating dinner Lucee told Father that Harlan Junior wanted to ask him something.

Harlan Junior turned real red and he looked at Lucee like he didnt know what in this world she was talking about. But then he stuttered a little bit and then just stuttered out real big that he wanted to know if he could get married to Lucee. I like to of died for him when I saw how awful hard it was for him to have to set right in front of all of us and ask that. I do not think that a person should have to ask somebody else if they are the one who is going to get married. But that is the way that things are.

Anyway Father asked him a lot of questions but you could already tell right off that it was goin to be fine with him for them to get married. The worst part of it all was that the twins giggled right through all of it until Mama told them to stop their eating right there and to go to their rooms for the rest of the afternoon. I think that was good enough for them both.

Harlan Junior told ever body that his grandmama had left her house to him when she died and that enough land went along with it for him to be able to make a living and support Lucee. And so now that they would have both a place to live and a way to live there was just not any reason for them not to get married.

It seems funny to me to think that old Missus Chambers dying made it to where Lucee and Harlan Junior could get married. But when I think of her I think that she wouldnt have minded dying at all if it would have helped out somebody else. But when I told all of that to Mama she said that was not the way to think about it. She said that things like people dying do not happen so that other people will get stuff and get to do stuff but that when somebody does die it is the duty of the people left to just go right on living and that is the way that life mostly works out.

I used to think that dying was the most confusing thing in the world but now I am about decided that living is just as confusing.

Anyway Lucee and Harlan Junior are going to get married the next time the preacher is in town and it will take from now until then to get used to the idea of all of that. And so now one more of our family will be grown up. And maybe we will get to go back to using the parlor on Sunday after this.

Sunday, July 31, 1910

Well Mister Roosevelt is back home in the U S A. He sailed into New York City and Father read it to us today. Except that I do not know why the news paper says that he sailed in when Father read that he was actually traveling in a steam ship. Maybe it is that he would of rather been sailing in a big sailing ship to make even a bigger impression on all the people watching him get home.

Anyway he came to New York City which is his big city home even if it is not his actual home town. He did not come back to Californya and then come all across the country to get home the way that Father thought he would in order to get people to vote for him again for the President. He will not even talk now about where or not he wants to be the President again or about politicks at all. I think that is a dead give away that he knows that is the way that politicks works. I just know that he is going to try to get it again.

There were many thousands of people to meet him in New York City and there was a salute of guns and a big parade with a lot of bands and old soldiers. The news paper said that he smiled at ever body and that some people took a chance on getting fired from their jobs by leaving their work just to go and look at him.

It also said that there was a terrible rainstorm right at the end of the parade and that ever body got soaking wet. I think that it is a remarkable thing that by way of the news paper we can not only learn what happened somewhere else but can even know for a fact that it rained on Mister Roosevelts parade.

Anyway he is back. The trip took fifteen months and I just hope that if Mister Roosevelt does get to be the President again that then Mister Taft will get to take a trip around the world like that so he will have a chance to be written about all the time and have his fair share of the attention. Besides that if Mister Taft is as big as they say he is then he would not have any danger of getting eaten by cannibals in Africa because he just would not fit into the pot.

Sunday, August 7, 1910

Tomorrow is the day that Lucee and Harlan Junior are to get married. Mama says that we all have to help to get ready for the wedding which will be here in our house. The parlor will not get to cool off yet.

It is a good thing that most of the crops are laid by now or Harlan Junior would not get to take the time to get married. But in August most of what we do is watch things grow so there is a little time now for the wedding.

Because today is Sunday and people are not even allowed to loaf good on Sunday we will have to do the getting ready that was not finished yesterday on tomorrow the same day as the actual wedding.

Mama has it all planned out. Some of the neighbors are coming and are bringing food for supper. Then of course all of Harlan Juniors family will be coming. That will be bad enough because he has three little sisters that are just one year apart each.

Mama will send some of us up into the woods to pick some flowers and she will have the rest of us either cleaning the house or helping her in the kitchen. I will just be glad when this is all over. It looks to me like in this modern world people could figger out a easier way to get married than all this.

I guess that I already know that next Sunday I will be riting about what happens tomorrow.

At church this morning Reverend Sharpe was there. He just gets to come and preach at the Pine Chapel church once each month for he has to ride the circuit to seven other churches besides ours. We have Sunday School and a speaker ever week but the real preacher only once a month. That is why the wedding is tomorrow while he is still here in Close Creek.

Anyway at church today he told us about the big Methodist Conference they just finished having in Asheville. It was for Southern Methodists from all over the country. And he told us that one of the things that they voted to do was to take the part out of the wedding service that makes the woman promise to obey the man. He said they also are going to change the words to make it say Husband and Wife instead of Man and Wife. I will bet that if Harlan Junior knew this a little sooner he would have tried to get married to Lucee a month or two ago instead of now so that she would still have to obey him. But the way I know Lucee it would take more than a little promise to get that across.

Reverend Sharpe said that sooner or later they would have to let women go to the church conferences and even vote because more of them are getting jobs and making money and once they start giving money to the church like the men do it will be impossible to keep them out.

Father said that they should let them in where or not they give any money because most of the men who give the money wouldnt be fit for nothing without the women to push them along anyway. I just dont know about all of that. I hope that men and women have settled their differences before I have to be one.

So we will just wait and see what happens tomorrow and then I will find out where or not it is worth riting anything about that wedding on next Sunday.

Sunday, August 14, 1910

I sure am glad that Lucee and Harlan Junior did not get married on a Sunday or I would not have got to rite about what happened at all that day because it took all up till the middle of the night to get it all over with. I have never seen such a day in my life.

People started getting to our house about before breakfast was over on Monday morning. I hope none of them had been planning to do any work back home that day. If they did it sure didnt get done. Harlans Mama and Daddy and ever body else we knew was there and they all stayed the whole entire day.

We like to have worked ourselves to death cleaning the house again and even Harlans mama helped with that. Ever body else of the relatives and neighbors came in the afternoon and we spread all of the food on the front porch so it would be ready to eat after the wedding. Finally the preacher came.

Harlan Junior had been out of sight for all the day and he came about just as the preacher did. I guess he didnt want to have to do none of the work so he stayed away as long as he could. Lucee had also been out of sight from all of the work but all of that time she was in her room getting ready. The twins was helping her and I think that they even helped her take a bath when she had already had one on Saturday the way that we always do.

At about four oclock it was announced to be about time for the wedding. There really wasnt much to that part. We just all got in the parlor and the preacher called us to pray and then he married Lucee up to Harlan Junior. The preacher forgot to leave out the part about her obeying him and she had to say that anyway. Maybe it is not official to leave it out yet since it was just decided at that Methodist Conference a little over a month ago to do it. Some changes are slow and anyhow I think myself that Lucee needs to obey.

When that part was over we started into the eating on the porch and in the yard. Youve never seen such food even at a dinner on the ground at church. We ate for over a hour without stopping for anything but to get more food.

The Mayfield brothers who we beat in the May Day relay race brought their musical instruments. There is two of them named Ledge and Bull who each plays one now that their brother Duck got shot dead by Mister Johnny Cambell. Nobody thought they would come out in public this soon after that happened but somehow Father got them to come. I guess maybe being part of the wedding might help them forget that bad day the way that Doc Grahams automobile helped us think about something else for a while. Mama says that Mister Mayfield has a wild look in his eyes and Father told her not to be surprised about that.

The brothers Ledge and Bull are the fiddle and the guitar. Their daddy sometimes is the mandoline. Duck used to play the banjer but now that he is shot dead there is not a banjer player. Harlan Juniors Daddy calls square dances and so the Mayfields played and he called and we had a real fine long square dance right there in the yard.

Ever body kept poking at Lucee and Harlan Junior about where or not they were tired and ready to go home but they just kept on dancing. Finally when it was on after ten oclock ever body went on home and Harlan Junior finally took Lucee on to her new home.

I thought that the day was over then but I didnt even know the start of it. The Mayfield boys had told Zeb and Merry to bring me and meet them at their house in about a hour. Even Champ stayed and went with us. Father did not say even one word about our going that late and when Mama said that we shouldnt he told her that people just get one Honey Moon and that it ought to be a good one and that we could go on up there if we wanted to. I didnt know what he meant by that because we were not the ones that was married.

Anyway we all got us some cow bells and Champ took along his shotgun and we met the Mayfields at their house. From there we went on up to Missus Chambers old house which is now to be Lucee and Harlan Juniors new house. The lights was all off when we got there and I figgered that after all that had happened that day they had got tired and gone on to bed.

We got out in the yard and Champ loaded the shotgun and then he shot it in the air right over the house. Then we all hollered and rung the cow bells and beat on the house with sticks. They all hollered Chivaree Chivaree and I hollered it too but I didnt know what I was hollering. Finally a light was lit and we saw Lucee and Harlan Junior look out the window. Go On Away was what Harlan Junior hollered and Lucee told me that I ought to be in bed. One of the Mayfields told

Lucee that she was the one who had ought to be in bed and she slammed the window shut.

After that the Mayfields played a lot of sad sounding songs and then we finally went home. It was a lot of fun and I hope that Lucee and Harlan Junior enjoyed the music. And I think the wedding day did cheer the Mayfields up a little bit as well.

So they are married. I will sometimes miss Lucee my sister and so I am glad that they do not live far away. I do not like it when I hear of people getting married and moving away off from their Mama and Daddy. If I ever get married I am going to just stay right at home with Mama and Daddy even so. I dont want to go way off.

Sunday, August 21, 1910

This afternoon we have had just about the finest day that we could have in the world. Lucee and Harlan Junior came home with us after church and ate dinner with us. I think that Harlan Junior is going to be a lot better now that he and Lucee are married. I mean that he talked to me and played around with me today instead of just spending all of the time looking at Lucee like she was some kind of a valuable cow.

It was a good hot day and after we had finished eating Sunday dinner Father said Lets go swimming. Mama said Cate it is Sunday. But Father just said that the preacher was not watching and besides it would be a good thing to do to get Harlan into the family with all of us and not just Lucee. So we did it.

The swimming hole that we like most to go to is about a mile and a half from home down on Wainwrights Creek. It is on the Wainwrights property but since they are our neighbors they do not ever mind if we go swimming there. Besides that they have said that people have been a swimming there since the Indians lived here and that was a long time before they ever owned the land.

Mama got out some old britches of Champs for Harlan Junior to wear and off we went. She did not go but said she would fix some food for supper and then come on down later.

At the swimming hole there is a big rock that you jump off of into the water. The water is cold all of the year and I have finally learned that it is better to jump right into it. When I was little I would spend the whole afternoon easing my way into it and just finally would get all of the way in there by the time it was time to go on home. Me and Merry and Zeb and even Harlan Junior raced down to the swimming hole and jumped right in off of that big rock.

There is a real deep pool right there by the rock and when nobody is a swimming it is sometimes a good place to fish for trout. Right above the pool there is what we call a slidy rock. It is where the water is shallow but runs down a slick rock into the pool. We can climb around to the top of it and slide down into the pool over and over again.

There is also a big rope tied to a tree limb which sticks out over the jumping rock. We like to swing on that rope and drop into the water. The rope is thick and three of us can swing out on it at one time and make a great splash. Father says that when he was a boy there was a grape vine there that you could swing on but it finally got too brittle and it broke one time when somebody was swinging on it. I do not know who put the rope up there but it is a good thing to have and I thank them for it.

Lucee and Annie Laurie and the twins mostly piddled around in the shallows where the pool is sort of dammed up at the lower side. It does seem like the water is warmer there because it is shallow and right in the sun. When I got close enough to hear them the twins and Annie Laurie were asking Lucee one question after another just all about being married. They were all three giggling fit to be tied.

Finally Mama came with a big picnic basket and we had a picnic supper right there on the grass while we were still wet. Boy it was good. Father said a long blessing before we ate but he did not even ask to be forgiven for swimming on Sunday. I dont see what is wrong with it myself and he must not either because it was his idea to do it to start with.

I sure do like the summertime and it seems like a lot better time for people to get married than in the winter when all they can do once they are married is just stay at home. But maybe once people are actually married they do not mind to do just that very thing.

Sunday, August 28, 1910

I do miss Lucee very much and maybe it is partly because there is now nobody to stop the twins from calling me Baby more than ever. I wanted her and Harlan Junior to come home with us from church again on this day but she said that they had to go home and eat with Harlan Juniors Mama and Daddy on this day and that we would have to wait until next Sunday.

I did set on the porch a long time with Grandpa though and he told me a lot of things about what it was like to live with Aunt Louise down there in Nashville Tennessee. I have never been to a place like Nashville Tennessee or to any town besides Suncrest and so I do not imagine what it is like very well. He had not ever told me much about it before but that is because I had never known to ask him about anything so that he could tell it.

When I had told him after he came here this year about seeing the automobile on the way to get him he told me that there was a lot of automobiles in Nashville Tennessee and there was a lot of different kinds there too. He said that a lot of the big streets had bricks laid out on top of them so that they wouldnt turn into mud when it rained and then all of those automobiles drove on those streets not to speak of the horses and wagons too.

He told me that on those bricked streets they also had what are called Street Cars. This means that they are just trains for the town but they go on electrick engines and not on steam like the real trains do. I have not ever seen anything run on electrick fuel and I cant imagine it. There might be electrick lights in Suncrest at some places but I do not know much about it. Grandpa says that before I grow up there will be electrick lights just about ever where.

He said that Aunt Louise has gas lights which run off of a gas line that goes all through the house and that she also has a stove that runs off of gas from that same gas line. He told me that the streetlights in Nashville Tennessee run off of that same gas line and he once saw a automobile run into a light pole and break the line and set it on fire and a long flame shoot out until the police came and turned the gas line off. I think I would just rather stick with kerosine than have to worry all of the time about something as dangerous as that.

Grandpa told me a lot of other things about the train ride and the stories and the people in the city of Nashville. He said they even had boats you can ride on the Cumberland River on there. Sometime I would really like to go to visit at a place like Nashville Tennessee. I do not think that Mister Roosevelt has ever been there even with all of his travels.

Sunday, September 4, 1910

Father has been reading to us in the news paper about the explorers trying to find the South Pole. That is a thing hard for me to think about.

I do know from what Mister Robinson told us at school that the world is round and that gravity keeps us from falling off. But it still does not seem like people could actually be right on the very bottom of the world and not fall off. But they are trying to do just that.

There are several different teams of the explorers all trying to get to the South Pole and they are having a race to see who can get down there first. One leader is Captain Scott of the English team and another leader is Mister Amundson of the Norwegians. There is also Mister Jean Charcot who leads the team of the Frenchmen. I dont know who will get there first. It said in the news paper that they are taking ponys which will carry their food and after that food is eat up they will then eat the ponies. That sounds just awful to me.

Part of what I wonder is how they will tell when they find the South Pole. Is there really a pole there that you can see. Maybe it goes all the way through the middle of the earth and the other end sticks out and is the North Pole. Grandpa says that he saw a model of the world at the public library in Nashville Tennessee and that is what it looked like to him.

Another thing is to wonder whether it is downhill all the way to the bottom of the earth. But if the bottom is all round how could it be downhill.

Maybe the reason they have such a hard time getting to find it is just that the snow has covered the South Pole up and none of them will ever be able to tell if they do get to it.

I am glad that I do not have to go there. Even though it is still real hot now I just do not want to even start thinking about cold weather yet.

Sunday, September 11, 1910

It has stayed real awful hot into this month and that heat was the start of what led to trouble.

Sometimes we go swimming at the Wainwrights creek when it is so hot as this on a Saturday but it is a little way down there and it takes some effort to do that. So sometime in the last week Merry and Zeb came up with a idea that they were going to build a swimming hole for us right here at our house. They did not talk to Father about doing this. They were just going to do it and then it would be done and would be a big surprise for ever body.

They were going to go up on the flat part of the yard close to the back of the house and dig out a big swimming hole right there in the ground. There is still not much farm work to do right now at this time of the year except to set and hope it will rain when it ought to and so they thought that they could slip up there and dig the swimming hole all day yesterday.

Zeb had got a mattock to loosen up the dirt and Merry had got a big shovel to dig it out. I dont know what they were going to do with all of the dirt as they never did tell that part later on. They were going to try to dig it all in one day and then show ever body about it when it was all finished and full of water.

About ten oclock in the morning we all heard screaming and Merry come running to the house with blood all running down over his face and about all over him. Zeb was running right behind him hollering Im sorry Im sorry over and over. I didnt mean to do it he kept saying.

Mama grabbed a hold of Merry and rapped a towel around his head and asked him and Zeb what happened. Merry was still screaming so hard that he couldnt get his breath long enough to talk and so Zeb told what had happened.

It was then that we all heard about the idea of the swimming hole for the first time to start with. Then Zeb told that he had been loosening up the dirt with the mattock and Merry had been shoveling it out and one time when Merry bent down to lift up a shovel of dirt he bent over right where Zeb was chopping with the mattock and before Zeb could catch hisself he chopped Merry right in the very crown of his head with the sharp edge of the mattock.

By this time Merry had stopped squallin and Mama had cleaned a lot of the blood off of him. Still whenever she took the towel off of his head he commenced back to bleeding like a stuck pig.

She sent Zeb to the springhouse to get a pan full of cold water and then she washed his head good with lye soap and cold water because she said she had to get all of the dirt out and there wasnt time to heat up the water and besides the cold would help to stop the bleeding. She told Father she could see clean to the bone and that she had better sow Merrys head up with a needle and thread.

She put Fathers straight razor in a pan of water along with a needle and some thread. After she boiled them she took the straight razor and shaved off part of the hair on Merrys head to make a good clear place around where the cut open place was.

He still was hollering a little but he was mostly whimpering and Zeb was a holding his hands and still telling him that he was sorry and that they could just finish that swimming hole on another day.

Merry didnt seem to care nothing at all about the swimming hole at this time. Then Mama sowed his head right back together again just as neat as sowing up a split space in some britches. By the time she was done Merry had done quit his crying but now he cut loose and vomited great big and Mama said that it was from all of that hollering and crying. He was just a shaking all over.

Now that the sowing up had stopped the bleeding Mama cleaned Merry on up and then Father took him in the buggy up toward Suncrest to Doc Grahams house so Doc Graham could look at his head.

After they come back Father said that Doc Graham had just asked if Mama had washed the cut and boiled the needle and thread. He had painted some red stuff on Merrys head and said to tell Mama that she had sowed him up just as good as any doctor could have done it.

Father did not even get mad at Zeb and Merry. I guess that he figgered that both of them had gone through enough. But he did ask them how they had planned to get water into the swimming hole once they had got it dug out.

They didnt look like they had either one of them even thought about that and then Zeb said that they could turn the creek into it. But when Father told them that where they were digging was above the creek and that the creek couldnt run up hill then Zeb said that they could just use buckets.

Thats when Merry said that he didnt think that we needed no swimming hole to begin with and that we could just go to Wainwrights creek if it was hot enough to go swimming.

Today Merry didnt want to go to church but he had to go anyway. Father did let him wear his cap though ever where except right inside the church house itself. Anyway nobody would tease anybody right inside the church house.

Sunday, September 18, 1910

As of yesterday we have a new person living at our house for the time. It is our new schoolteacher who is going to live with us until she finds a place to live all of the time. She is a lady and is not going to move about each month like Mister Robinson did but will get one place to live for all of the year but for now she is living here.

Her name is Missus Henrietta Melville and she is a Yankee from Boston Massatusetts but she is real nice anyway. Yesterday I went with Father in the wagon to get her from the Narrow Gauge in Suncrest along with all of her stuff which seems to me to be a lot. School is a little bit late in getting started but I guess that is because the new teacher had so far to come to get here. I think maybe they couldnt even find a teacher until last week.

Missus Melville is not a very old woman but she is a widow woman. She looks to be about as old as our Mama is. Her husband was sailor on a ship that got destroyed in a ocean storm and he got drownded I guess. Father says that her husband was related to the family of Herman Melville who rote the story of Moby Dick and also a lot of other sea books.

Anyway the truth is that after her husband was lost in the storm she decided to become a missionary but she was really already a trained schoolteacher. I do not remember all that they said about how she came to get from Boston Massatusetts to here but she is here and Father and Mama are glad.

I sure do hope that Missus Melville can handle some of those boys like the Mayfields especially Ledge Mayfield and also Tommy Dooly. I will hope the best for her but I know she will have a hard time getting started because she does talk so very funny and I can already hear some of those boys making fun of her. I hope that she is tougher than she looks.

Sunday, September 25, 1910

Our new school year started on Tuesday and there is a lot of things to tell about Missus Melville and the new year but today I cannot even think about that for Father has just read to us about the most unbelievable invention that has surely ever been invented in the history of the world. It is called the Talking Motion Picture and the man who made it is Thomas Edison.

That Thomas Edison must be a real genius and this is the proof of it though I have not actually ever seen any of the things that he invented. I do know about electricity and electrick lights and that they will soon have electrick lights all over Suncrest because they are building a electricity plant on the Allen river over the mountain and will run wires all over the place. I also know that Mister Edison has made a way to take sounds and record them and play them out loud over again just like they were made but this new invention is more than even that.

I have tried and tried to figger out how the machine that makes plain moving pictures can work. I have never seen one of the moving pictures but in thinking about it it must be something like a shadow made on the wall by a light. If you could make a shadow with enough detail it would after all be a whole picture and I think that it works like this.

Anyway now Edison has made a machine that puts the recorded sounds and the moving pictures together at the same time. Putting the two together does not seem to me as hard a thing as making each of those machines to start with. So now people in the cities will be able to go see moving pictures with sound in the theatres there.

Maybe Grandpa will get to go see a talking picture when he goes back to Nashville pretty soon before cold weather comes. But when I told him this he said that he could live a long time without that. I think he has already lived a long time without that and that maybe he doesnt care much about some new inventions.

I sure would like to see one of them though and tomorrow at school I am going to tell the whole school about it because one of the new things we do with Missus Melville is to tell the things we have learned.

Sunday, October 2, 1910

It has been a hard week for Merry and Zeb. Merrys head has hurt and Zeb has suffered something awful over what happened.

On Tuesday Doc Graham came in the Ford automobile and looked at Merrys head again. He gave Mama some of the red stuff called Eyedine to paint onto where it was swelled up now around the sowing. The sowed up place has turned into a purple pump knot but Doc Graham said that it still looked as good as it could. By today it looks a lot better though. Doc Graham says that he will come back this week and take out the thread if it is healed up enough. I dont know exactly how he will do that. I know that will hurt Merry again. His hair is starting to grow back out just a little bit. He wants Mama to cut all of his hair off short so that it will pretty soon look about the same all over as it grows back out.

Zeb has gone up behind the house and filled the hole back up where they were going to build the swimming hole. I dont guess we need that swimming hole now but when we are putting up hay it would feel awful good to jump into the water when you get home itching at the end of the day. I guess that we can just go to the Wainwrights creek then though.

Sunday, October 9, 1910

Father has read to us today that Florence Nightingale has died. I do not know when I first heard tell about Florence Nightingale being the inventor of nurses but I do know that when Mister Robinson read about her in school last year I already knew about her from Mama. Maybe Mama would have wanted to of been like Florence Nightingale if she had not had all of us to take care of or maybe if she had been born back in Scotland or England like Florence Nightingale.

Anyway one time Mister Robinson read us a poem that Henry Watsworth Longfellow rote about her as a nurse. She was a English woman who went with the English Army to the wars in the country of Turkey and she taught them how to make hospitals all real clean. She stayed right in there and took care of the hurt soldiers right in the actual time of the real fighting I think.

After that she started up a school to teach other women how to be a nurse like she was.

When Father read to us about her being now dead he read to us that she was ninety years old when she died. I guess that keeping clean kept her alive to be a old woman. But Missus Elizabeth Chambers lived to be older than that when she died and left that house to Harlan Junior and Lucee and I dont think that she was so very clean. She was just normal. So maybe being clean helps and maybe it dont.

Father read to us about a lot of prizes Florence Nightingale had got for being a nurse. I think that Mama is a nurse without either knowing Florence Nightingale or going to get trained either one. After all if she wasnt a nurse she wouldnt have known to sow up Merrys head and she did know so she must be a nurse. At least she is to me and also to Merry. Also Merry got the stitches took out of his head by Mama before Doc Graham even came back to do it.

Sunday, October 16, 1910

This week we have been trying to finish making hay and on Friday you would not believe it but another bad thing happened to my poor brother Merry just after his hair is barely growing back over where his head got cut open.

Champ had come over here each and ever day to help out with the hay making because in the winter we share hay with him and he shares hay with us. We do that because he is our brother but I believe that any real neighbors would do the same thing brothers or not.

Anyway the hay making goes like this. Father and Champ work with our horses who are King and Outlaw because they are quick and smart. Merry and Zeb work with Robert E Lee and U S Grant who are our mules as I have already told about. The mules are slow but they are strong and steady.

Father helps Merry and Zeb hitch up the mowing machine. The mowing machine has two metal wheels and a long bar with a sickle that has teeth and blades. One of the boys rides on the machine and drives the mules while the other one walks along at the end of the long sickle so he can lift it up if it gets hung up or clean it out when it gets clogged up.

While the boys mow the hay Father and Champ do the raking and the stacking up. Since Grandpa is still here this year he helps Father and Champ but not very much.

On Friday Father and Champ were raking and stacking the hay from the flat field beyond the barn. At this same time Merry and Zeb were mowing the hay in a new ground we cleared last fall where the pine woods used to be above the barn. This is the first hay crop we have got there at the newground and mowing it had been put off till the last.

Mowing in a newground is awful hard because a lot of the stumps are still in there in the hay. That means whoever is driving the mowing machine has to go around all he can and that whoever is walking has to lift the sickle bar over ever stump that is in the way.

While Zeb was driving Merry was walking and they were a doing fine until Zeb run the sickle bar into a stump with a yeller jackets nest in it. The yeller jackets come out of the stump and started to sting Lee and Grant and then Zeb jumped off the seat and run off and left poor Merry standing right there.

Those mules was getting stung and having a fit but they couldnt run off because the mowing machine was hung up in the stump with the yeller jackets nest.

Well Merry just stood his ground. He stood right there and got that mowing machine loose while he was getting stung all over. Then he led the mules out of there until they got on off to where the yeller jackets left them all alone. But they did get stung awful bad and so did Merry.

Mama put wet soda all over him where he was stung. He even got stung right on the head where his head got sowed up and that just is not fair at all.

I thought that Father was going to whip Zeb for running off but he finally told him that he would just have to mow that new ground the rest by hisself because Merry does not have to help until he is well.

So Zeb will have to stop the mules and get hisself off the mowing machine and lift the sickle bar over ever one of those stumps and that will just take forever.

Father told him if that seemed too hard to do he could just mow it by hand with the scythe. When I think about it I guess that is worse punishment than getting whipped to begin with. Father is awful smart about things like that in the long run.

Grandpa decided to go on back to Nashville after that day was over. He is tired of what he calls the Antics. He left on the train on yesterday. I miss him already.

Sunday, October 23, 1910

Mrs. Melville certainly is one remarkable new teacher for us to have at school. First of all she taught us that the correct way to rite Missus is <u>Mrs.</u> and Mister is <u>Mr.</u> and almost ever day she teaches us something helpful which I will gradually be able to use in the riting out of my own life and a lot of useful new words also.

But the best thing of all that she did since school has started back was the way that she handled Ledge Mayfield. She has proved that she can handle the entire room full by her handling of that one worst bully in all of the class.

Ledge is only twelve years old but he is worse than any two sixteen year olds in the whole school. He picks on ever body and always causes a awful disturbance.

Well Mrs. Melville had already heard all about the Mayfield boys I guess from our Mama. Anyway she had gone up to see Mrs. Mayfield one afternoon after school. We heard about it this week that she had gone to talk about those boys with their mama. I guess she heard all about Duck getting killed while she was up there.

Mama told Father that Mrs. Melville had found out that Mrs. Mayfield is a good woman herself who tries hard with the boys but that Mister Mayfield the daddy is just as mean as a snake and likes for all of his boys to be just that mean. Anyway Mrs. Melville and Mrs.

Mayfield made a plan and Mrs. Melville borrowed something from Mrs. Mayfield to help make the plan work. We heard about all of this after we saw what happened.

On the third day of school Ledge kept teasing Rebekah Hannah because she had grown so much in the summer that her dress had got too short and he kept poking her and saying that he could see her underwear. She sets right in front of him at school. She kept squalling ever time he said it.

Finally Mrs. Melville just told him. She said Ledge you are acting like a baby and I am just going to ask you one time in front of this class to stop acting like a baby. If you do not stop then I will just have to treat you like a baby to be sure. Is that clear to you she said.

Ledge didnt say anything. He just set there and sort of grinned at her. She went back to her teaching and in no time he was picking at Rebekah Hannah again and she was squalling again too.

Mrs. Melville stopped the entire class and then she said Ledge you come up here. And he did. He was grinning all of the way. At the front of the room she told him to set up on her big stool and he got right up there and grinned just like he was proud of hisself.

Then she said Ledge I told you that if you keep acting like a baby I would have to treat you like one and now I am going to have to keep my promise. First of all I must show these big boys and girls what you have brought to school in your coat pocket. Then she went to the coat pegs and reached in the pocket of Ledges coat and pulled out a nursing nipple baby bottle full of milk.

Ledge stopped grinning and looked like he couldnt believe what was happening. Mrs. Melville went on talking to the class. She told that Ledge had to act like a baby because he didnt get to finish his bottle before he came to school. Then she walked over to Ledge and told him he could just drink that bottle of milk right there in front of the class since thats what it seemed like he needed to do. She said if he wanted her to she would hold him and rock him while he nursed the bottle.

Ledge said right to her face that he wasnt going to do it. Then she told him that if he didnt do it she would have to let the whole school out right then and there so she could go straight up to Ledges house and show his daddy that he was sneaking baby bottles to school.

When she said that Ledge got pale as a sheet. He begged her not to tell his daddy and said that he would drink the bottle. He drank ever bit of it right there in front of the whole class.

So Ledge drank the bottle. We laughed until Mrs. Melville told us that this was a private matter and that if any of us ever told about Ledge and the bottle she would think up something just that bad for us. She told us that when we solved our own problems at school that should be the end of it. But riting is not telling and so I am riting it all out because this story should be preserved.

And I do not think that Mister Ledge Mayfield will ever try another trick in Mrs. Melvilles room again. Neither will anybody else. Ledge needed this lesson I do know. But I cant help from feeling some sorry for his life given his family and his brother Duck getting shot to death.

Sunday, October 30, 1910

Today we are celebrating Annie Lauries 12th birthday which was actually on Thursday. This means that Father has told me that I should not rite on my life but just give attention to my sister which I do not mind at all to do.

I will just tell that Mama has made a spice cake for her with butter icing on it and that Father has bought her a dress for a present on the last time that he went to town.

It is a pretty day and so we will now eat the cake out in the yard to celebrate.

Sunday, November 6, 1910

Father is very excited today because this coming Tuesday is election day. This morning was our preaching Sunday for the month at church but all of the men were more interested in standing in the church yard and talking about the coming elections than in going in to hear Reverend Sharpe preach. They say that politicks and religion dont mix but they sure dont mind to talk about politicks in the church yard. Anyway ever body who lives here in Close Creek is a Democrat and so I guess that it is safe to talk even at church.

One time Father told us that he once saw a Republican on display in a cage in Asheville. He laughed like that was a joke but Mama didnt act like it was funny. Anyway we will not have to go to school on Tuesday because the schoolhouse is where all of the voting takes place. It shouldnt take all day. But with all of the talking that is the main part of politicks I guess that it will be all day long before it is over.

Now besides the elections there was another interesting thing in the news today. About three weeks ago a man in New Jersey named a Mr. Wellman set out in a lighter than air aeroplane to try to fly over the Atlantic ocean to the continent of Europe. The airship is called a dirigible and this one is named the America.

Anyway today Father read that the dirigible went down in the ocean out from North Carolina about four hunderd miles. I guess it got a leak. Maybe a bird ran into it and poked a hole that let the lifting gas leak out. They did not get drownded though because a mail ship called the S S Trent came along at just the right time and rescued Mr. Wellman and all of the others with him. I dont know how many there were.

It is exciting to think about floating up in the air and looking at ever thing. But I dont think that I will try it.

Sunday, November 13, 1910

Well Father is very happy about the results of the election day and so are about all of the voting people here in Close Creek. We did not even have to wait for the Nashville Banner news paper to find out what happened. Father and some of the others took the local ballots to Suncrest and then waited right at the telegraph office all night long to hear ever thing that they could about the result of the elections.

The good news about the election to Father and the others who waited up is that the Democrats have won most of the races for Congress just about all over the whole U S A. Father said that it is the first time since 1892 when Grover Cleveland was elected the President for the second time that we have won so big. He is pleased about it.

Father and the neighbors are thinking that there may be a chance to get a Democrat for President of the U S A in the 1912 election. He has been real interested in two of the elections in the House of Repersenatives. One is a man called Thomas Woodrow Wilson who has been elected in the State of New Jersey. This man has been the President of a College and Father says that he is the smartest man to be in politicks since James A. Garfield in 1880. Of course poor Mr. Garfield who Father says could rite Latin with one hand and Greek with the other got shot just after he got started and didnt get to do much. I dont know if Thomas Woodrow Wilson can rite either Latin or Greek with either hand. I sure cannot.

The other election that Father is interested in is the one with Mr. Franklin Delano Roosevelt in the state of New York. Father says that he is some kind of cousin to Teddy Roosevelt and what could be better than a Roosevelt who is actually a Democrat. He is a very young man to go to Congress and he is married to his own cousin.

The other thing in the news is that President Taft is going to take a trip to Panama. He says that he has to fix some trouble there.

The U S A has been digging a canal through there from the Atlantic Ocean to the Pacific Ocean. It is not supposed to be finished for many more years. But the trouble is that those people in Panama think that this country wants to take them completely over and make their country another state of the U S A. I guess the canal is one thing but that being a state is something else to them.

I think probably that Mr. Taft is actually going to try to attract some attention after so many of the Republicans have just got beat so bad. It is not as good as going to Africa but at least poor Mr. Taft is going to get to go somewhere.

Well Lucee and Harlan Junior have done it again. They have now told us at dinner today that Lucee is going to have a baby. Now that is something.

The most interesting thing about it so far was watching how they did tell us about it after Sunday dinner on today. They came home with us after church. Most of the time they ride to church on horseback with Lucee riding side saddle on her horse. But on today they came to church in a buggy that Harlan Juniors grandmother left in her barn when she died and made a place for them to live by giving them her house. I got to ride all squeezed in with them in that buggy to get home from church.

At the end of the day Mama said that she should of noticed all along that something was going on what with the buggy and Harlan treating Lucee so particular and all. But I notice that people can always say that they should of seen something when they look back that they never say nothing about at all at the time when it is happening.

Anyway we did not really notice anything to speak of until after dinner when Lucee said for Harlan Junior to tell us. I have never seen nothing more pitiful since back on that day when he had to ask Father and Mama if he could marry Lucee to start with. He got all red and shaky and was just about sweating right out on his upper lip.

Lucee giggled and said to Harlan to tell them. Then he said that they were going to have a baby in the springtime when the lambs come and was it all right to do that.

It was such a shock that the twins couldnt even giggle for a minute or two. Finally Father said that of course it was all right but what did the lambs have to do with it. And he laughed. Harlan Junior didnt laugh but he looked relieved to have it known and over with.

I dont know what is so embarrassing about having a baby. After all if the animals that dont think can have babies without no trouble at all then people that do think should be able to have a baby OK. I guess that it is the first time that it is hard.

Sunday, November 27, 1910

Today I begin to rite out my life better than before because of a wonderful thing that Mrs. Melville has this week fully explained to us. She says it is properly called the Apostrophe and we even learned how to spell it.

The Apostrophe looks just like this ' and she has explained to us that it has two uses. One is to shorten two words into one word like when you rite Don't instead of Do Not. This is a good thing because it helps you to make your riting sound like the way people really talk instead of just sounding like riting.

The other use of this apostrophe is to show who something belongs to when you put it before the 's at the end like to say a Dog's bone. Without that it just sounds like a lot of dogs just got one bone instead of what you actually meant to say.

Mrs. Melville says that ever thing we learn about riting ought to help us say what we want to say and that we shouldn't just learn a lot of rules unless we also learn the way that they are helpful to us. Now that I think about it I think that I may have already heard about that apostrophe before but I never did remember it because I wasn't riting out my life at the time and so I didn't need to know stuff like that to help me out.

Anyway I think it is good to learn the stuff that will be helpful to you and maybe OK to forget the rest. Whether it is OK or not it does offen happen like that.

Sunday, December 4, 1910

Boy am I sore today all over. All day yesterday we spent cutting wood.

We have been cutting some wood all along but on yesterday it was a real pretty day and we just chopped all day. It has been a clear week and so back in the week Champ came one day while we were all at school and he helped Father cut two trees and bring them to the house. One was a walnut tree that had blown over last spring and had a split trunk so it wasn't any good for anything else. The other was a white oak that had got hit and killed by lightening in the summertime.

Champ and father sawed them with the crosscut and with King and Outlaw they pulled them back to the barn in big pieces and waited for yesterday to come.

Yesterday morning we started early when Champ came over in time for breakfast. All the day long it was the same thing. Champ and Father used the crosscut saw to cut the trunk into smaller pieces and the big limbs up into short rounds. Merry and Zeb worked the maul and wedge to split the rounds into sticks of firewood and sometimes used a ax on the littler pieces. My job was to stack up the wood.

I counted the pieces that I was stacking until I got to 164 and then I lost count and did not start over again. We cut and chopped and stacked the whole entire day except for lunch time when Champ's wife Sallie Jane and their Junior came for dinner.

It was a lot of work but it was a necessity. I do hate being cold in the wintertime.

Father told us a story about a man who had a ax with words carved into the handle. The words were My Wood Warms Twice. In the story it was a kind of riddle I guess. It meant that the wood you chopped with that ax warmed you up once when you chopped it and then again when you burned it. I thought that was pretty good.

Anyway today we are all as sore as can be and that does include even Father and Champ. Father says that cutting wood helps you find all your lost mussels. I'd as soon leave some of mine lost but I do still want to keep warm in January.

Sunday, December 11, 1910

Well it surely is a good thing that we cut all of that wood last Saturday a week ago because on Tuesday night it seemed like that wintertime just came all on one day. It started raining before we got home from school and we had to walk home in the rain without being ready for it and it was awful cold. Mama let us take off our clothes and stand up close to the stove in the kitchen until we got warm all the way through before we put on our new clothes.

By then that rain was turning into ice and before it was dark we could actually see that ice hanging from the trees and building up on the ground. But the worst was still coming. In the night it turned to pure all out snow just falling right on top of that froze ice. By the morning the snow was laying seven or eight inches thick on top of that ice.

When Father came back from feeding that morning he said it was so slick to walk with ice under that snow that it was hard to stand up. He said he wouldn't dare get a horse out into it for it was liable to fall and break a leg for sure.

It turned even colder the next day and the snow got so hard that I could walk right on top of it. It is still here even today.

Tomorrow is the birthday for Champ and Sallie Jane's baby Junior. He will be three years old. Today they walked over here and carried that baby for a visit after church. Junior can walk real good but they didn't want him to get froze to death in that snow. The baby can even talk to where it makes some sense most of the time.

Harlan Junior and Lucee did not even come to church. Harlan Junior is scared to death to let her do about anything since they are going to have that baby in the spring even though she does not even look like it yet. At least I am not confused by having two people named Junior over here at the same time even if one of them is a baby. But if they didn't call that baby Junior then we would probably of had two people named Champ. Maybe Lucee should of married somebody with a different name.

Anyway Father says that it is awful early in the year for us to have such weather as this. I can't remember from year to year when it snows the first time but Father always rites it down and so he remembers. I do know this. I do not like the wintertime. If I would ever leave home it would be to go to a warmer place.

Sunday, December 18, 1910

Today was a good day because of two things. The first is that it is warmed back up a lot and all of the ice and snow is long gone. It is even sun shining outside today.

The second thing is that this afternoon we had a special party at school which was called the Old Folks Party.

Mrs. Melville said one day that it is too bad that people think that only children need to get stuff for Christmas. Her idea was for all of the pupils at school to give a party for the old people. We made a list of all the old people we could think of and then we rote a private invite to them all to come and said that even somebody would come to each house in a buggy to get them.

Twelve of the old folks said they would come including Mr. Linseed Woody who is ninety five years old and does not have a hair on the outside of his head or a tooth on the inside of it.

We fixed up the school house with a cedar Christmas tree and strings of strung up pop corn. All of this was Mrs. Melville's idea which I guess she got in Boston where she is from.

We brought food which most of the mamas made. Mama sent a chicken pie which she said old people could eat easy even if they didn't have no teeth. When the old people were there we had recitation and sang and then ate supper at about three o'clock in the afternoon so they could get home before dark. Father gave each one there a stick of peppermint candy.

This was another one of Mrs. Melville's good ideas which never do run out. Some of those old people had tears in their eyes when they got those sticks of candy. I guess ever body likes to get a present at Christmas time.

Sunday, Christmas Day, 1910

Santy Clause did come. On Yesterday we put up our Christmas tree. It is a cedar tree which we popped popcorn and strung on thread to decorate. We also folded scraps of paper and cut out snowflakes and paper stars for the tree. It is beautiful.

We got up real early this morning so we could get our stockings down from the mantle and see what we got. They were full. Each one of us got two oranges and a stick of peppermint candy. Zeb got horehound candy because he don't like peppermint.

Then in the bottom of our stockings we found something else. Each one of us got a penny for each year old that we are. I even got eleven cents since I will be eleven in just one week and now I am rich.

Right now I have tied that money in my stocking so I won't lose any of it and I have tied the stocking to the bed post beside my head. I have been looking all day for a good place to hide it for the future. Santy Clause must be rich.

Mama cooked a lot on Saturday to get ready for today. Champ and Sallie Jane and their Junior came after church and so did Lucee and Harlan Junior and a lot of food was needed for that.

We went to church and even if it was not our preaching Sunday we got all the ages together and Father read the Christmas story from the Bible to ever body. Then we came home and ate all afternoon.

We will keep the tree put up in the house for twelve days because that is how long it took for the Wise Men to find their way to the baby Jesus. Then we will have another Christmas day on January the sixth in the honor of that. Some of the Old People don't even think it is Christmas until then and they call it the Old Christmas. Anyway that just means that we really get Christmas twice. The modern one and the old one.

I think it is too bad that Jesus had to get born in the winter when it is cold. Of course I got born about now too and maybe that is why I hate cold weather. I do not remember.

1911

My Birthday, Sunday, New Years Day, 1911

Today I am eleven years old and Father is sixty one. I cannot remember a time when my birthday was on a Sunday before but Father says that it has happened once in my life at least. It has been a fine day like it was on Christmas and as good as that was in ever way.

When we came home from church I found that Mama had fixed my favorite Sunday dinner. Fried chicken of which I got the pulley bone. I actually got two pulley bones since Mama fried two chickens in case either Champ and Sallie Jane or Lucee and Harlan Junior got to come. They did come to visit on in the afternoon but they did not get to come to eat because they came last Sunday and today they all had to go to the inlaws instead of here.

Anyway after the chicken and beans and mashed potatoes and fried apples Mama brought out my favorite spice cake which she had made just for my birthday. It was real fine.

Besides all of this Grandpa sent me a book called Plutarch's Lives from Nashville Tennessee. It is about the stories of some old Roman people and it is my first book of my own.

In the afternoon Father said he wanted to talk to me about the riting out of my life. He said that I had passed the first great test of riting which is called Discipline. I have passed it because I have written ever single Sunday for one entire year.

Now he says that I should start to pay more attention to what I rite. That means first of all that I now have to decide when to rite instead of just riting ever Sunday. This is because he says that good things to rite about could happen at any time on any day of the week and a riter should be ready to rite when things happen and not just because it is Sunday again.

It has made me feel very good to know that I have accomplished this and I will try to do my own very best to keep on the lookout for good things to rite about and then to do it at the right time.

I feel much older than when I was only ten.

Tuesday, January 3, 1911

Already I have started to rite about things when they happen because when we went back to school on today something happened. Mrs. Melville gave a Christmas present to the school.

She told us that she had ordered it from Boston Massatusetts and wanted to give it to the school at the Old Folks Christmas party but it did not come in time to do that so she brought it today. She could of waited for Old Christmas but today is OK. Her present is called a Globe of the World.

Now we have been learning that the world is round ever since Mr. Robinson was our teacher. But I still thought that the countries were on the front of the world and the ocean was what went around on the back or on the bottom at least. Now with the globe of the world we can see that countries are spread out completely around the world.

The Globe is like a small ball which is about as big as my head if my head was actually round which it is not. It sets on a wooden base but you can pick it up and look at it all over. The oceans are blue and the countries are all painted in colors except that the North and South Poles are painted white for all of the snow and ice that is there. It must of been a expensive thing for Mrs. Melville to get but she says it came from a benefacter and she only had to pay to have it sent in the mail. It is surely helpful for teaching about the world.

I could already point out the U S A because we did already have a map of that on the wall and also a old flat map of the world. So I could identify the U S A by seeing the state of Florida sticking out into the ocean.

It is not the same though to see the countries where they really are. We can see Panama and now I understand why it will be a helpful thing when they can go through that canal instead of all around South America. We can also see Nicaragua where the war there is still happening.

I can hardly wait to see if I can trace the way of Mr. Roosevelt's trip around the world.

Mrs. Melville asked us if any of us would like to go somewhere on the globe besides here where we live. I was surprised as anything when Ledge Mayfield was the first one to say yes. Mrs. Mellville asked Ledge where he would like to go and he said he would like to go to Anywhere. After that I got to thinking that maybe a bully is someone who has it so bad at home he can't act up there and so he has to do it at school.

Anyway there are many places on the Globe that I have never heard of at all. It is strange for me to think that there are whole nations of people living that I have never even heard the name of or do not know one single thing about. Do they know anything at all about us here in the U S A I wonder.

I would like to be able to close my eyes and put my finger anywhere on that Globe and then to see what it looks like there. It is a good thing to have at school. It is the first school thing that I have seen Ledge interested in.

Sunday, January 8, 1911

Well I am riting on Sunday as usual but today it is a particularly good thing to do. Today is a special day for Father for the eighth of January is the anniversary of the Battle of New Orleans. Ever year Father tells all of us about this over and over again. It was in the War of 1812.

General Andrew Jackson was leading the Americans and he did not know that the war was really already over because it was in the year 1815 and they did not have any telegraphs back then.

When the British started attacking the Americans Father told us that General Jackson told the Americans not to shoot back at them until they got so close that you could see the white parts of their eyes. That was to save bullets I think from missing too many long shots.

Anyway General Jackson's men won and now that war was really over and in a few years General Jackson would start to running for the President of the U S A. It took him until 1828 to really win even though Father says that he got more votes than John Quinsey Adams got in the election of 1824. I sure do not at all understand politicks.

While I am riting on today about war I must rite that the war in Nicaragua is now over. Father read about it in the Nashville Banner today. President Taft is back in Washington now. He has called home from Nicaragua some American soldiers who were sent there to keep the peace and he has said that now General Estrada can be the President there.

Since we have that Globe of the World I can see how close to Panama the country of Nicaragua is and I think that the reason that Mr. Taft is interested in Nicaragua to start with is to keep trouble away from that canal the U S A is digging across Panama.

In politicks there is always some reason for ever thing and very offen you cannot understand that reason at all from what you can see at the start.

Sunday, January 15, 1911

This afternoon a thing happened which is both funny and terrible at the same time.

Reverend Sharpe came home with us for dinner after church. Today was our preaching Sunday. He lives in Suncrest and goes to preach at eight churches during ever month. He is here at our own church ever second Sunday on this go round.

Reverend Sharpe is a young man who is not married. He does not get paid much for preaching and we bring him home and feed him ever once in a while. This is thought to be as good as paying him as a preacher. His clothes always look worn out and so does he.

Pretty soon after Reverend Sharpe arrived Mama told that the dinner was ready and that we could ask the blessing and then bring our own plates by the stove and she would dish out the food. She has discovered that if she does it this way when we have company she can be sure that none of us takes out too much. Father asked Reverend Sharpe if he would ask the blessing.

Since all of us were standing around Reverend Sharpe asked us all to get down on the floor on our knees to pray. We did and he prayed. He prayed and prayed and prayed and prayed about ever thing and ever body until I just knew that the food was going to be either burnt or cold depending on where Mama had left it when she had to shut her own eyes for the praying.

All of a sudden Reverend Sharpe let out a big holler and jumped up and kept hollering while he danced around on one foot. The praying was over all at once and he didn't even get to say Amen. Finally he settled down and pulled off one of his shoes and there was a cooked hot apple all smashed down inside of it.

What had happened was this. While he was down and praying one of his old brogan shoes had dropped down loose from the heel of his foot. Mama had a row of hot apples roasting on the hearth in front of the fire in the fireplace. Somebody who didn't have their eyes shut had picked a hot apple up by the stem and dropped it into the preacher's shoe. Boy did he dance around a lot after that. It is a good thing that he is not a Babtist or he would be in trouble just for the dancing around of it.

Father tried and tried to find out who had done it but ever one of us just swore that we had our eyes closed and didn't see a thing.

Finally Father said the Amen hisself and we all ate. But Reverend Sharpe didn't eat much. He kept looking around out of the corner of his eyes like he was not sure what might happen next and then he left pretty soon after the eating was over.

When he was gone Father gave us a good talking to about the apple business. He said that he would like to punish whoever had done it but that he didn't want to punish a innocent person. He said that if whoever did it didn't fess up that there would finally be a way to find out who it was and that then there would be trouble for sure. Nobody still said a word.

I guess that I will likely have a hard time going to sleep just trying to figger out who of my brothers or sisters might of done that. I just can't figger it out.

Monday, January 16, 1911

The truth is out. Father has found out about the apple business just like he said he would.

When we all got home today from school Father gathered us together and told us that he had a way to find out who did it. He told us to all come out on the back porch and he would show us. While we waited on the porch he went out to the hen house and came back with a chicken under his arm.

Father told us that chickens do not lie and that is why they cackle when they lay a egg so that they won't even be keeping that a secret. He took the chicken and put her under the big black washpot which Mama has in the back yard. Then he told us to all come into the kitchen.

Father told us what we had to do. He said that one at a time we had to go out in the yard and go up to the washpot where the chicken was. Then we had to put our hands on the pot and say our name and say I did not do it over and over three times. He said that the chicken could tell from your voice and your hands if you were lying and that it would cackle when the guilty one was there and that we would all hear it because that chickens do not lie.

We went out there one at a time while nobody else watched the one who was there. But we did listen. I was scared to death at my turn for fear that the chicken would make a mistake or not know for sure which one I was. It never cackled.

The chicken never did cackle at all and when we were all back inside Zeb said that it looked like nobody did it. Then Father said for us all to show our hands. I saw right then what had happened.

Ever one of us had black hands from the washpot but not Zeb. His hands were plumb clean because he was scared to death to touch the pot to start with since he was the guilty one and he just knew the chicken would holler. Father pointed to Zeb's hands and said that it looks like somebody did do it too.

He didn't whip Zeb because he said that a caught liar's conscience is the worst punisher there is. Zeb wanted a whipping so it would all be over with but Father told him to just think about it.

Later he took the pot off of the chicken and the old chicken was plumb asleep in there in the dark. I do not think that chickens care one thing in the world about telling the truth. But it was a good trick all right.

Sunday, February 12, 1911

Today is the first time that I have written on my life in nearly a whole month. I guess that I just can't think of noticing interesting stuff to rite about when I don't already know that I am going to have to rite ever Sunday afternoon to start with. When I had to do that it seemed like there was always plenty to rite about.

What I have decided from this is that from now on I will make my own self rite on Sunday afternoons just because I think that this is the best thing to do. If I do not make myself do something like this I may not hardly ever come up with nothing to rite about at all.

Anyway I am going to promise myself right now that I will rite on next Sunday so that all this week I will keep it in my head and then it will work. That is about the best plan.

Sunday, February 19, 1911

Well I am riting again. Last Sunday was Abraham Lincoln's birthday and I could have written about that but that is not what I am going to rite about now. I am riting today about what has happened this week to me.

On Friday night I had the most wonderful and I think the longest dream that I have ever had in my life. I dreamed that I was flying and it was so real that I thought that it was all actually happening until I woke up.

I was in the bed and going to sleep. I had moved my pillow and was turned over on my stomach because that is how I like to go to sleep a lot of times.

All of a sudden I was just as light as a feather and was just floating right up out of the bed. It was so amazing a thing that I don't even know what happened to the bed covers or whether I was wearing my nightshirt or anything like that. Also I do not know how the window got open there in the bedroom but it sure was open in the dream.

Anyway it was sort of like swimming in the air. It seemed like I sort of felt around with my arms and legs to see if I was going to fall and then when I knew I was going to stay up there I could just think of the way I wanted to go and I would just go flying off exactly in that very direction.

After I flew around the room a little and saw that Merry and Zeb didn't see me then I just flew right out of the window. It was dark outside but I could still see everything real good.

It was like the moon was shining down and lighting up the whole earth. I did remember thinking that I was glad it was at night so that if anybody looked up they wouldn't be able to see that I was up there a flying.

I flew around the house and out over the barn and back. Then I flew up toward the schoolhouse and over around by Champ's house and then on up by where Lucee and Harlan Junior live. I remember still seeing some lights burning in both of those houses because it was not real late at night.

After that I got a idea to just see if I could fly to where I saw a town with electrick lights. I flew fast and long and pretty soon I saw a big town all lit up and with people out on the streets in the night and with automobiles with lights on them moving in the dark. I don't know where it could of been. It could have been Nashville Tennessee or New York City or even Californya for all I know.

I thought about trying to fly to the ocean to see if I could see some ships with lights on them but I got worried that maybe there was a aeroplane up there where I was and if it didn't see me it might run right into me in the dark before I could get out of the way. So I flew on back home.

In the dream it was almost morning when I got back to the house and when I started to fly back into the bedroom somebody had shut the window in the night and I couldn't get back in. I couldn't find a window open nowhere because I started to realize that it was cold and of course all of the windows was closed. Then I started to freezing my own self. For some reason I couldn't get down to the ground out of the sky in the dream and I knew that I would have to try to stand up in the air and then I could fall to the ground.

Finally that is just what I did. I fell right down and just as I hit the ground I woke up with a big jerk and there I was right in the bed and it was time to get up. I couldn't hardly realize it was a dream for a while and I sure didn't tell nobody about it.

At the breakfast table Zeb wanted to know if I had got up and raised the window in the night because he said that he got cold and it was up and he then put it down. I said that if I did put it up I sure didn't remember it but now I do know how it got shut in that dream.

I have not told nothing at all about this to nobody but I sure would like to tell Mrs. Melville and see what she thinks about it. Also I would now not be scared to fly in a aeroplane anymore because I do know for sure what it looks like from up there.

Also I say Happy Birthday to Abraham Lincoln and also to Mama since she was fifty one years old one week before Mr. Lincoln.

Sunday, February 26, 1911

Am I ever glad on this day that we chopped all of that wood in December. Father went to Suncrest yesterday and when he came home he had bought something that we have never had before. It is a temperature thermometer that you can use to tell just how cold it actually is out of doors.

This morning when we got up it said on that thermometer that it is three degrees below zero. Now just knowing that has made me so cold that no matter what I do I just cannot get warm.

I already knew that it was freezing because all of the water in the watering trough is frozen clean through to the bottom almost. Father has to chop it out with the ax or the livestock has to drink in the creek where it runs too fast to freeze. But we have learned at school that water freezes at a temperature of thirty two degrees on the thermometer and I just did not have any idea in the world that it got a lot colder than that.

What I had always thought is that once it got down to freezing that you did not feel any colder but that the coldness just went deeper into the insides of ever thing. Now I think that I know that it really can just get colder and colder and that you can feel it finally clear through.

Father said that it may not of been a good idea to get that thermometer because he said that he was sure that it had been this cold before even during this winter but that when we didn't know how cold it was we didn't act so foolish about it. He may be right about that.

At any rate I sure am glad that we cut plenty of firewood and I am glad that Father has us to stack a lot on the porch when the weather breaks so we have it for the bad times.

The good thing about today is that Mama made the last cracklin bread of the year. She has been saving the last cracklins that are the little bits of meat left when the lard is rendered. She always saves some for the late winter when the other meat starts running out. She puts them into the batter for the cornbread before it is baked. I do love the way that the cracklins make the bread taste. I am willing to endure a little bit more of the cold weather knowing that is the time when Mama always makes that cracklin cornbread.

Sunday, March 5, 1911

Well now the Republicans are having more problems than ever. Father has read to us that a man named Mr. Robert LaFollett who is a Senator from the State of Wisconsin has actually convinced a lot of the Republicans who do not like Mr. Taft to split off from the main Republicans and form a new organization of Republicans. They call it a new party but it is actually a kind of politicks club and not anything like a party that would be a occasion to go to. Anyway it is called the Progressive Party.

It sounds to me like this is something like when the Babtists get mad at one another and then they split up and make new churches. Sometimes they get back together again but most of the time they are happier when they are all split up.

The Babtists argue about stuff like angels and how much water was used on Jesus when he got baptized. I don't know what the Republicans argue about. Maybe some of them are mad about how much water it takes just for Mr. Taft to take a bath in the White House. I don't know.

Father says that he wonders which bunch of Republicans Mr. Roosevelt will join up with. If the new Progressive Party would run him to be the President I bet he would go over to them. But Father says that he thinks that Mr. LaFollett wants to run for the President and that is the reason he started his own party to begin with. So maybe Mr. Roosevelt will just stay on as a regular Republican.

Anyway I am still sorry for poor old Mr. Taft. He can't seem to get anything actually going his way. I don't think that he is all to blame that all of the other Republicans got beat. But Father is happy about it all. He says that the more ways the Republicans divide up the better chance it is to get a Democrat for the President in 1912. That is the way it works in politicks.

Sunday, March 12, 1911

I have missed a few days of school this week for the first time this year. I have had just a terrible bad case of the grip and though the grip will not kill you Mama is so scared from that new monia that I had last winter that she has made me stay home from school since Wednesday. Now I am a lot better and am sure that I will get to go back on tomorrow.

It has been bad to have to miss this week because we have been learning a new thing from Mrs. Melville which I know will surely help me in the riting out of my life. It is called Quotation Marks for the making of talk in your riting. This is a thing that I have tried to figger out a way to do in riting in the past but could not figger out. Now that she has told us about it I realize that this is seen all of the time in books that you read but nobody had ever told me what the marks were for or what they were called.

Quote marks look like this ".

Now when you want a character in your riting to say something hisself all you have to do is to put these marks before and after what he says and then tell who is saying it. This will be most helpful to me in my life riting.

Today when Father was reading the news paper to us I was thinking of a way to use the quotation marks in telling about what happened. Father was reading to us and his reading sounded like Quotes to me. He read this report to us from the digging on the Panama Canal.

This is what I learned. A Colonel George Goethals which is a name hard to spell is the man in charge of the digging of the canal. He said "I think that we ought to fortify the area where the canal is being built." He said "It just takes too much money to build this canal and it is too important to leave it unprotected and let somebody who is just mad at the U S A come along and tear it up. It ought to be fortified."

Now that is the way to use Quotes to make your riting sound like people are talking.

It is now time for me to go to sleep and besides Mama has just come in and said "Med if you feel better in the morning it will be OK for you to go on back to school."

See that is good riting for sure.

Sunday, March 19, 1911

The best news of the day all week was that we got a long letter from Grandpa. He is making his plans to come on back from Nashville Tennessee to spend the summer with us. I was afraid that pretty soon he was going to get too old to keep coming back and forth. If he got too old while he was here and had to stay here all of the time that would be all right with me. But if he got too old while he was in Nashville Tennessee and had to stay there with Aunt Louise even through the hot summers that would not at all be fair to anybody.

Anyway he wants to come on back earlier than he came last year and the most exciting thing is that Aunt Louise has written too and said that why don't we just come to Nashville Tennessee for a visit and bring him home with us. That would not be a thing for me to believe if we were to go to such a city.

Father and Mama have both said that it is a good idea but that we just cannot afford to do such a thing both as to spending the time and the money it would take. But Father has another idea. He has said that if we know exactly when Grandpa is coming that we could go to Suncrest and all ride the Narrow Gauge to Erwin Tennessee and meet the main Clinchfield Train line there and get Grandpa.

I have seen the Narrow Gauge train almost ever time I have ever been to Suncrest. But I have never actually thought about getting to ride on it. I see people get on and off of it but I thought you had to have somewhere to go to do that. But Father says that we can ride it to Erwin even if we don't have anywhere to go because we can take it down there just to get Grandpa and have the experience.

It is not sure if we will really do this and I am not sure who all will go if we do. There will be Mama and Father of course and also me and Merry and Zeb and the twins and Annie Laurie. What I don't know is if Father means to take Champ and Lucee or if that would mean having to take Sallie Jane and the baby and also Harlan Junior. I don't know when your family is not your family anymore where things like this are concerned.

Besides that I know that Lucee could not ride on a train because she will be having that baby in less than two months and even if somebody could help her get up on the train I think that it would be too dangerous for her to ride on a train.

I am not sure when this trip is going to happen but it seems certain that it will happen. I will tell Mrs. Melville about it and will think some about it each day. Maybe another year we can go all the way to Nashville Tennessee.

Sunday, March 26, 1911

This week Father plowed the garden for the spring and on yesterday we planted peas and turnips and greens and onions. Soon another time of warm weather will come and I will be very happy for that.

It is settled. On next Friday I will get to miss school and we will go to Suncrest and ride the Narrow Gauge to Erwin to get Grandpa from the L and N line that gets to Erwin Tennessee from Nashville Tennessee. When I asked Mrs. Melville if I could make up my work early and get to miss on that day she told me that a trip like that would teach me more in one day than she could tell me in school in more than a week and that there would not be any work to make up. She certainly is a good and smart teacher.

Anyway all of us are going and this week the hardest thing to do is to keep from just thinking about nothing at all but that all through the entire long day.

Sunday, April 2, 1911

We did it. We rode the Narrow Gauge from Suncrest to Erwin Tennessee and back home again.

We got up early Friday morning to get into Suncrest before nine o'clock because the train we were riding leaves at 9:20 ever morning. We took King and Outlaw with the wagon to haul us all and then we left them at the blacksmith's shop since we wouldn't be back until today. Mama had got up real early and fried some chicken and made up a picnic to eat on the train.

We got our tickets and waited on the platform by the railroad station. This train is a freight train mostly but it does have some passenger cars on the back end of it. It is a big steam locomotive that says "Baldwin" on it and is partly painted green but mostly is just plain black.

Our whole family got in a car with wooden seats that had backs that folded back and forth so you could fold them to look either way in your seat. We fixed two of those seats on each side of the aisle so we all faced each other and we rode that way. It took nearly four hours to get to Erwin.

Grandpa's train had not got there yet from Nashville and so we took our picnic which we had not ate on the train and we ate it under some trees in the middle of town. After that we walked around the town some and looked into windows until it was time for Grandpa to come. There were automobiles ever where and wires were strung up on poles which Father said were called telegraph poles even if some of them did have electricity wires on them.

Grandpa's L and N train was a lot bigger all over than our train and we were glad to see him. After he came we went to a boarding house and got a room with four beds in it to spend the night in. The woman that ran the boarding house fed us our supper. Her name was a Mrs. Miller and she was a widow woman.

Yesterday morning we went back to town and walked all around some more and looked at ever thing there. The stores were all closed but the train was going to run anyway even if it was Sunday. The only thing we saw that was open besides the train station was the Post Office and Father says that they are open ever day.

The train back to Suncrest left at 10:15 and took as long to get back or even longer than it did for us to get to Erwin to start with. That Mrs. Miller where we stayed fixed us some food to eat on the train and this time we did actually eat on the train ride itself. We even had a birthday cake for the twins that Mama and Mrs. Miller made. Tomorrow is their birthday and I guess the whole trip feels like a kind of birthday present to them.

We got back to Suncrest about 3:00. Since it was Sunday Father had to go to the blacksmith's house to get the horses and wagon back. Then we rode home.

I feel pretty sore from that train riding and Grandpa says that he is just wore out. He looks a lot older than he did last year. I think that I remember how he looks when he gets here ever year more than what he looks like when he leaves and he does surely look like a old man.

But I am glad to have him back and I will never forget riding that train or going to the big town of Erwin Tennessee either one.

Sunday, April 9, 1911

This week Grandpa went to school with me on Wednesday. He did not go to learn anything but instead he went to tell all of the pupils about something which he did while he was in Nashville Tennessee. He had told us about it at home after he got back here and when I told Mrs. Melville about it she said that he should come to school and tell ever body so they could go there in their minds. What it was was a aeroplane show.

Just about two weeks before he came back to be with us for the summertime Grandpa went to a aeroplane show in Nashville Tennessee. Aunt Louise did not want to go and she did not want for him to go either because she said it was dangerous. So he slipped out of her house and rode a streetcar out to the fairgrounds where it was to be held. It did cost fifteen cents to ride that streetcar but I know that was worth it all by itself. It runs on electricity.

At the fairgrounds he paid another twenty five cents to get in to see the aeroplane show.

Grandpa told us that there were six different aeroplanes there. He said that there was one aeroplane made in France and called a Bleriot or something like that. Most of the aeroplanes were Wright Aeroplanes named for the Wright Brothers who I guess made them or at least had them made. But the best aeroplane of all was called a Curtiss Biplane and had two wings and belonged to a flyer named Mr. Lincoln Beachy.

Grandpa said that they got to walk all around the fairgrounds field and look right at the aeroplanes and even touch them. He says that they are made out of frames of wood and wire and are covered with cloth which is painted so it is stiff from the paint. I just cannot imagine how something made of cloth could be strong enough to hold up a man in the air. He also said that he got to see the engines of the aeroplanes and that they are not like train engines but burn gasoline and make a terrible noise when they are started up which is done by one man turning the propeller while the pilot is inside ready to take off.

After all the looking was over Grandpa said that they did the flying show. Each aeroplane flew one at a time and some of them even did some tricks. He said that one of the aeroplanes flew down and into one door of one of the buildings at that fairground and went right through it and out of the other door and then back up into the air again. He also said that they could turn way up on their sides in the air when they made curves in the air.

The great finalley of the aeroplane show was a race at the end. Grandpa said it was like a figure eight race around two big poles at different ends of the fairgrounds. All of the six aeroplanes got into the air and they all flew around and around the course. I don't know if one of them won or not or if it was just all a show.

Anyway I am glad that he came to school because that meant that I got to hear all about it again without even asking. And my Grandpa is now a sort of hero here since he had both seen and touched a aeroplane. He is the oldest one in our family and he has done and seen more things of the modern world than any of the rest of us.

Easter Sunday, April 16, 1911

Today is Easter and it was a very beautiful day. Sometimes Easter is as cold here as the wintertime but on today it looked like summer had come.

After church we had a big dinner and both Champ and Sallie and Junior and Lucee and Harlan Junior got to come. Lucee looks just like she is about to pop. They are saying that it still may be another month before that baby is born but I do not see myself how she can stand it more than another day or two.

After dinner we had egg fights. Mama had let us boil some eggs. Then Grandpa brought out something he had got in Nashville

Tennessee for us. It was called Food Color. We put some of it in water with the eggs and they came out in colors. They were real nice for playing hide the eggs.

The egg fights were at the end. Each one of us would pick out one of our eggs. Then we would hold it by the big end and crack the little ends with another person. The one whose egg cracked the other one got both eggs to eat later.

Zeb got about all of the eggs until he slipped and dropped his fighting egg and then we all saw that he had slipped a hard shelled guinea egg in on us to fight with.

"That's as unfair as fighting with the knot off a maple tree" Father said. He made Zeb divide up all of the eggs he had won and give them all out to all of us. Mama brought some salt and we peeled the eggs and ate ever one of them right up.

It seemed almost a shame to peel and eat those pretty colored eggs. But they wont keep and so we ate them. We saw that some of the eggs had leaked some of the Food Color and with those even the white inside of the egg shell was a little bit colored in spots. I didn't know that eggs could leak but I do now.

Sunday, April 23, 1911

This day is a great and important day. Because this week we have got to be what Father calls "News paper subscribers by the mail." Father has paid a dollar and fifty cents to get the Asheville News and Gazette news paper sent by the mail right to our house here at Close Creek ever single day of the week except on Sunday for three months. That means that by spending six dollars in a year we can get the news of the entire world right here in our own community only one day after it is written up in that Asheville News and Gazette News Paper.

I do not understand a lot about how the U S mail works. What I do not understand is this. How is it that the people at the Asheville Citizen news paper learn about the news of the world as soon as it happens so that they can put it into that news paper ever day.

When I have asked Mama about this she wants to know too and so she asked Father. He and Grandpa have both told us that it is what is called the Wire Service. What that means is the telegraph. There are news paper riters all over the world who work for that Wire Service and they send the news of the world on the telegraph to all of the news papers who pay to get it.

Father says that if a news paper doesn't pay to get the Wire Service then their news is out of date before they even tell it but that the Asheville News and Gazette pays for it and so we get up to the day news.

I do love to look at the advertisements in that news paper. Now that we get a paper ever day there are plenty of them around the house for all of us to look at as much as we want to. My favorite thing is the advertisements for the automobiles.

The Asheville Motoring Company has a advertisement for a Maxwell automobile for six hunderd dollars and a Overland Model 51 automobile for $1250 dollars. They do not sell any Ford automobiles there and so I don't know where Dr. Graham got his or how much he had to pay for it.

There are also a lot of advertisements now about Easter clothing and shoes and Easter hats for ladies. Easter is next Sunday. There is even a advertisement in that news paper with a actual visible picture of a woman's corset shown right in it. But it is not shown on a woman.

Sunday, April 30, 1911

I sure do like it now that we get that Asheville News and Gazette news paper ever day. When we just got the Nashville Banner news paper once a week Father was so particular about it that none of us could touch it until he was all through with it and then if one of the neighbors happened to stop by on Sunday afternoon once he was done reading it he was likely going to give it on to one of them.

Now we get a paper almost ever day when the mail carrier comes and most of the time they are just one day old. That means that we have so many newspapers that Father doesn't even care if any of us looks at them even before he does.

I like to read the cartoon pictures in the news paper but mostly I love to read the advertising pictures. This week I have been looking at the advertising for bicycles.

I have seen some bicycles in Suncrest and there were a lot of bicycles when we rode on the train to Erwin Tennessee but I have not ever rid on one. The springtime must be the time to sell bicycles because they have had a lot of them in that newspaper. I sure would like to have one of them but even if I had the money I would not know how to go about buying one way out here in Close Creek.

There was another advertisement in the news paper this week that was a puzzle to me. It was a advertising for a State summer School for Colored Teachers and that sounded to me like it was something funny and so I asked Father what that meant. He told me about Colored People.

I have learned about slaves in school and also about President Lincoln and the War Between the States but since I have never actually seen a Colored Person I guess that I thought that was just something in a history book and not something right now. There are not any Colored People here or in Suncrest either one and if there are any in Erwin Tennessee I did not see any of them when we were there.

Father has said that there are Colored People in Asheville and then Grandpa told me that they are all over the place in Nashville Tennessee.

I have seen Indians sometimes when we go to town in Suncrest because there are Cherokee Indians not too far from right here. I wonder if I will ever see a Colored Man or Woman or a Colored Child my own age. Father says that surely I will.

Sunday, May 7, 1911

Today has been a very interesting day for learning about other people. When we went to church today nobody in all of Close Creek could of guessed who was going to be there. It was the entire family of the Mayfields. Right there sitting inside the church house were Mr. and Mrs. Mayfield along with Ledge and his big sister Darling and their other living brother who they call Bull because he is so big. That is all of the Mayfields right now since Duck was shot and killed dead for being the firestarter for all of those barn fires. Bull quit school and joined the Army a while after Duck was shot and since he is home for a visit maybe that is the reason that they all came to church on this particular day.

There wasn't nobody setting close to where they were when we got there but Mama said to Father "Cate let's us go set up there where Mildred and Whitey are." We never do set in that part of the church but we went right up there and set down right in the same row almost with them. I do not know why they had come on that one day because they never do ever come to church.

When church was over I knew that it was the day for Lucee and Harlan Junior to come home to eat with us. But Mama got Lucee over in the corner and asked her if they could go to Harlan's Mama's house for dinner and when she found out that they could do that then Mama invited all of the Mayfields to come home to our house to dinner.

Mr. Mayfield who is the one that Father calls Whitey looked like he could have just been shot with a squirrel rifle but their Mama who is called Mildred told Mama "Why thank you that would be a very nice thing to do."

The Mayfields do not have any horses and they had all ridden to church in a ox cart and so they rode on to our house right in that same ox cart.

I played out in the yard with Ledge while Mama was getting the rest of the dinner ready and without anybody else there to show off for he wasn't even so bad to have to play with.

When Mama called us all to come in and eat Mr. Mayfield would not come inside of our house. Mrs. Mayfield said that could he just eat on the porch as he got to feeling hemmed in on the inside of houses and sometimes in strange places. So Mama fixed two plates and both Father and Mr. Mayfield ate out on the porch. I have never seen anything like that happen before.

There has never been anybody in our house to eat like the Mayfields. Ledge and Bull ate like they had never had anything to eat in a year and even Darling and Mrs. Mayfield did a good job in cleaning out ever bit of food that we had in the entire house. After it was all over Mama said that she was sure that was the first real meal they had had in a long time.

I listened a lot while Mama and Father talked for a while about the Mayfields. They tried to figger out why they had come to church to start with and I wondered why Mama and Father didn't just ask them if they wanted to know but they never did do that. It all sounded to me like they were awful sorry for the Mayfields but in spite of that I am awful scared of them and especially that daddy. He may of been calmed down for one Sunday but I wouldn't want to have to be around him for much time at all. Ledge is not as bad as I thought though.

Sunday, May 14, 1911

Well this week we have learned about something very interesting at school which I have never heard of before. It is called the Census.

What that means is that ever ten years somebody counts all of the people in the country and gives a report on how many people there are to the goverment in Washington DC. What I do not know for sure is who the somebody is who does the counting but I would guess that there are a lot of counters and one person who is in charge of all of them. I do not remember being counted though.

Last year was the thirteenth time that the census had been counted in the U S A since the first time the people was counted was in 1790 right after George Washington got to be the President. They count the census ever ten years on all the years that end in a 10 or two zeros.

After all of the census people was counted last year it took until this year to add up and decide that there are 93 402 151 people in the United States of America.

What I do not know is how they account for what happens between the counting to start with and the adding up in the end. I mean that if Duck Mayfield or Mrs. Elisabeth Chambers got counted to start with then they was both dead before they were added up in the end. But when I asked Mrs. Melville about this she said that with new babies getting born all of the time that it balances out in the end.

Now the most interesting thing of all to me was this. At the same time that the counting was going on here in the U S A they were having a census in Great Britain which means in all of England and Scotland and Wales but I am not sure about Ireland.

Now I always thought that England was a big country since the U S A came out of England but that census told that only 45 216 665 people live in all of Great Britain and that is at least three countries in all and maybe four. It is just amazing to me that as new as the U S A is that there are already more than twice as many people here as in all of Great Britain. But with what is about to happen at Lucee and Harlan Junior's house I guess that I should not be surprised.

Sunday, May 21, 1911

Today Father has read to us a article in the news paper which came from the wire service in our own state capital of Raleigh. It is by the State Geologist whose name is Joseph Hyde Pratt.

The article tells that they are going to build a actual highway right through here in the mountains from the state of North Carolina into the state of Tennessee and maybe even connect into Virginia. The plan then would be to connect it somewhere to a road that is supposed to already exist and goes from New York City to Atlanta Georgia. If that is done people could go anywhere.

The reason that the state geologist is the one riting is because the road would be a natural wonder. Not only would they have to just about move entire mountains to build it but then people would see the beauty and wonders of the mountains and the waterfalls and all ever time they came through here. That geologist says that our mountains would be as famous then as the Grand Canyon or Yellowstone Park.

At first it seems like a very exciting and good idea to build such a road as this. I mean that we could go anywhere that we wanted to go and we could even save up and have use for a automobile. I am not sure that Father would be the one to learn to drive the automobile because he is so old but maybe Champ or Harlan Junior could do that. Then we could take Grandpa and all of us all the way to Nashville Tennessee if we wanted to.

But that highway also would mean that a lot of strange and maybe not so good people would be able to come right here into our mountains just if they wanted to do it. I haven't met very many strangers but from what I have heard that would not be a good idea.

I guess that the best thing all in all is that it will take a number of years to build that road if they decide to do it and they haven't even decided to do it yet. If it takes all those years then I guess we will all have time to get prepared for it and get ready to handle it. Maybe it won't happen at all and if it does we will just have to learn to live with it. I think that the Narrow Gauge ought to be good enough for anybody.

Sunday, May 28, 1911

Well today is a day that none of us in this family will ever forget. This is because that last night Lucee had that baby.

It all actually started on yesterday morning when Harlan Junior sent word to Mama that it was coming. Father said "Don't bother Martha. You ought to be calling for Doc Graham."

In spite of saying that Father and Mama and all of us packed up and went up to Lucee and Harlan Junior's house. We got there just about exactly at the time that Doc Graham got there.

"Well" Doc Graham said "At least there will be somebody to talk to while we wait."

Doc Graham went in and checked out how Lucee was making out

and when he came back out he told us that she had a long way yet to go but that we might just as well wait. We all sort of settled on the screen porch and in the kitchen and Mama wouldn't dare let any of us go in there where Lucee was getting ready to have the baby.

We stayed there the entire blessed day. About ever hour or so Lucee would start to hollering. Mama was in the room with her and Harlan Junior was out in the kitchen with the rest of us.

When Lucee hollered Harlan Junior wanted Doc Graham to go in there and do something but Doc Graham told him that Mother Nature was doing all that was necessary. Still he went in and talked to Lucee and to Mama ever long while.

After supper we all settled down to spend the night. About midnight Lucee started hollering and yelling something awful. She was not calling for Harlan Junior which was a mystery to me since he seems to have been the cause of all this what with marrying her and all. She was hollering "Mama" and Mama was already right there.

Doc Graham put some water in the stove to boil and he disappeared into that room and this time he stayed. After a good long while we heard what sounded like a slap and a baby started squalling its little head off.

In a little bit Doc Graham came out and said to Harlan Junior "It's a boy." Harlan Junior danced around and wanted to know if we could go in there. Doc Graham said that "I reckon so since the baby is yours."

We all went in there and Lucee was holding the baby in the bed with her and acting like she had not even screamed for Mama to begin with. She said "We are going to name him Cato Jefferson the Second after Father and we will call him Little Jeff."

That made ever body happy and we all stayed up just about all night long with Lucee and that baby. On this morning we did not even go to church and that is really a unusual thing for our family to do. I guess having a baby is worth a week of church.

So now we know what all that courting leads to. All I can say is that if the twins get married I sure do hope that they don't have a baby on the same day. If they do they'll be able to hear the screaming in Suncrest.

Sunday, June 4, 1911

School is out as of last Friday and I guess that it is a good thing because with that new baby getting born there has not been one single bit of attention given to school work this entire week. I do not think that Mrs. Melville cared though because we went outside a lot and she told us over and over again how much we had learned this year.

I am very happy that Mrs. Melville is going to come back to be our teacher again next year. For the summertime she is going to ride the Narrow Gauge to Erwin and catch the train up from there to Washington DC and on to New York City and then home to Boston Massachusetts to visit for awhile with her family. I guess that she will visit with the family of her drowned husband too if they are still living there. She has showed us on the globe of the world exactly where that trip will take her and we have seen it much closer and better on some more maps that are in our room.

What I think is that maybe Mrs. Melville is as anxious to get out of school as we are and that is why she has not made us work so much this last week.

Anyway we went up to Lucee and Harlan Junior's house just ever single night to take some food and look at that baby called Jeff. Father is very proud of that name and calls him "Jefferson" but Lucee and Harlan Junior just call him "Jeff."

He does seem to be a pretty nice baby but he is still not able to walk or talk. I guess that takes a while but I am not sure how long. Since I am the youngest one in our family I do not remember being around any other babies and somehow even though Champ and Sallie Jane have Champ Junior who is four years old we never did hang around him like we are doing now. I guess that is because we are related to his daddy and not his mama.

Also Merry got his diploma and got out of school for good this year but that did not get any attention at all beside of that baby. So school is out and the baby is in and that is about all there is to it.

Sunday, June 11, 1911

Well Friday was Merry's birthday. He was eighteen years old and he got a present for his birthday from Grandpa which ever single person in our family is glad that he had his birthday to get.

What he got was a baseball and a baseball bat. Actually Grandpa said that the baseball was for Merry and that the bat was for Zeb whose birthday is not until the 29th day of July but he needed to get it now to go with that ball. I hope that Zeb remembers that when his birthday comes.

We do not do much around here on birthdays except to have them and maybe get a cake from Mama. I guess that is because there are so many of us all in all that especially with husbands and wifes and new babies we could not afford to stop and have celebrations and buy presents all of the time.

Anyway we have put out bases in the yard and have got two teams. Father even said that since we went to church it would be OK if today we even played on Sunday just this one time. Ledge Mayfield came and so did Hallie Wainwright and with all of them and Harlan Junior and Champ and Father that made two good teams. Me and Ledge and Champ and Zeb played against Hallie and Father and Harlan Junior and Merry. We won the game fifteen to eleven since we were at bat first and it seems easier so far to hit the ball than to catch and throw it.

So it was a good day and from now on I will pay more attention to what it tells about baseball in the news paper since we now have a team or really two teams right here in Close Creek.

Sunday, June 18, 1911

It just seems to me like there is nothing much in the news these days except train wrecks and murders. At least one time a week there is a big story about a murder. Then a lot of times the story goes right on until the murderer is tried and hanged or put to the electrick chair.

A lot of the murders are in cities like New York City or Chicago but about once a month there is a murder story from here in North Carolina and not just in the big cities either. It seems like most of the murderers are men and they seem to murder somebody they know and usually somebody they used to even like.

Murder is a funny thing to think about. I don't think that killing the murderer stops it one bit. Because when somebody murders somebody else that is all that they are thinking about and not what might happen to them for doing it. Besides they are usually boiling mad.

Then the train wrecks. Well those do seem to happen a lot. But I guess with all of the trains that run on the rails that is bound to happen some. Probably if there ever gets to be as many people traveling by automobiles as by the trains then there might be that many automobile wrecks as well. It does not scare me any from riding the train though.

Sunday, June 25, 1911

My brother Zeb is in terrible trouble again. He has now done something which is worse than putting the hot apple in the preacher's shoe because it will take longer for it to get over with. He has given Merry a haircut.

It happened on Thursday in the afternoon when we were about to go back out to hoe in the corn and Merry got to talking about how hot it was getting to be and how he was miserable working out in the heat and the sun.

Zeb said "I can take care of that. What you need is a ventilater haircut."

Merry said "What is a ventilater haircut."

And Zeb said "I will just have to show you. It will make your head feel cooler than it has ever been."

And so Zeb went into the house and slipped in the kitchen and when Mama wasn't in there he got up in the cabinet and slipped out the hair cutting set that Father uses on us ever Saturday it seems like.

Zeb came out into the yard where we were and told Merry to come over with him behind the big rock. Once we were all there Zeb took out the hand clippers and told Merry to set real still.

Then he cut a swath right across the top of Merry's head which went from his forehead across and to the nape of his neck and made a strip just as naked as a Jaybird.

Then he ran a swath around the base of Merry's head just above his ears. Then he said "Now I am finished. Isn't that the best ventilater haircut you have ever seen."

Of course Merry couldn't see anything but when he put his hat back on he said that he could feel cool air circulating all around his head even with his hat on. He told Zeb that it was wonderful and thanked him for the haircut.

Nobody thought much about it until we came in for supper. We stopped and washed in the horsetrough before we went into the house and when we went in the kitchen door Mama hollered "Lord God somebody's scalped Merry." I think she was remembering about that time he got his head cut open with the mattock.

I never had heard Mama say anything like that before even when somebody was hurt. She seemed like she knew right off that it was Zeb that had done it.

Well all that I can say is that there was a awful lot of hard talking after that and the end of it is that Zeb has to go to church twice ever Sunday until Merry's hair grows back out and Merry doesn't have to go at all. I guess that Zeb has to go for the both of them.

Anyway it was the most interesting thing that has happened in our immediate home in a good while and until the hair grows back it is still yet a interesting thing just to see.

Sunday, July 2, 1911

On yesterday the Goat Man came through Close Creek.

At sometime nearly ever year the Goat Man comes. It is usually in the warm weather but it can be at about any time of the year and after he comes it gives us something to talk about in the other times of the year.

The Goat Man has about forty goats of different kinds and sizes and they are what he lives with. He has a little covered wagon with four wheels and that is what he lives and travels in. More than half of all the forty goats are harnessed to that wagon in a long line and they pull him along for his travels. He sleeps and lives in the wagon. The rest of the goats are tied on behind and we have seen and heard him call on them to push when the going gets rough.

The Goat Man calls out "Need a little help" and the goats tied on in the back put their heads up against the back of that wagon and push for a while.

The Goat Man smells awful. Actually you cannot really tell whether it is the actual Goat Man who smells so bad or just that the smell of all of those forty goats just goes right through everything that is around there. He has a long beard and looks like he has been wearing the same clothes for longer than he has had some of those goats.

Nobody knows where he lives or even if he has a home. He comes along and starts asking for a place to camp. When he finds a place he sets up camp and milks some of the goats and cooks his supper and spends the night and goes on the next day. If anybody wants some he will give them some of the goat milk. He does not sell it for money.

The Goat Man is actually a tinker for a living and after he gets his camp set up people take their pots and pans to him and he fixes them. He heats up what looks like a big fat wire and melts some metal to make solder and somehow he patches the holes. I don't know why the patch doesn't come out when you cook with the pan again but it doesn't. The Goat Man's hands look so hard that I think he could drop that hot solder right on him and not get blistered. He looks tough as the bark on a tree.

Father says that a lot of people think that the Goat Man is a escaped criminal or at least somebody who has been in trouble and has to stay on the run. He says that some people think that the Goat

Man has a lot of money in the wagon since he gets paid some for tinkering but doesn't ever seem to spend any of his money.

I don't know what the real truth is but I just think that the Goat Man is a man who likes to wander around and see different parts of the world and he has figgered out a way to do just that. I don't feel so sorry for him at all with all that he has probably seen and even done. I might even be like that if I had not got used to drinking cows milk and besides I have also got used to having a bath ever week dirty or not. Maybe Ledge would like to join up with him and they could go see Anywhere.

Sunday, July 9, 1911

Well now after doing all of the work of the King for one full year and getting over his daddy dying at the same time King George the Fifth of England has finally got crowned official.

They had a big party in England on Friday and at eight o'clock in the morning they did the crowning so that they would have plenty of time to do all of the other stuff that needed doing before the day was over.

I asked Father how they got the news over to this country so fast even if the crowning just happened on Friday. He said that part of the reason is that the newspapers already knew what was going to happen and so they just rote about it like it was already done and over. The other part of the reason is something that I have never heard of.

Father said that because of the turning of the earth that it gets to be eight o'clock in the morning in England six hours before it is that time here and so the news gets a six hour head start to begin with. He has tried to show me with a egg and a candle what he means by that and I get that part in my head about the sun and the earth turning but I don't understand the time part. Maybe Mrs. Melville can show me in the fall of the year on the globe of the world.

Anyway we do now know that George the Fifth is the official full king and that his wife is called Queen Mary even if she is not really the ruler.

This is another strange thing about the Kings and Queens. If the King is the actual ruler then his wife is called the Queen but if the Queen is the actual ruler then her husband is just called a Prince like with Queen Victoria and Prince Albert. I don't understand this but I do know that it is just one of the ways that men and women do not seem to be called on as equal in the world. My Mama however is the equal to anybody.

Father read that at the crowning there were a lot of threats and protests from people who do not want a King anymore. I asked him about this and he said that all over a lot of the world there are revolutions and people are wanting to get to do what they think is best for them instead of following a King even if the King is a good one. I guess I can agree with that idea.

Besides that all of the other Kings and Queens and Princes in Europe were at the crowning except one from Portugal. That is because they have had one of those revolutions lately and I guess that there was not a king left to go to England after that.

Father said that he did not think that Mr. Taft went to the crowning but that there was probably somebody there in his place. I think he might have sent Mr. Roosevelt since he is about the closest thing to a King that the United States has had for a while and I guess he already knows most of those other Kings and Queens.

Anyway it is interesting to me and I also think that there may be a new world coming where ever body will get to do what they want to do.

Sunday, July 16, 1911

Yes the world is changing. Early this week Father started getting very excited reading the news. He says that there is a new amendment to the constitution of the U S A and that from now on the voters will get to elect the senators.

Of course I used to think that this was the way it was done anyway but it turns out that it was not. In truth voters elect the state Legislature and those men then pick the senators from that state to serve for the next four years. What was happening on the day that senators were elected was that ordinary people were just watching to see what the state ones were going to do. This new way is much more fair and the other new thing is that once people elect a senator he is in for six years.

There are only men senators and I guess that is because Father has told me that women are not allowed to vote. They never have been. But in the world that is changing even that may change because Father read to us of big groups of women marching around in cities pushing for the right of women to vote.

This part I think started in England where there had been women Queens in the past and with their Congress which is called the Parlament the women there want to get voted in just like the old Queens heired their way in. That is only fair.

Now the idea is come to the U S A and women here are marching around for the same reason. I think that women like Mama and Mrs. Melville could certainly vote as good as men could and besides they would not put up with some of the silly ways of politicks that go on now. Maybe it will come to pass.

Sunday, July 23, 1911

It is always so much fun when Grandpa is here. He wanted ever body to have a big picnic for the Fourth of July and so we did. Grandpa said it is because he is getting so old that he thinks that ever time he comes for the summer it may be his last time so he wants to get the family together ever time we can. I do not like to think about his reason for wanting to do this but I am glad that we do it just the same. And besides this year we had a new family baby for ever body to play with.

Besides the Fourth of July this week Grandpa has taught me how to make a knife. He said that the knives we make are always better than modern store bought knives and besides that a boy like me could learn to make his own knife when he could not afford to buy one.

Out in the barn on the wall is a piece of a old crosscut saw blade which is saved for the steel to be used in making knifes. We took that old saw blade and laid it across a stump in the yard and Grandpa let me trace out with a pencil the shape of the knife blade I wanted to make. He said to make one side of the blade run right along the edge of the metal so we wouldn't have so much cutting to do.

Then we went to the anvil and Grandpa got a cold steel chisel. We took turns striking the line I had drawn with the chisel until finally we had cut off the rough knife blade from the rest of the old saw blade. That chiseling seemed like it took half a day.

The next thing was to make the handle. We did that out of walnut because it is my favorite wood and that part was not very hard. The hard part was sawing in a vise the slot for the blade to go into. I asked Grandpa to do most of this part.

After we got the blade to fit Grandpa drilled two holes through the handle and the part of the blade that was in it. Then he cut off two nails until they just fit through the holes and braided the ends down tight until that blade is now in the handle. He said "That's just as tight as Dick's hat band and that's the way we want it."

Then the sharpening started. After showing me how to start he turned that part over to me and I have been working on it for three days. I have spent almost all of that time working with a file to bring that sawmetal to a edge. I have filed until I have blisters on my hands and finally it is coming sharp. The hardest part is keeping it even from one end to the other.

Grandpa says that when it is as sharp as I can get it with the file he will show me how to start honing it on the whetrock. Then it will be finished.

After the knife itself is finished Grandpa said that Mama can teach me how to make a leather sheath to carry it in.

This has been a good thing to learn how to make something that I didn't know how to make before. Especially something that I have wanted and needed for a long time. Besides this I now know why people take good care of their knifes. Because they do not want to have to make another one.

Even so Grandpa says that if the knife sharpening man ever comes through we will get a real tempered edge put on the knife that nobody else could do. Until then I still think that it is really fine.

Sunday, July 30, 1911

It seems like it is getting to be the middle of the summer now and it is really good and hot. I sure do like the summertime.

This past week the blackberries really got ripe and we spent two different days picking blackberries and working with them. Grandpa is the leader of the blackberry picking but Mama also went with us and Father went on one of the days.

Ever body in the family has a bucket or a tin when we go picking. We have our favorite places which we watch all through the year and wait to go back to when the ripening time comes.

Our biggest and favorite patch is up on the side of Horse Field Mountain. There is a huge open space where there have not been any trees for a long time and the blackberries have taken over. In the wintertime Father and Zeb and Merry go up there and cut paths through the blackberry briars so that there will be trails for us to get to a lot more ripe berries when the time comes. This is important because the blackberry briars are so prickly that you couldn't get actually through them if you had to and you miss a lot of berries that way. It is OK though because the bears surely get the ones that we miss.

There are three things to watch out for when you are picking. One is bears which you actually never hardly ever see but there is always the possibility of it and besides Zeb and Merry are always shaking the bushes close to the twins and hollering "Bear got you."

The real thing to watch out for that I do not like is snakes. I guess that the snakes know that birds and mice are around those ripe berries and they sometimes crawl right up in the blackberry briars to wait and you can run right into one of them face to face. It does not matter to me if it is a king snake or a black snake instead of a poison one because in that first minute before you can see what kind of snake it is it has already scared the life out of you.

The third problem thing is one that you cannot really watch out for. That is chiggers. They are so little that you can't even see them but if they burrow up under your skin it is the most miserable itching thing in this world. This year Grandpa has brought us some sulphur powder from Nashville Tennessee and we tied strings around our britches legs and our sleeves and shook some of that sulphur powder inside our clothes and I did not hardly get any chiggers at all. Mary Adeline did not want any of that powder on her and so she got the chiggers meant for all of us and is in bad shape. Mama rubs lard on her and she says that will smother the chiggers to death.

Anyway we got a lot of blackberries and we have eaten all of them that we want to eat. We have ate them plain and we have ate them in a pie and Mama has made a lot of blackberry jelly for the wintertime. Also Grandpa and Father have started some blackberry wine but not very much of that and we have bottled up some juice to keep because it cures the diarrhea when you get that.

I actually like raspberries better than the blackberries but we just do not have many of them to find. Usually we just eat the raspberries as we pick them a little earlier than this. But blackberries are almost a staple food for us both now and in the winter jelly time.

Also yesterday was Zeb's birthday so now the ball bat is officially his.

Sunday, August 6, 1911

Well it seems that this house cannot be without politicks for even a single day. All this week Father and Grandpa have been talking about who ought to run for the next President from the Democrats.

It all started when Father was reading about the new rules for electing the senators and the news paper story said that about ever one of the members of the Congress who talked about the new rules said something about the next President who they said ought to be Champ

Clark.

Champ Clark is the Speaker of the House of Repersenatives which means that he is like the President of them. He runs the House of Repersenatives and tells each person when he can talk and when he has talked enough. It sounds like ever one of the Senators in Washington wants him to run against Mr. Taft from the Republicans.

Father and Grandpa are both for Champ Clark it sounds like but still Father wants to know more about Woodrow Wilson from New Jersey.

Now this is what beats all. Grandpa said that maybe Father ought to run hisself for the North Carolina House of Repersenatives in the elections next year. Grandpa said that ever body in Close Creek and about all of Suncrest County would vote for him and that he could do a good job. Grandpa said that he would even stay here all winter and help take care of things while Father was gone to Raleigh if he was to run and win.

I don't know what to think about all of this. Up until right now it did not sound like politicks was real but just almost like a story for people to read and talk about. But if our own Father should run and even get elected and go off to Raleigh for several weeks then maybe politicks will turn into something real and we would have to believe it. Father might even get written about in the newspaper. Whatever way it comes out it does make hearing the news more interesting. And if it should happen the way they are talking about it then I would surely like it if Grandpa could stay here all through the winter whether we need his help or not.

One other interesting thing is that since I have been paying attention to the baseball news after we got that ball and bat I have heard that some men actually get paid for playing baseball. I have never heard of the idea of anybody getting paid for playing something. It is a modern world if that can happen.

It certainly is a lot of good help having Grandpa around here for sure. I just hope that Father does get in the Legislature so that Grandpa will have to stay. For example this week he has directed the planning and making of a new outhouse for Lucee and Harlan Junior.

Grandpa said that with the new baby here and with the old outhouse left behind by Mrs. Elisabeth Chambers when she died being fallen in and for just one person anyway it was time to build a new and proper outhouse for Lucee. He said it was like a present from him to her and since this month was the anniversary of her and Harlan Junior getting married the present could just be for that.

He got me and Zeb and Merry to help and we went on up to Lucee's house and he told her not to look out the back window until he told her to look and he would have a surprise for her. It took three days of not looking for the surprise to get built.

First Grandpa picked the place. It was uphill from the house and a little behind it but still considerably below where the springhouse is so that the outhouse wont interfere with the good water from the spring even when it rains and soaks the ground.

Then he marked off the hole and all four of us took turns digging until we had a hole that was just about square and deep enough that the last one digging couldn't get out without some help from somebody else. We threw all of the dirt down in a gully over behind where we were digging so it wouldn't make a lot of mud around the new outhouse when it rained. All of that digging took up the first day of our working mostly because it was hot and especially Grandpa had to stop over and over again to rest and drink water.

On the early morning of the second day we started the serious carpentering. Grandpa put together the outside ledger boards and held the floor joists in place while Zeb and Merry got down in the hole and nailed everything together. Then we built most of the actual outhouse itself right up to putting a slanting roof over it after leaving a little air space for ventilation up near the top.

I asked Grandpa why we weren't making the outhouse like it was square and he said that for a family outhouse you ought to have a two holer and that's what we were making. We put in the part of the floor you would stand on and then quit for the day.

On the third actual day we did the finishing. Before we even went out there Grandpa showed us how to cut the boards that would make the sitting places and the holes. Then we built up like a sitting box with boards with the two holes on top spaced out so that there was plenty of room for two people. You could see right to the bottom of those holes down through them.

Finally Grandpa made two lids to cover the holes and put them on with hinges. I have never seen a outhouse this fancy in my life but he said that a lady ought to be able to keep one lid shut while she used the other one in privacy if she wanted to. Last of all we made the door and hung it. Grandpa bored some holes up high in it in the shape of a star instead of sawing a halfmoon the way it is in our outhouse.

Zeb and Merry thought we ought to go get Lucee to come and try it out while we watched to see if it worked all right but Grandpa wouldn't allow that. The funniest thing about the whole thing was how Grandpa told Lucee about the new outhouse. He threw some old wadded news paper down the hole of the old outhouse that was falling in and he struck a match to it and set the whole thing on fire. Then he went to the door and knocked and told Lucee to look at the outhouse that something was wrong out there.

Lucee screamed and like to of had a fit and then she saw the fire that was burning up the old outhouse. She said "What in the world is going on out there." Then she saw the new outhouse. She then like to of hugged Grandpa's neck off like she had been wanting that outhouse awful bad but couldn't say anything bad about the old one since it came with the house and with Harlan Junior. Anyway she does like it.

After that we filled up the hole of the old outhouse and by now I know that Lucee has broke in the new one. As soon as I can get to go up there for some reason I surely am going to use it to see how good it really is. It is just another wonderful thing that Grandpa has made happen since he is here.

Sunday, August 20, 1911

Yesterday we all went into town to Suncrest and on the way home Father told all of us some of his ideas about building roads from different parts of the country into the towns. It seems like a funny time of the year to talk about improving the roads because this time of the year is the time when the roads are all in the best shape of any time. It is dry and hot and except for the dust there is no problem at all in going to town or about anywhere else.

I think that the time to talk about improving the roads would be thought of in the wintertime when it freezes and mushes up all of the time or in the spring when the raining makes one solid mudhole which goes from Close Creek all the way to town. What I think is that maybe Father is practicing some of the ideas that he might try out as a politishun if he decides to really run for the Legislature in 1912. That is what I think.

Anyway he told us that there are plans to build a actual highway all across the whole state of North Carolina and that if it is finally built it will come surely all of the way to Asheville and may connect on over into Tennessee. If that should happen then it could not be too far away from where we live and if we could get to it we could go anywhere.

Father's idea is that the state ought to build up this one main state road and then that the people in all of the small towns and communities ought to raise money to build their own roads to that big road. Father says that it would take a lot of money to do that and that if he were in the Legislature he could call for a local road building tax to take care of all of that.

I remember that he read to us in the paper about a idea for using prison convicts for the labor of building roads. The article said that since all convicts have to work anyway it would be a good use of their work. It said that at the present time the prison convicts work on farms to raise their own food but some people have the idea that it would save more money to buy the food since our state raises plenty of that and then to get those convicts to do the road building work. I think that would work since a lot of them are mean and would have to be pretty strong. I would bet that it would do killers and robbers more good to shovel on the road building than to just hoe corn and beans which is not like being in prison at all but just like real life.

Anyway Father says that the idea would be fine for the state road but that people would not want those convicts working right in local communities on our small roads. Whatever happens though it would be a good thing in the wintertime to think that we might get better roads to help us go to town.

I have never thought about where the roads we have now come from. It seems like that they must have just been here to begin with. Maybe they started out as trails by the Indians and just got wore out into roads. But in the modern world we will have to have actual planned and built roads even if convicts have to do the work.

Maybe Father should run for the Legislature and get some of his ideas started down there.

Sunday, August 27, 1911

I do like living very much right where we live here at Close Creek but over and over again there are times when Grandpa tells about things in Nashville Tennessee that I would like to get to do or try out some of the things that you could do in a city.

One of the things that I would like to do in a city is to go to a moving picture. I know that they have moving picture shows in Asheville and there may even be one in Erwin Tennessee but I do not know about that. Anyway I sure would like to see one of them.

Grandpa told us that he has been to see more than one of those motion pictures in Nashville Tennessee. The last one that he told us about is just about the most interesting thing that I have ever heard of in my life. Grandpa went to see what he told us was called a Double Feature moving picture. He said that it was a education all by itself.

One of the moving pictures that Grandpa saw was called The Blowing Up of the Battleship Texas. In the moving picture the

Battleship Texas was used as the target for a made up battle held by the United States Navy. The made up battle was used to teach fighters how to do a war if they ever have to do it for real. I know that they learned from it but I just cannot imagine just taking a real ship and blowing it up for learning even if it is a old and out of date one.

Grandpa said that you could see the flashes and the fire shoot out of the big guns and that it was so clear that you could almost imagine that you could hear the sound of it. I can just imagine that if Mr. Thomas Edison really does get sound into moving pictures that it would really be something to see and hear the sound at the same time.

The other moving picture that Grandpa told us about on that Double Feature Moving Picture was one called The Panama Canal. It showed all about the building of the canal and you could see how much of it is finished and a lot about how the canal is getting built.

I did not understand how you know what is going on in the moving picture and wondered if somebody was there to tell about it. But Grandpa said that there is printing on the bottom of each of the pictures to tell what is going on and even has the quotations of what some of the people are saying. He said that there is a organ player up in the front of the theater and that the organ player watches the moving picture and plays music to go along with it.

With those words and all of that music I now do not know what the purpose would be in having sound to go with the moving picture. I did not understand before Grandpa told me that there is already sound there without Mr. Edison's invention.

Anyway I sure would like to see one of those moving picture shows. Maybe one day I will get to go to Nashville Tennessee and Grandpa can take me since he knows how and maybe in the modern world of the future there will even be a moving picture building in the town of Suncrest.

Sunday, September 3, 1911

We had a interesting visit this week from part of the Mayfield family.

On Wednesday about the middle of the morning I was out in the yard playing with Annie Laurie when up came Mrs. Mayfield and Ledge and his sister whose name is Darling. They were not in their wagon the way they usually travel but were walking.

Mrs. Mayfield came up to me and Annie Laurie and asked us if Ledge could play with us while she visited with our Mama. That was fine with us because on that last visit I had learned that Ledge was not so bad if you had him out of school where he couldn't show off and at this time of the year he has been out of school for the whole summer and is probably not so bad.

Anyway Ledge did play with me and Annie Laurie and their mama and sister knocked on the door and set on the porch for a long time and talked with our Mama. Ever time we got up close to the porch Mama told us to go on away that they were talking and acted like it was real private talking on top of that.

One or two times when I looked up there toward the porch it looked like Mrs. Mayfield was crying. She seemed like she was wiping her face with her apron and she would put her head down like she couldn't talk and look at Mama at the same time. Some of these times the sister Darling would set real close to her and sort of hang on to her.

Anyway Ledge and Annie Laurie and I got along right well. We played rollybat with that new ball and bat and then a little hide and seek. He is not such a bad boy and this year in school I am going to try out being his friend. I do not know about the sister at all. I have never heard of anybody with the actual name of Darling before.

I don't think I have ever heard grown up people do such quiet talking as Ledge's mama did with our Mama. They talked about all of the afternoon and I did not hear them laugh for a single time and that is just not natural at all. I am afraid that it must be real hard living at that Mayfield house and I sure do wonder what the talking is about. But I guess that it is not any of my business.

After a long time of that private talking she gathered up Ledge and they went on off. I heard Mama ask all three of them if they would stay and eat dinner with us. Ledge looked like he hoped that they would but their Mama said "No we better get back home before Whitey knows that we are here. He wouldn't like it a bit."

I do not understand why a man would not like for his wife and children to share a meal with neighbors. The Mayfields are funny people.

Mama did not say one thing to Father about the visit and it didn't seem right for me or Annie Laurie to talk about it until she said it first. It was a funny time all right.

Sunday, September 10, 1911

I just cannot decide what I actually think about aeroplanes. The idea of flying through the air is certainly a exciting thing to think about. And the mechanical interest of these machines that I have heard about and heard Grandpa tell about from that time that he went to the aeroplane show in Nashville is something to think about. But then I do also think about the dangerousness of that flying through the air and even of being close to aeroplanes.

Father has read to us in the Asheville Gazette about a terrible aeroplane accident in France. It seems that a number of French aeroplanes were starting a aeroplane race which was to go from Paris in France to Madrid in Spain. It was a big thing and a lot of politishuns and other official and important people were there to look at the aeroplanes start the race.

Four of the aeroplanes took out and got on their way just fine. The fifth aeroplane was one flown by a flyer named Mr. Train. His aeroplane took off just fine and started climbing up into the sky.

The news paper story said that just then Mr. Train seemed like he lost control of the aeroplane and it first looped back around and then crashed straight down into the crowd of people who were on hand to watch the beginning of the race.

Now the very place where it crashed down was where the French government officials were gathered to watch the start of the race. The crash of the aeroplane killed the Minister of War on the spot. His name was Mr. Bertow. The crash also injured the Premier who is like the President of France. He is Mr. Monis and the news paper said that he is hovering between life and death.

The funny thing about the news paper article is that it did not even tell whether Mr. Train who was the pilot either lived or died in the crash of the aeroplane. But it was in all certainly a terrible thing.

I guess that ever good new and modern invention has some basic problem that comes with it.

So that is why I can not figger out what I really think about aeroplanes. I guess that I am glad that there are not some of them around here so that I might have to decide whether to ride on one or not as that would be hard to decide. It would not be easy like deciding to ride in Doc Graham's automobile. If the aeroplane day ever comes I will have to decide then. But I will always think about the dangers of getting killed even from just watching.

Sunday, September 17, 1911

School starts back on tomorrow and this afternoon we have had a time that makes me happy to be getting on back to school. Our entire family has been for a picnic down to Mrs. Melville's house.

This year Mrs. Melville really has a house of her own. There was a Mr. Rogerson who died just up above the Babtist church and he didn't have any wife or children either one so that there was not anybody to heir his land. He left it to a nephew of his and the nephew had a house already and so he sold it to Mrs. Melville. I guess that she must have some money from her family in Boston Massachusetts.

Anyway it is a real nice little frame house and it has a fine big yard in the back that goes down to a pretty little creek. There is a white wooden bridge over that creek and it is just a fine place for a picnic.

Mrs. Melville just bought the house and got it fixed up to live in about a month ago and last week she sent around and invited all of the families which have children in school to bring some food to share and have a big picnic at her house on Sunday afternoon which was today.

I got to see some friends from school that I have not really seen all of the summer and it was really good to see Mrs. Melville and realize that she will be our teacher again this year.

Anyway she said that the parents and the children ought to all play games together. That was a new idea to a lot of those there but we all did it because she is the teacher and you do what the teacher says. So kids and parents both played kick the can and a big game of hide and seek. We also played Zero and Sally Down the Alley and Down to Cairo. Boy was it fun to see the grown ups play and it was fun to play with them. Father can really kick that can.

The Mayfields were all there but Mr. Mayfield wouldn't play the games. In fact after the eating was over he rounded them all up and took them home. I wanted at least for Ledge to get to stay. But he did not.

Mrs. Melville made a little speech about how she was looking forward to school and then our Father made a longer speech about how we were all glad to have her for our teacher. I think he was practicing some more for politicks.

So there will be twenty two children in school this year in all and tomorrow we will get our start. I am going to try to work up into the seventh reader as soon as I can.

Sunday, September 24, 1911

It is a good thing to be back in school for a new year with Mrs. Melville. I did get put into the seventh reader right from the start of the first day and so that puts me as a seventh grader overall. Ledge is only in the sixth reader and he is two years older than I am. I wish that he would work harder in school so we could have the same reader. But maybe he's not allowed to do school work whenever his daddy is around.

This year Mrs. Melville wants me to read a lot more than just the reader we have for school. She says for me to read the news paper each day and that I can make what she calls reports on the news of the world to our entire school about what is happening. I started that this week.

My first report I decided to call We are Living in a Modern World. In this report I told about two things that are the proof of this. These two things are Inventions and Science.

On the subject of Inventions I have told the class of reading about a new electrick starting automobile that you do not have to crank by hand. There is a voltage battery which stores electricity and that voltage battery is hooked to a little motor which does the cranking for you. Once the automobile is running it sends the used up electricity back into the voltage battery so it can start the car up again the next time.

Now the people who need the automobile most will get to use it. What I mean is that up to now anybody strong enough to crank up a automobile was probably strong enough to walk to start with. Now this new invention means that old people and women can use automobiles and they are the ones that need them. This is part of the modern world.

A lot of the students did not even know the word Science. But I told them about it. It is not about inventing but about discovering new things about the world that have been there all of the time.

The example of science is what is called the Vitamin. We have eaten food forever but only now has Science discovered about what is called the Vitamin. The vitamin means that food is not just to fill us up but to give us particular things that we need for our bodies to work right.

They fed rats rice with the hulls rubbed off and the rats got full but they weren't healthy. Then they fed other rats rice with the hulls left on and they were fine. This means that the hulls had vitamins in them which make you healthy.

I am not sure what this all means but it does mean that it is not just eating that we need but certain kinds of eating are better than other kinds. This is science.

Anyway that was my first report on the news of the world. I should say News of the Modern World because it seems more and more like that is the right thing to call the times we are living in.

Sunday, October 1, 1911

I do not even know how to start to tell about what has happened this week. If I say that it is the worst thing that has ever happened in all of the world that would not be bad enough for how I feel about it. Let me just start and tell you the whole story.

On Tuesday of this week Zeb and Merry were mowing hay. Father and Champ were doing the raking and the stacking and I was helping out there by raking up stray bunches by hand and putting them on the piles.

Zeb had been driving the mowing machine with King and Outlaw and Merry had been walking the end of the sickle bar so he could lift it over stumps and keep it unclogged and all of that. The time came for them to swap their jobs so Merry could ride and Zeb could be walking for a while.

We do not really know why it happened or I guess even exactly how. But instead of getting off of the mowing machine on the left side and walking around the back of the mowing blade Zeb got off right in front of the sickle bar on the right hand side. I don't know why he would of done that and I wonder if he actually did get off on the left side and walk around like he was supposed to do to start with and then for some reason just stepped in front of the blade to do something with the horses or something.

Anyway he was there in front of the sickle bar and had his back turned to it. Then for some reason just as Merry climbed onto the seat the horses jerked forward all of a sudden. When this happened the mowing blade hit Zeb right in the back of his left leg just exactly above the top of his shoe and the sickle cut through right to the bone.

I cannot even imagine what that must of hurt like but he did not cry at all. He hopped over into where the hay was already cut and just fell on the ground and hollered for Father. When Father picked him up and tried to help him to see if he could walk that foot was already hanging there just as limp as it could be.

We got him to the house and Mama rapped it so it wouldn't bleed. She didn't try to do anything else to it and I think that was because she knew that it was something awful bad. Right then and there Father carried Zeb to the wagon and took off in a hurry to Doc Graham's house.

When they finally got back Father was almost crying. "He cut the leader in his leg" he told Mama. "There wasn't anything Doc Graham could do but sew up the skin. That foot won't ever have any control again."

At this time none of us knows exactly what that means. I know that the leader is that part that runs from your heel up to the back of your leg but I do not know what it is for. And by now Zeb's foot is still just rapped up to heal from the sewing that Doc Graham did.

To say that this is bad is all there is to it. I am only glad that Merry did not even have any accidental thing to do with it. It would be even worse to have to worry about whether something like this was somebody's fault or not.

So that is it. All I can do is write down what happened and start hoping and praying for the best. We all went to church today except Mama who stayed home with Zeb.

Sunday, October 8, 1911

There sure are a lot of things in this world that I do not understand. And right now a lot of those things have to do with the crippling that has happened to our brother Zeb.

What I mean is this. In the news paper today Father has read to us about some criminals in the city of Greensboro who finally got caught selling a poison drug called cocaine to a lot of people. They had been selling it for a long time and it was hard to catch them. Now when they were finally caught they were tried in court and the judge gave them a sentence to work at hard labor on repairing the roads around Greensboro for six months while they are in prison.

This is my thinking. These men who were selling the poison had been doing something that was both bad and wrong for a long time. And besides that they were doing it on purpose. Now they got caught and they are in prison. But this is the thing. These men will be back out of prison in six months. My brother Zeb never did nothing wrong at least not on a mean purpose. He never did anything to deserve getting cut by that mowing machine.

Now those men who did wrong on purpose will be out of prison in six months but my brother Zeb who did not do nothing wrong at all is going to have to be a cripple for life for something that happened in less than a minute.

I have spent the whole week thinking about this idea and when I heard about the cocaine business I figgered out how to say it to myself.

Maybe there is something wrong about just being in the wrong place at the wrong time. I would surely like to talk with Father or Mrs. Melville about this but I do not even know if it is the right thing to wonder about this. I will for now just keep thinking.

Sunday, October 15, 1911

On Friday Doc Graham came back to check on Zeb. The doctor took the bandage off of his leg and pulled all of the stitches out that had been there for two weeks.

The leg looks awful much like it is healed up except for one thing. Zeb can not move his foot around at all.

Right now it is just stiff but Doc Graham says that when the stiffness works out of it it will probably flop down and hang loose because without that leader in connection Zeb will not have any control over lifting it up. Doc says that the hardest thing will be learning to walk without being able to push off a step with his toes. I never thought about that but since he said it I have been noticing and that is the actual way that you walk.

Right now Zeb is not walking at all. Doc brought a pair of crutches for him to use until he starts to learn to get around but so far he is too proud to use them. He just hops and tries to hang on to stuff when he has to get from one place to another.

Doc told him that he had to try to walk but he just doesn't do it.

He also told him that when he got some better that he would measure him and order a brace to hold that foot out stiff and that would help him in walking a lot.

Father told us that back in the times of slavery when a slave was like to run away that sometimes the owner would cut through the leader on purpose so that the slave couldn't run anymore. That is a awful thing to think of but the good thing about that story is that the slaves must have still been able to work after that or the owners wouldn't have done it. So maybe Zeb will still be able to work for hisself even if he is a cripple.

One of the strange things is that it is always usually Merry that gets hurt. He is the one who always gets hit in the head or cut or broken. I do not remember a time that Zeb has ever got hurt before this. Maybe he just got all of his hurting at one time.

Sunday, October 22, 1911

One of the hardest things in the world to do right now has been to finish getting all of the hay in after what has happened to our brother Zeb. Father has got Champ to come up and help and he and Father went right back out there where the actual crippling happened and took right up to mowing right then. I don't think that I could have done that. That place itself now seems scary to me and I would have just left the hay out there alone and got it somewhere else. But Father says that we have to keep going always no matter what and that is what he does.

Sometimes when Father reads the news paper to us it sounds like the modern world is not all progress but actually sometimes going backwards. You would think that more people and more new inventions would make more business for the Post Office. However this must not be the way that it is since Father read to us today that the Post Offices of the U S A are thinking about not opening for business on Sunday.

It said that the church ministers were for the closing. I guess they just want people coming to church instead of reading their interesting mail.

Now I know that a lot of stores in cities do not open on Sunday and that is a all right thing to do. But it seems like to have the Post Office closed is like trying to go for a day without milking the cows. It just seems like ever thing would get all backed up and you never would get straightened out after that.

Imagine now if Zeb had got hurt like he did but he was off somewhere like in New York City. Imagine that the doctor there wrote Mama and Father a letter and told them what had happened and that Zeb needed some help in getting home. Then imagine that the letter got almost here by Sunday and then it was laying up there in the closed Post Office. Why I reckon Mama and Father would have to just stay up all night not knowing anything at all just because that Post Office was closed.

Annie Laurie was thirteen on Thursday but we didn't have a party.

Sunday, October 29, 1911

On Friday Father told us that he had heard that there was a man in Suncrest who was buying potatoes and that since we had a whole lot of extra potatoes this year we ought to try to sell some of them. We had dug all of the potatoes in the past two weeks and there were over a hunderd bushels of them and Father figgered that we needed not more than a bushel a week to do us.

He said that Merry and I could hitch King and Outlaw up to the wagon and haul the potatoes to Suncrest to sell them. He said that the man was supposed to have a railroad car down close to where the Narrow Gauge comes in and that was the place to go to sell them.

Well we started off. I have never been to town with just Merry and Merry has never been in charge of a trip to town all by hisself before. We were both scared but we didn't talk about it to one another or show it to anybody else either. We got into Suncrest by late on in the morning because Father told us to hurry and get home early.

The thing is that when we went to the train depot to find out about the potato man the agent told us that he was not there. He had already left. We were told that he had got the Narrow Gauge to pull his train car about four miles on down the track to Bluffton where the big lumber company is.

Now I did remember that we passed through Bluffton when we rode to Erwin Tennessee to get Grandpa but I had never actually been there. Merry had not been either and we did not know what to think or do either one.

We were afraid that if we went on to Bluffton we would be in trouble because Father had not told us to do that and also we would get home late. But we were also afraid that if we went back home without selling the potatoes that we would be in trouble for that. We talked and talked and then Merry thought and thought. There was not anybody you could ask to get any help.

Finally Merry said "We're going to Bluffton." I think that is what Zeb would of done. We asked around how to get on the right road and then we went. It took us over an hour to get there. There is the biggest saw mill there you have ever seen in your life. It is spread out all over ever where and there are mountains of logs and big stacks of lumber all over the place and there is a regular shifting yard to hold all the train cars that come in there to haul the logs in and the lumber out.

We asked around about the potato man and found out that he was down in the railroad yard off on the end of one of the sidings. It was pretty hard getting the wagon down there but I guess that is where the lumber people put him so that he would be out of their way.

So we got on to where he was and we sold the potatoes. He even helped us unload them into the railroad car. It was the first freight car that I have ever been in.

Just as we got the wagon turned around to start back out of there we heard a awful noise. It was the screaming of a steam engine and there was a engine coming right down the line toward where we were. I knew it would not run over us because we were off on the side of the track. The trouble is that the horses were going crazy. King and

Outlaw started rearing up on their hind legs and I was sure they were going to take off running and that the wagon would just fall apart if they went across those railroad tracks.

When they reared up the next time Merry hollered "Pull." Both of us pulled on the lines as hard as we could and Merry rapped them around a stanchion on the wagon bed. The horses were pulled up so short that they couldn't put their front feet on the ground and they couldn't run that way. Merry then set on the brake handle and pushed his feet against the wagon frame to lock the wheels.

King and Outlaw danced and danced but they couldn't run. That steam engine came on by and screeched some more loud as could be and then it was gone. We let the horses down but that is about the scaredest to death I have ever been in my life.

Then we went back home. We were awful scared we were late and would be in trouble but Father just wanted to hear all about what had happened. We gave him the money and told him the whole thing.

I thought he was going to cry when he heard about all of it. Then he said "I'm proud of you boys" and he gave each one of us a dollar.

I took my dollar and gave it to Mama and told her to save it to help to pay for that brace that Doc Graham is going to order for Zeb. I would rather in a thousand years try to get Zeb to where he can work again with Merry than to go through another trip like that.

Sunday, November 5, 1911

The Mayfields have come again.

On Monday Merry and I were pulling fodder down in the cornfield below the big barn and so we were not at home for all of the day except for dinnertime. It was Zeb who told us about it that night after we were going to bed.

He said that about the middle of the morning Mrs. Mayfield and Darling came up to the house and wanted to talk to Mama. Ledge didn't come this time.

Since it is getting pretty cold outside by now they had to talk in the kitchen instead of out on the porch and with him up in the bedroom that means that Zeb could hear ever thing.

I do not know exactly what all of the talking was about because Zeb said that it just didn't need to be repeated but I do know this. That night Zeb tried to walk more than he ever has since he got in the crippling accident. What he said was that after listening to Mrs. Mayfield and Darling he realized that he wasn't bad off at all. He said that there were a lot of things worse than having a little hurting in your body. He said that he thought the worst hurting in the world would be the kind that happens in your mind.

I do not understand what he is talking about since he just would not tell me and Merry more than that. But what I do know is that he is now using those crutches that Doc Graham brought and he is working for hours at a time to put that foot on the ground and learn to walk on it.

Things do happen in unusual ways. Mrs. Melville says that the right word for it is "Mysterious."

Sunday, November 12, 1911

When father reads the news paper to us he usually starts with politicks. But today the first story he read did not turn out to be about politicks at all.

It seems that President Taft has a cow named Pauline Wayne the Second. Pauline Wayne the Second lives on the back yard of the White House and is the cow that provides milk for Mr. Taft and his family. That would seem to be a reasonable thing in ever way because the President of the U S A needs milk just like anybody else does.

The funny thing is this. They have now built Pauline a brick house just like people live in and the brick house has what the news paper called a Shower Bath where that cow can actually be washed by people who I guess you would call the President's cow washers.

It says that she gives a lot of milk but I think that this is the most silly thing I have heard of. Besides the shower baths there is a special

Swedish cow trainer who takes her for walks and gives her a special rub down so that she will not get too fat. Maybe Mr. Taft does not want Pauline to get fatter than he is. The cow also has a fan to keep her cool at night and she sleeps in straw that has been heated in a oven to kill all of the germs in it. The other thing is that this cow house has electrick lights in it.

Part of what makes this so funny to me is remembering about having to make Mr. Taft that giant bathtub so he could take his baths. If they had this cow shower at that time the two of them could have taken their baths together.

When Zeb heard of this his sad face brightened up and he started laughing. Mary Adeline and Margaret Angeline started laughing until they were crying. Then Mama and Father and all of the rest of us got to laughing until it hurt me so bad that I couldn't get my breath and tears were running down my face. We laughed and laughed and I fell down on the floor and had to curl up in a ball to try to get my stomach to stop hurting. We must have laughed for a hour.

When we all calmed back down Mama looked at Father and said "Thank you Med we needed that." I think that I understand exactly what she meant by that because exactly what we did all need was to just laugh our heads off.

For the rest of the day we have been still laughing off and on and Zeb is getting to where he can get around so fast on those crutches that sometimes he can catch me before I can get away from him. I think what we need is a good dose of laughing ever week from now on.

Sunday, November 19, 1911

One week ago Saturday we killed a hog. The weather has now got cold enough for that and I did not think anything about it at the time because we always kill a hog as soon as we have enough of a cold spell. But when I said something about it to Mrs. Melville she looked at me and said "Med you have got to make a report to the class on that."

I said to her that killing a hog is not news of the Modern World and that ever body knows about killing hogs. What she answered me was a interesting thing. She said that she for one did not know about killing hogs. Can you imagine that a grown woman who is smart enough to teach school did not know about killing hogs.

Then she told me that just because we knew how to do something did not mean that ever body in the world knew how to do it. And she said that part of moving into the modern world was going to be realizing the older ways of doing things that may not be the same in the future. She said it is important to remember the old ways of taking care of ourselves.

So I did the report on hog killing. I told about getting the water hot in the scalding tub to start with by heating rocks in a fire and dropping them in the water. I told about the block and tackle where we hoist the hog up to clean it. I told about Father hitting it in the head with the go devil to kill it. I told about bleeding it and cleaning it and about cutting up the meat right down to making sausage and then getting the hams and shoulders ready to cure in the smokehouse with salt and ashes.

At the end I told about getting the hogs bladder to blow up and make a ball out of. Mrs. Melville had never heard of that in this world and then a lot of students in the class filled her in on some of the different ways they did parts of the hog killing at their houses.

She liked it and it was fine to get to teach the teacher something. Even some of the students that never hardly say anything felt like they had something to say because they all knew about hog killing. Mrs. Melville told us she learned a lot and that no matter how much somebody knows ever body they meet could teach them something new because we all know different things. I never thought about that.

One thing about the hog killing I could not tell about. That is that the way we hoist the hog up is by cutting a opening between the leader and the bone in the hog's hind legs and running a rope through there and up to the block and tackle. When I started to tell that part all I could think about was how Zeb got crippled and I just could not tell it even about the hog. When I thought about it I saw how strong that leader is and I knew more than ever that Zeb has really lost something that is as strong as one of his bones.

Anyway that was the report and Mrs. Melville told us all to tell her more about what we did at home because some of it she might need us to teach her about.

Sunday, November 26, 1911

A woman has got her aeroplane pilot's license.

Father read the news to us right out of the news paper first thing today. A woman named Miss Harriet Quimby who is a flying student at a flying school on Long Island New York is the second woman in the world to be a flyer. The first was of course in France. This is the first in the U S A.

To get your flyer's license one of the things you have to do is to land the aeroplane within a certain number of feet of a target. The world's record for closeness in this trial is five feet and four inches from the target. Now this Miss Quimby who is both a woman and a beginner in flying landed her aeroplane only seven feet and nine inches from the target. I think that is very good.

When you think about it there is actually no reason in the world that a woman should not be able to fly a aeroplane just as good as a man. After all somebody else spins that propeller to start the engine and after that it is just knowing what to do. I think she can do it just fine.

But when I think about it what could be easier than deciding who to vote for for President and then voting for him. But women are not allowed to do that. It does not make me mad that my Mama and Mrs. Melville do not fly aeroplanes but it does make me mad to know that they are probably as smart as anybody that I know and the men of the world do not think they know how to vote for who is to be the President.

If Father runs and gets in the Legislature I am going to try to get him to fix it to where Mama and Mrs. Melville and all of the other smart grown women in this country will get to vote. Maybe if Mrs.

Mayfield could vote she would not have such a hard life. I will think about it.

Sunday, December 3, 1911

This started out as a hard week for all of us. It was because it was supposed to be Thanksgiving but this year it did not seem like we could possibly have anything to be thankful for because of what has happened to our brother Zeb.

We did not have school on Thursday and besides that we had to go to church at the Babtist church because there was what they called a Community Service there for Thanksgiving. The Babtist preacher talked about all of the things we should be thankful for and as I listened to him there was not one of those things that our brother Zeb can do at this time. I felt like hating the very idea of Thanksgiving.

At home in the afternoon we were awful quiet at the Thanksgiving dinner even though both Champ and Lucee and their families got to be with us. It was like there were extra people to feel sorry for Zeb.

In the afternoon Father and Zeb disappeared into Father's bedroom for a while. After a while they came back into the living room and Father said "Zeb wants to tell something." Then Zeb my brother made the best speech I have ever heard in my life.

He told us how the second the accident happened he knew that he was crippled for the rest of his life. He told us about how mad he was at ever body after that. About how he blamed Father for making him cut hay and Merry for wanting to swap jobs and even blamed just living here in Close Creek and having to work to make our way.

He told about being mad at Doc Graham for not being able to fix his leg and mad at the idea of using crutches to walk on.

Then he told us about hearing Mrs. Mayfield talking to Mama about what a awful life they live at their house. About how mean and hateful Mr. Mayfield is to her and Ledge and Darling. That is when he says he began to be thankful for not being one of the Mayfields.

That he said was the start of his new thinking. Zeb said that over against what he heard about the Mayfields he got to thinking about what a good life we have and then he said the most remarkable thing. He said that finally he realized what a good life we have even without even thinking about the troubles the Mayfields have. He said that we have a good life even without comparing it with anybody else's troubles.

Zeb said that maybe this was the most important Thanksgiving in his life because he had learned to see all of the good things that we just think are always there and so we don't ever pay any attention to them.

Finally Zeb said that the thing he was most thankful for was that he lives in a home where we could overcome any hardship and that he was going to overcome what had happened to him and we better stop spoiling his day by whining about it anymore.

It was better than any speech that I have heard in school or in church. After it was over I was about to cry from just listening and Mama and Father both had tears in their eyes.

What I think is that if Father decides to run for the Legislature that he better hire Zeb to make up his speeches for him. He could not lose after that.

Finally Zeb said "Let's play rollybat. I'm the first hitter." We went out and found out that Zeb can balance and hit the ball just fine. And in rollybat you don't have to run when you hit it.

Maybe the trick is to always be sure you find a game where the things you are not good at are just not a part of that game. Anyway we did have Thanksgiving after all in the end.

Sunday, December 10, 1911

All of a sudden this week after that speech that Zeb made to us all on Thanksgiving Day I have figgered out the solution to all of his problems. Zeb does not have to worry about not being able to do farm work because what he can do is that he can just become a politishun.

Politishuns work with their mouths and not with their physical strength and there is surely nothing the matter with Zeb's mouth.

The way I figgered this out is this. On last Sunday a lot of what Father read about in the paper was another big speech that Champ Clark made in the House of Repersenatives. The speech was a direct attack on President Taft and the high cost of living in the U S A. In the speech Champ Clark declared that the Democrats would fight it out until election day of 1912 and that he was the best man to lead that fight.

Maybe he was just talking about his job as the speaker of the House of Repersenatives but when he said what he said all of the congressmen cheered "Champ Clark for President" over and over again.

The article in the news paper said that Champ Clark started out his life as a barefoot country boy behind the plow on the hills of Kentucky and now said that he is on the last leg of his trip to the White House. He is now called "The Big Missourian."

So what I have figgered out is that if a barefoot country boy from the hills of Kentucky could get to be the President then our Brother Zeb could certainly do it since North Carolina is a better place to be from than Kentucky. That is all there is to it.

I think the best thing is for Zeb to get in with helping Father in politicks. Then he can start to make a name for hisself when ever body sees how good a speechmaker he is. I can hardly wait for him to be in the White House. Maybe he will give me the job of giving shower baths to his cow.

Sunday, December 17, 1911

This afternoon was the school Christmas party for families. The party was held at the school house and was held on today so it would not interfere with class during the week.

Mrs. Melville made all of the cookies and had hot cider on the heater stove. We put up a tree and decorated it with pop corn and strung up berries and clipped some candles onto it. Then we sang some Christmas songs and each of us did a recitation we had learned.

My recitation was "Ever Where Ever Where Christmas Tonight" by the same man who wrote "O Little Town of Bethlehem." I can remember the poem and all of that but I just can't remember his name right now.

Mrs. Mayfield came with Darling and Ledge but Mr. Mayfield did not come at all. The three of them hung back from the others there and looked shy and even scared. Ledge sure is different this year. He isn't a bully at all and always seems kind of sad at school. Between Duck getting killed and whatever else is going on there it must be a hard life.

After it was all over Mrs. Melville told us to work hard for one more week and we would be out for Christmas. Then she gave us all a orange.

I have been holding and rubbing that orange ever since I got it. It makes your hands smell so good. It is hard to give up holding it and think about eating it because then it would be all gone even the smell. I wonder if Ledge got to eat his or if his Daddy ate it.

Christmas Day, December 25, 1911

Since yesterday was the Eve of Christmas I decided to wait until tonight which is a Monday to write since I surely could not figger out what to tell about before ever body got their Christmas presents. Besides Christmas seems a lot like Sunday anyway.

First of all this was such a good Christmas because Zeb is doing so well and second it was good because about all of our family was here today.

On Sunday Lucee and Harlan Junior had gone to Harlan's Mama's house and Champ and Sallie Jane had gone to be with her family and so on today both of their families were here with us and that made ever body here and that is even Grandpa who says that he just never did get around to going to Nashville this year.

At the first of the day Father said "Let's take a Christmas Roll Call and remember this day as a time we are all together. These times are good and do not go on for ever." I was afraid that would hurt Grandpa's feelings since he is the oldest one of us and I am afraid he will not be here forever. But it seemed to make Grandpa happy to be the oldest and to have the roll called.

First there was Grandpa who since his birthday is eighty one years old. Then there was Father hisself who is now sixty one years old but will be older in one week like I will be too. Next came Mama. She is only fifty one years old.

Father made all of us children stand in a row and he went down the row from the top to the bottom. He called out "The Champ Family" and there was Champ and Sallie Jane and their baby Junior who is just about not a real baby anymore since he just turned 4. Then he called "The Lucee Family" and he meant Lucee and Harlan Junior and their true baby Jeff who could not answer for hisself.

After that it was down the line "Zeb age 19. Merry age 18. Margaret Angeline and Mary Adeline age 17 each. Annie Laurie age 13. And finally Medford age 11 and nearly 12." And that was all of us.

Then Mama said "Cate don't forget the ones that we lost."

And Father said "Let us remember Flora Dare and Arthur Moody." That was a good thing to me because I know that once you are dead most people just forget about you. And I would like to know that somebody still remembers you even after you have been dead a long time. Besides that I would not even know about my dead brother and sister if I had not been told since I never was born until after they were gone. Even after all of that nothing was said about Mrs. Elizabeth Chambers being dead and gone even though Harlan Junior and Lucee are even living in her house. But I remembered her.

After that we got a real Christmas present. Champ said "Father next year you will have another name to call. Me and Sallie Jane are going to have another baby in the summertime."

Sallie Jane must of turned as red as blood and we knew that she had not agreed to tell it yet. But Lucee run over and jumped up and down and hugged her and so did Mama and the twins.

After all of that I do not even need to tell about any of the

Christmas presents because between all of that remembering of the past and all of the excitement about the future there is nothing we could get that could be any better. Zeb is getting stronger and a new baby is coming. What could be better than that.

Sunday, December 31, 1911

It is New Year's eve and Grandpa has just surprised all of us more than any surprise he has ever brought yet. He brought something from Nashville Tennessee which he has saved all the way up until now and it is the most wonderful thing you can imagine. We have just seen it and it was fine.

What it is is called a Roaming Candle. I guess that it is called that because the fire of it does not stay in one place but roams all over the sky.

Grandpa said that he had something to show us about how people in the cities celebrate for the New Year. He went into his trunk and brought out a paperboard tube with a block of wood on one end and a fuse like a blasting fuse on the other end. None of us had ever seen anything like that.

The paperboard tube was covered with colored paper and it had little designs on it. Grandpa said that it was made by the Chinese and that the little marks were Chinese writing that only the Chinese could read. We wanted to know all about what it was for and he said to wait until it was real dark and we could see.

After it was real dark we went outside. Grandpa said to blow out all of the lights even in the house so it would be pitch dark and we did. We got way out in the yard and he stood it on the ground on the wood block end and told all of us to get way back. When we got way back Grandpa struck a match to that fuse and then he ran back to where we were like he was a boy running from a bad dog.

We just watched as that fuse burned down out of sight and then the entire world just blew up all at once. A great big hunk of red fire flew up in the air with a whoosh and then a hunk of blue fire flew up and then hunks of ever color of fire you can imagine flew up one after the other. That Roaming Candle was spewing fire and making whooshing sounds and lighting up the sky and Margaret Angeline and Mary Adeline got to screaming and running around like it was the world coming to the end.

Then we all got to clapping and laughing and just dancing around. That thing must of blew fire for five minutes before it was all wore out. I have never seen such a thing in my life.

When it was all over Grandpa gave me the burned out tube and I have it right here with me. It smells like a shot out shotgun shell and now all of the colored paper is blackened but I am glad to have it and will always keep it to remind me of this day.

That Roaming Candle was so wonderful that I am now ready to go to sleep and have just now remembered that tomorrow is my birthday.

1912

It is now 1912 and that means that I am now 12 years old. Monday was my birthday and also Father's birthday number 62.

Usually I have got some present for my birthday but this year I got two presents and either one of them would be enough to last for several birthdays. All year long Father has been teaching me more and more about shooting guns and now for my birthday I got a single shot 22 rifle all my own.

It is a blue Remington with a short stock that just fits me. It has a bolt action and you put a bullet in it one at a time. Father says that you have to be able to kill a squirrel with one shot anyway because after that it has already run away. He says that if the gun would shoot more than one bullet you would just waste shots by shooting twice when the squirrel has already run off after the first shot.

Yesterday we went hunting. Father and Merry and I went and between all of us we shot eleven squirrels. That was enough to make a real fine dinner for today with fried squirrel and gravy and biscuits. I shot one of the squirrels myself.

Father says that it is not fair to hunt for squirrels with a shotgun and besides that it would just mess their meat up. He says that a shotgun with buckshot is for deer hunting but that for squirrels and rabbits we use 22 rifles.

The hardest part of squirrel hunting for me is cleaning the squirrels that you shoot. Gutting them is just hard to do and it is hard to pull the skin off besides that. But Father says that you have to clean what you shoot or you are not old enough to shoot to begin with.

I do love fried squirrel and also squirrel pie and so I am glad to go to the trouble of cleaning what I am lucky enough to shoot.

For two years or more I have been hoping and dreaming about getting that rifle and now I am old enough to have it.

After getting the rifle and a box of bullets I certainly did not expect anything else for my birthday or for anything else for the rest of the year. But then Grandpa came out with a paper sack and handed it to me and when I opened the bag there in it was another Roaming

Candle. It was just for me.

Grandpa said that I could shoot it off anytime that I wanted to but I have decided to keep it unshot for the rest of my life. That way I can imagine ever day what it might look like if it went off but if I did shoot it off it would be all over with and I would pretty soon forget about it. I put it in the bedroom on the dresser where we can all look at it and imagine.

A funny thing happened then. I told Grandpa that I had figgered out why you called it a Roaming Candle. He laughed and said "That's good Med but it is called a Roman Candle." I asked him what that meant and he said for me to get Mrs. Melville to tell us about the Roman Circuses and I would figger it out. I will do that.

So I am now both a hunter and the owner of my own Roman Candle. This is what happens when you build up enough birthdays to start to be grown up.

Sunday, January 14, 1912

As of one week ago schoolchildren have more to learn about the U S A than they did before that. Now all schoolchildren will have to learn about forty seven states instead of forty six because on the sixth of January the state of New Mexico became number forty seven.

Since we live here in North Carolina in a state that was one of the first thirteen colonies it is hard to think that there is a place in the U S A where a state is just now getting organized. But Father told us that in that new state of New Mexico there are only two people on the average for ever square mile and that includes the cities. I guess they don't see enough of one another to get very organized.

We have learned from Mrs. Melville at school that New Mexico is a lot of desert and that it goes to the border with Mexico itself. She said that five or six years ago there was a plan to bring the Territories of New Mexico and Arizona into the U S A as one state but the people in Arizona couldn't agree to it. So now New Mexico is a state of its own and in all of the U S A Arizona is one of the only Territories left.

What that means is that in a Territory the U S A goverment is still in charge of ever thing but when you get to be a State then the state has its own goverment and gets to be in charge of itself but still a member of the U S A.

Grandpa says that it is so far to New Mexico that his traveling to Nashville Tennessee is nothing beside of that. He said that you would have to ride a train for a week to get there. I do not understand how so many different places so far apart can be a part of the same country. What I think is that the politishuns know that aeroplanes are coming more and more ever day and when aeroplanes are ever where then the country can be held together a lot better.

Most of this is a mystery to me. It is enough to think of Father helping to run North Carolina if he gets into the Legislature let alone thinking about the President running forty seven states. Whatever they say about whoever gets to be the President I think it would be a awful hard job. It would be like being a teacher with forty seven children in your class all at one time.

Sunday, January 21, 1912

Well it is now official. Father is going to run for the Legislature of North Carolina for sure. He told all of us on Monday and then on Wednesday he had to go to Asheville to do what is called Filing and paying a fee to get to run. I don't understand why the word Filing is used but that is what they call it when you want to run. I will ask Mrs. Melville instead of guessing at the meaning like I did with the Roman Candle.

Ever day Father is trying out his ideas on us. He is most interested in two things. These two things are schools and roads. He is for what he calls Schools for All. Our school with Mrs. Melville he says is a subscription school where those who go have to pay a fee to support the teacher. Father wants schools to be paid for by a tax so that ever body will then go to school for free. That explains to me why some children do not go to school.

What I do not know is now how Ledge and Darling Mayfield go to school since I know that the Father at that house would not pay for it. Our Father says that it doesn't matter who pays for it as long as somebody does.

Anyway he is for raising a tax to build roads and run schools because he says that individual people just cannot do those things and that since they are for the good of the whole community ever body ought to share in paying for them. I think it is a good idea and it would be cheaper for ever body to pitch in than just those who are really interested.

Father has also said that he will work hard for the nomination of Champ Clark as the Democratic candidate for President of the U S A. He will try to get our part of North Carolina to go for him at the party meetings. He says that Champ Clark understands being from the country since he is a country boy and besides he was born in the same year as our Father was born so they are bound to share a lot of the same ideas.

So Grandpa will stay here as long as we need him and Father will start to travel around and politick. He will have to go over seven counties in all to try to get votes and he will have to take either King or Outlaw to do it. He says that he will try to do as much as he can before time to start plowing so that he won't break the team up then but that we will have to use the mules more this spring than ever before.

So we are now a family into politicks.

Sunday, January 28, 1912

Yesterday we went deer hunting. We had a heavy snow on Wednesday and Father said that it was not good weather to start his politicking so on Friday at supper he said that he and Merry would go deer hunting the next morning. Zeb said that since he had a shotgun but could not go why did they not take me since with my new rifle I was now a marksman. He said that I could take his shotgun since you can't kill a deer with a twenty two.

Father said "Maybe it is just time for that. Med needs to learn about shotguns and about deer hunting." I had never been before because deer hunting is hard but now I was going.

Before we went to bed Father got Zeb's twelve gauge and got me to hold it. He said to be sure that you hold the gunstock real tight against your shoulder because the shotgun has more kick than a twenty two and it could break your shoulder if you have it too loose. I wanted to shoot it but it was dark by then and he said I would just have to remember and that shooting the twenty two was sort of like practice for the shotgun anyway. Then we went to bed early.

I was so excited that I just could not get to sleep. About all night I rolled around and thought about shooting a deer. Just about the time I got to be asleep Father shook me and said to get up. It was about four o'clock in the morning.

We got all our clothes on and ate some leftover food and set out in the dark. It was Father and me and Merry. We went up over Cedar Ridge and way up into the oak woods beyond where you can look down to the Socoee River.

Father picked out a big oak tree that was wide enough for two people to hide behind. Even in the dark we had been seeing a lot of deer tracks in what was left of the snow and there were several sets of tracks coming together around here. He put me on the side of the tree that was out of the wind. I thought that was to keep warm but he said that there was no point in being out of sight if your smell gave you away.

Father told me to just stand with my back to the tree and wait. I was not supposed to move. He said that the only way to get a deer was if it was to come to you. He said to not shoot a doe but if a buck came to shoot it if I was sure I could hit it with the first shot. He said there would not be a second chance.

I said "How long do I wait." He just said "Until a deer comes or until we come back." Then he and Merry went on off to find their places to wait.

So I stood there. I stood there with my back against that big oak tree for what seemed like two or three hours. Gradually it got light and then a few sounds started to sound like the woods was waking up. There was a bird or two singing and it was so quiet besides that you could hear the birds' wings hit the air when they flew. I heard a squirrel or two but I wasn't out to hunt squirrels.

Finally the sun was coming up over the ridge. I was glad for this because I had been purely freezing to death up until then. The sun was warm because it was coming right toward me but it did blind me somewhat with a lot of snow still on the ground and all.

Finally I thought I heard Father coming back. I could hear steps. But the steps sounded awful light and they would go fast and then stop. All of a sudden I realized that there might be a deer coming up behind the tree where I was.

I could hear the sound and I was dying to look around the tree but Father had told me not to do that whatever I did but just to wait. Then I got scared. What if it was not a deer. What if it was a bear or a painter or another deer hunter who might shoot me if I scared him. I couldn't move. I just stood there and listened with the sun still half blinding me.

Gradually the sound came past the tree and off to the right I could see them. First out of the corner of my eyes since I was scared to even turn my head and then as full as could be. There was not one deer but there were two. There was a buck with four point antlers and right beside him there was a doe. I just couldn't believe my luck.

I watched while they circled right around in front of me. They were nuzzling in the snow and ever once in a while finding something to eat. Maybe it was some moss or some kind of green shoots or something. I got the shotgun up to my shoulder and started to line the barrel right up on the chest of that buck. He had his head down and I thought that as soon as he lifted it up from the ground that I would pull the trigger.

The buck lifted his head but as he did his eyes came up and he saw me. He did not move. He just stood there and looked me straight in the eyes. He made a little noise and when he did the doe looked up and she looked me straight in the eyes too. There I stood with the shotgun all loaded and aimed with those two deers looking straight at me and not afraid at all of me.

They were the most beautiful thing I have ever seen in this world. And besides that I had just heard them talk to one another and I knew they were a family. They looked and I looked and I knew that I could not pull the trigger. I just let the muzzle of the shotgun ease down toward the ground and I just kept looking at them.

I could see their sides heave when they breathed and their breath would steam in the air when they breathed out. They were not twenty steps from where I was and I could see the buck's pulse in his neck when his heart beat just like the pulse in a horse's neck. We just looked and looked at each other.

What I did not realize was that the shotgun was sinking down lower and lower and that it was beginning to hang by my finger which was on the trigger. All of a sudden the weight of the shotgun against my finger pulled the trigger and that twelve gauge went "Blam." That thing jumped backwards and the stock hit me in the armpit and like to have knocked me right up into that tree. It blew a hole in the ground about six feet in front of me and when I could look both of the deers were gone.

By then I could hear Father and Merry come running. They were hollering "Did you get one Med. Did you kill it."

When they got there I was hopping around and holding my armpit and the shotgun was on the ground. With that hole shot in the snow there wasn't any point in lying so I told them just what had happened.

Father smiled and then both he and Merry laughed. Father said "I couldn't have shot it either son. Let's go on back home."

So we went on home for the day. We didn't get a deer but I sure did get a good story to tell. I have told about it at school and I guess I have told it to Zeb about ten times. He sometimes calls me The Great Deer Hunter but he also has said that Father ought to get me to shoot moles in the ground when we start the garden in the springtime.

Sunday, February 4, 1912

Well the news is out. Mister Roosevelt is running for President for sure. He said in a meeting in New York City that he would run "If forced." Then later on in the very same week some of the men who are trying to support him actually announced their plan to get him the Republican nomination.

These men figger that when the convention comes that Taft will be the strongest with the Republicans but if they can slow down the convention and talk it around enough that Taft can't win then Roosevelt will get nominated. That way Taft's friends can be loyal to him in the beginning and it won't be anybody to blame if they are just outvoted in the end.

There are two problems to me. One is that I like Mister Roosevelt and wish that he was a Democrat. I do not know a thing about Champ Clark except what Father says but I would hate to be for somebody besides who my father is for.

The other problem is that there are now a whole bunch running to be President from both parties. There is Roosevelt and Taft and LaFollette from the Republicans. Then there is Champ Clark and Woodrow Wilson and even William Jennings Bryan for the Democrats. Maybe it will all get solved in the end. I am going to get tired of politicks before this is all over.

The real news of the modern world is that Mr. Glenn Curtis who is the best aeroplane man since the Wright Brothers has built and flown what is called a "Flying Boat."

For several years he has been working to make regular aeroplanes so they could take off and land on water. Now he has made one with a actual bottom like the bottom of a boat and he has flown it in a place called Hammondsport New York.

With all of the trouble that looks like it is coming with Germany and the countries of Europe it may be that a armed aeroplane needs to come next. Who knows.

Today was Mama's birthday. She was fifty two years old on today and Father has bought for her the finest present you have ever seen. It is called a Sewing Machine.

The Sewing Machine is called a National Two Spool and it is wonderful. Father had ordered it a few months ago and when it came to the railway station in Suncrest he got it there one day and had hidden it in the feed room of the barn right in the crate it came in.

This morning when we got up there was a big crate right in the kitchen and Mama herself had to open it to find out what it was.

The Sewing Machine itself is built into the top of a little oak table. Under the table is what is called a "Treadle" which is a pedal connected to a belt which runs the machine. I have heard of sewing machines but have never actually seen one.

There is a needle that goes up and down when you pedal the machine and there is a spool of thread on the top and another one out of sight underneath. You run cloth through where the needle goes up and down and somehow that needle connects the two threads through that cloth and sews it right together in a instant. There is a hole in that needle that works one of the threads but I cannot figger out where the other thread comes in.

The sewing machine is black but it has some silver and gold parts and it is just beautiful and it makes the finest sound when it runs. It sounds like a little tiny train coming down the track.

Besides the machine Father gave Mama ten spools of thread. There are six black spools and four white spools.

Even though it is Sunday it seemed to be OK to play with the new machine. Mama didn't actually make anything but she did just practice at sewing some pieces of cloth together. I will bet you that tomorrow morning Mama starts right up sewing on that machine. I just cannot imagine how much time it will save or how many things Mama will be able to make with it.

The only trouble is that if you can sew this fast then the limit on what you could make must be having enough money to buy thread and cloth. Mama does weave woolen cloth and she always uses all of the feed sacks but this machine sews so fast that she could in one week use up all of the cloth in this house.

Sunday, February 18, 1912

It snowed again this week on Friday. The snow started while we were at school and at lunch time Mrs. Melville told us that we ought to walk on home to be sure that the smaller children made it since not ever body had come prepared for that snow. It snowed about a foot deep before it quit in the night after that.

On yesterday morning Merry said that maybe he and I should take our rifles and go rabbit hunting. He said to me that it was good to go rabbit hunting in the snow because unlike the squirrels that can stay in the trees rabbits have to stay on the ground and so you can track them in the snow.

We did not take any dogs with us because we did not want them scaring rabbits before we had a chance to shoot at them. We figgered we could follow their tracks as good as dogs could follow their smell and that we would be smart enough not to bark like the dogs would.

The first rabbit tracks we saw were up toward the county road to town. We tracked the rabbit up the ridge and through a barbed wire fence. Then we tracked it down through the pine woods and into the oak trees around from where I had seen those deers.

All of a sudden we could see exactly where the rabbit was. The tracks disappeared in a hollowed out tree stump and it was for certain that the rabbit was in there. Merry and I waited for a long time for the rabbit to stick its head out of the stump so that we could shoot it but it just stayed down in there out of sight. I wanted to throw rocks at the stump and make it come out of there but Merry decided that maybe we could catch the rabbit and take it home alive. He said that we might could make a pet out of it.

We sneaked up to the stump and slowly looked over the top and down into the hollow where the rabbit had to be. Right there in the bottom of the hole we saw the prettiest little brown rabbit that you have ever seen. It was just sitting there and looking at us like it wasn't scared of us and it didn't even try to hop or run.

Merry took off his gloves and eased down to the stump. He was going to try to grab the rabbit by the nape of the neck with one hand and by the feet with the other hand. That was the plan.

Just as Merry got a hold of the rabbit that little feller went into action. That rabbit twisted its head around and sunk his big front teeth right into the heel of Merry's hand and bit right through the thickest part of his hand meat.

Merry hollered and slung that rabbit right up through the air. The rabbit hit the snow and it was gone in a instant over that snow and out of sight.

I looked at Merry's hand and it was bleeding bad. He rapped his handkerchief around it and we decided that the rabbit hunting was over. We went back home just as fast as we could with Merry sort of crying and holding his hand.

Mama thought that maybe she ought to sew up Merry's hand but he hollered so much about that idea that she just gave up on it. He did squall like a wild animal when Mama cleaned it up with turpentine. But then she rapped it up tight and said that she thought it would heal up all right. We didn't get to fire a single shot on the entire hunting trip.

Today Father was reading about a plan to recruit new soldiers for the Navy of the U S A and Merry said that if anything else happened to him around here that he would just go on off out of here and join the Navy. Zeb could not hardly keep from laughing at him since this rabbit bite was not much compared to his getting crippled. Still I am glad that he can laugh about it. But I do hope that Merry does not get serious about joining the Navy. Then I would have to do everything around here.

Sunday, February 25, 1912

Mister Roosevelt is now one step closer to running for the President and it is not because of anything either he or his men have done. It is because that Mr. Robert LaFollette is sick and has dropped out of the race with Mr. Taft.

Up until now it looked like LaFollette was going to be the chief one for Taft to actually fight. This was because he was a senator and he started saying some of the same things that Roosevelt is now saying while Mr. Roosevelt was still supporting Mr. Taft. That made it kind of hard to look like Roosevelt was really saying something new especially since Father said that he was the one who picked Taft to be the President this time anyway. I do not begin to understand all of this since most of it is what I have heard Father talking about with other people. But I do understand that with LaFollette out of the race that makes it a lot easier for Roosevelt. Besides the news paper said "Roosevelt Men Cheer that Lafollette is Out." I am cheering too because for the Republicans I would choose Roosevelt too. I do not tell Father though since he says that Roosevelt would be hard for the Democrats to beat. I guess when you are a Democrat you want the worst Republican to run against instead of the best one. That is politicks.

Sunday, March 3, 1910

Well Merry's hand is a lot better this week. Mama said that it healed up without stitches. He wants to go back rabbit hunting and is eager to go. He said he will "Blow the head off of the first one he sees."

Also Doc Graham came and gave Zeb the final measurement for the leg brace. Zeb's crippled leg is getting smaller than the other and that is why he has to be measured over and over. Doc says that is because some of the mussels are not used anymore. But he also said he is proud of Zeb and that he is doing very well. I think so too.

Sunday, March 10, 1912

On Monday Darling Mayfield did not come to school. When Mrs. Melville asked Ledge if Darling was sick he just shook his head to say No and didn't say anything else. Mrs. Melville didn't ask anything else from Ledge. She just nodded back to him and acted like she was sorry she asked to begin with.

When Darling didn't come to school Tuesday or Wednesday Mrs. Melville sent a note to Mrs. Mayfield and our own Mama and Mrs. Melville got together after school on Thursday and went up to the Mayfield house to find out what was going on. Mama said that Mrs. Mayfield looked like she had been crying for a week when they got there.

Mama and Mrs. Mayfield asked if Darling was sick and Mrs. Mayfield went back into the house and got a note that had been left and showed it to them. Mama said that the note said "I hav gon to see the world. You wont see me agin. Signed Darling." That was all there was for Mrs. Mayfield to tell them. She didn't know anything else.

When Mama and Mrs. Melville tried to ask questions Mama said that Mrs. Mayfield acted like she wanted them to leave instead of stay anymore. She wouldn't even answer them when they asked her when she found the note or how long Darling had been gone.

I don't understand why she was so scared acting because when Mama asked her if Mr. Mayfield was at home she said "No Whitey isn't here." I don't know what she could of been scared of if he was not there but Mama and Mrs. Melville felt so funny about it all that they did leave instead of asking any more questions.

Darling was at school all of the week before so as of now she could not of been missing for much more than a week. I don't know where somebody would go if they wanted to see the world. I guess I would start out by going to Nashville Tennessee but I cannot imagine where Darling would start out since she does not have a Grandpa to tell her about that place.

Anyway I sure hope that she either has a good time or comes back soon. Even if she does not come back soon I hope that she writes to her Mama. That woman will have even a harder time without Darling there and so will Ledge.

Sunday, March 17, 1912

Zeb has got his brace. On Friday when we got home from school Doc Graham's Ford car was in the yard at the house. I was afraid at first that something bad had happened or somebody was sick but it turned out to be good news instead of bad. The brace for Zeb's foot had come and Doc Graham had brought it.

The brace is not what I would have imagined. First of all it has a shoe at the bottom of it. In fact there was another new shoe for the right foot so that when Zeb wears the brace he has a matching shoe for the good foot to go with the one the brace is hooked on to.

First he puts on the shoe. The shoe has a steel rod that goes through the heel of it and then the rod turns and comes up the calf of his leg on both sides. Just below his knee there is a leg strap which straps the top ends of both rods against his leg. I guess that inside the bottom of the shoe the rod must be welded to a place or something because when you hold the brace by the rods the shoe stays sticking straight out and does not hang down. That is the way that it holds Zeb's foot level so he can walk without it dragging all of the time.

The most amazing thing is this. You can push up on the shoe and it gives. Then it must have some kind of a spring that pushes it back down until it is level again. That way when Zeb walks forward his foot can push up and then it moves back down for the next step. It is a simple looking thing and it must be wonderfully made inside. Zeb can already walk about like you wouldn't know he was cripple just after a hour or two of practice.

Doc Graham says that the shoe part can be replaced when it wears out and that this very shoe can be resoled and heeled. It is a wonderful invention.

Merry is the one of us who has talked about wanting to be a lawyer sometimes in the past. But I think that since Zeb is cripple and couldn't make a farmer anymore and since I have heard him make that Thanksgiving speech about his own self that maybe he ought to think about making a lawyer. It could be a good thing. Besides Merry has been threatening to run away and join the Army if he gets hurt anymore. Maybe if Father gets elected he could help Zeb find somebody to read law with.

Anyway it is now almost like Zeb is not cripple anymore. I do know that there are certain kinds of work that he cannot do but somebody who didn't know would never guess unless they could see the ends of that brace sticking out of his britches leg.

Sunday, March 24, 1912

Darling Mayfield is back. Actually she was not ever gone anywhere as it turns out. She was found dead this morning.

The whole story is that Mrs. Melville was the key to finding out what had happened to Darling. When Mama and Mrs. Melville went to see Mrs. Mayfield they both saw the note that was supposed to of been left by Darling when she ran away. The first thing that Mrs. Melville noticed was the spelling. It said "I hav gon." Mrs. Melville knows that Darling is or was a good speller and that she would never write like that as far as spelling goes.

After she noticed that spelling then Mrs. Melville looked close at the note and saw that it did not look at all like Darling's writing. So she talked with Mama about this.

Later in the week Mama talked with Father and as soon as he heard this Father went up to the Mayfields and had a talk with Mrs. Mayfield that he wouldn't tell any of us about. After that he went into Suncrest to tell what he knew to Sheriff Black. Sheriff Black said that it sounded to him like there was some kind of foul play maybe involved. He organized what Father said amounted to a possie and that possie spent three days and then into the fourth looking for what might of happened to her.

Father was in the possie and he said that they combed the woods ever where around Close Creek looking for a sign of either where Darling might be hid or that a grave might of been dug. They couldn't find any sign at all of Darling or a grave either until on Sunday morning one of the Babtists on the Possie noticed that a lot of big rocks had been pushed off into the edge of the Socoee River right above where they have Babtizings. When the possie moved all of those rocks from the edge of the river there they found Darling dead.

I heard Father tell Mama that she had been rapped in a big log chain to hold her body down and that Doc Graham thought right off that she had been choked to death.

Father says that Doc Graham will do what is called a Post Mortem examination which means a check up after you are dead to see what killed you. That is what will tell more of the whole story.

Right now nobody had been arrested by Sheriff Black. Both Mr. and Mrs. Mayfield have said that they stick by the story of the note that was left and that as far as they knew Darling had really run away to see the world. Nobody can get anything out of them and of course Ledge has lost his only sister and so he does not say one thing at all about it.

There has been so much suffering and meanness up in that Mayfield house that I am afraid to even guess what might of happened. Zeb said tonight that he could guess what Doc Graham is going to find but he wouldn't tell any of it until it is official news.

All of this has happened just this day. When we got home from church where Father didn't go since the possie was working non stop in case they might find Darling alive then we found it all out.

I will have a hard time sleeping after this day. Darling is the first person I know personally who has died without being a old person and she is the first person of any kind who looks like she was deliberately killed by somebody else. I hope that Sheriff Black finds out who did it very soon. Maybe that will help the rest of us to at least not be so scared.

Well I guess that the whole truth is out now. Sheriff Black has arrested the one who murdered Darling. Actually Father says that you are supposed to say "Suspected of murder" but it sure sounds to me like there are not any questions about that.

The whole story goes again to Mrs. Melville and to Doc Graham. After Mrs. Melville told that she was sure that the note was not written by Darling then Sheriff Black started trying to find samples of a lot of people's writing to compare it to. He got a warrant to search the Mayfield house but did not find anything there that was written by Mr. Mayfield.

Then up at the Sandy Bottom store Mr. Woody who runs it said for him to look at the credit account records. If you have a credit account there you have to write on a paper what you have bought and sign your name to it. That did it for the Sheriff. He told Father that over and over again the credit record said "I hav got" so and so. And besides the "g" where Mr. Mayfield had written "Sugar" was just like the "g" in the word "Darling" in the note and not at all like Mrs. Melville's papers from school show that she wrote it.

After that the biggest news of all was Doc Graham's report on the Post Mortem examination of Darling's dead body. Father told Mama that that examination showed that Darling was going to have a baby and Father said that was the motive since Mr. Mayfield was the daddy of his own daughter's baby.

Now I know why it was so awful to live up there in that house and when Zeb heard this report he said that was what he had suspected all along after hearing all of that talk the day Mrs. Mayfield came and did all that crying. Mama said that she thought it too but all of the talking was just about meanness in general and not specific about making the baby.

So Mr. Mayfield is now in jail. He of course is saying that he did not do it but I believe that it looks like he did. I have not seen Ledge since the arresting and I do hope that he does not stop coming to school. Right now he needs school for the regularity of it as much as for what he can learn there. It would not be good at all for him to set at home and just think about what has happened.

Mother says that she must go up and see Mrs. Mayfield but right now she just does not know what to do. It is a good thing to find the murderer but a puzzling time. I had thought before that we would all be happy to catch who did it but nobody at all is happy about the way it turned out. Sheriff Black and Doc Graham and Father are all very quiet and sober about this. It is a time almost too terrible to think about.

Sunday, April 7, 1912

It has been over a week now since Mr. Mayfield was put in jail for murder. During that time Ledge has kept coming to school and his brother Bull who is in the Army has come home on a leave and then gone back to the Army. I got to meet him and I remember him from before he went when he played the banjer for dancing. He looks and acts a lot better now than he used to look. Maybe if Merry did join the Army or Navy it would not be too bad for him.

Anyway during this week Father said that we needed to do something to keep Ledge cheered up and why did I not plan some little April Fool even if it is a few days after April Fools day that would make him laugh and maybe get him to come over. I thought and thought and I could not come up with something to do.

When Champ my biggest brother was over here on Monday I told him what Father had said and he said he had a idea that would cheer up not only Ledge but Merry and Zeb and even our own father. I asked him about it and he told me his plan which he had been thinking about for some time it seems.

Up at the store at Sandy Bottom Mr. Woody who owns the store has a big stuffed bear up in the front of the store. The bear was killed by Mr. Woody and he had it stuffed so it is standing on its back legs and growling. This was Champ's idea. He thought we ought to try to borrow that stuffed bear and put it in the feed room at the barn. Then we would all go out to feed and see what happened when somebody opened the door. He said that he would go try to borrow the bear and that nobody but me and him would be in on it.

I told Mama that maybe I could ask Ledge to come home with me from school on Wednesday and stay over for the night and she thought it was a good idea. I asked him and his Mama thought it would be just fine cause I guess she wanted him cheered up too.

So on Wednesday Ledge walked home from school with me. Also on Wednesday Champ borrowed the bear and on Wednesday night he slipped over here and set the bear up inside the feed room so it was growling straight at the door when you opened it.

On Thursday morning Father and Merry started out to the barn to feed and I said "Maybe Ledge and I could go and help you." Father thought that was fine and we all started out. I ran on ahead and Ledge caught up with me and I acted like I was going to open the feed room door. Then I bowed to Ledge and said "After you" and he pulled the door open with Father and Merry right behind.

When Ledge saw the bear it was just too much. He slammed the door back shut and started jumping about ten feet straight up in the air over and over again. He was screaming "Bear in there Bear in there" over and over again.

Father opened the door a crack and when he saw the stuffed bear he started to laugh and ever body saw what it was. We laughed and laughed but Ledge was pouting and still thought it wasn't funny. Champ came out of hiding then and told about the plan.

Just about that time Sallie Jane who had been hiding in the barn loft to watch started to climb down into the feed room. She had on a brown coat and when Ledge first saw that brown thing moving he started screaming all over again.

By now I realized that maybe we had done the wrong thing. It seemed that while in normal times it would have been a joke that Ledge would have laughed about and liked OK maybe this was not a good time for April Fool's to come along at all.

I told Ledge I was sorry we had fooled him and he finally settled down and said that it was fine. Still I did see that no matter how tough a person looks when something happens like what has happened to him lately it is hard on him all around. I have learned something from this.

Sunday, April 14, 1912

There is a new invention which is called a Parachute.

Father read two stories about this to us from the news paper today. One was a story of failure and the other one a story of success.

In the first story a man named Franz Reichalt who is from the country of Austria was killed when he jumped down from the Eiffel Tower in Paris France. He was not trying to kill hisself. Instead he thought that he had invented a thing he called a parachute. It is a thing that is supposed to make it possible for a person to jump off of a high place and not die. It is a thing that opens in the air like a big bag and the air it catches is supposed to make you fall slow.

Anyway this one did not work. When Mister Franz jumped off of the Eiffel Tower the bag did not open up I guess and the news paper said he "Plunged like a stone to his death." A sad story.

The second story was better. It said that less than a month after this death another man in Saint Louis Missouri did it. His name was Mister Albert Berry and he built a parachute too. He had a aeroplane pilot take him up into the sky and then he jumped out of the aeroplane. The parachute worked and he landed safely on the ground and was not killed or even hurt.

Now this is amazing. It means that the aeroplane is a lot safer. If all people in the aeroplanes will just get those parachutes then they will not keep getting killed. This also means to me that now the aeroplane can be used in war. If the pilots were all scared of getting their planes shot down like horses in the Indian wars then they would not go up there and fight. But now if their plane gets shot they can just jump out with their parachute and land.

Several times Father has read about the Army and the Navy doing experiments with aeroplanes especially in France. I have told Merry that if he really wants to get in the Navy that maybe he could get to fly in one of those fighting aeroplanes.

The real modern world is just about here now. There are not many more things to be thought up.

Sunday, April 21, 1912

The modern world is not here yet. The ship that was supposed to be so modern that it could not be sunk has gone down.

The ship was called The Titanic and it was made for the White Star Ship Company of London. It was just built and had not ever crossed the ocean before. The news was that this ship had air rooms built into it so that it could not ever sink and would float forever. It was thought to be so safe that there were not even many lifeboats on it.

Anyway the story is that it started out on its first trip from England to New York and the people who owned or ran it were determined to set a new speed record in the crossing. There was a weather report that there were a lot of icebergs in the path but the captain thought the ship was not to be sunken and was so much in a hurry for the record that he went on.

The news paper said that it was just a little bit before midnight on the fourteenth day of this month that the Titanic hit a big iceberg. The iceberg split a long split in the bottom of the ship that broke open all of the air rooms. It was less than two hours that it took for the whole new ship to go under.

Some of the people got into a few lifeboats and some were rescued by another ship but the story is that more than fifteen hunderd people in all drownded. It is a terrible thing to imagine how it was to be there.

There were some famous and wealthy people who were on board of the Titanic and they drownded right along with the regular people.

There is another story ever day in the news paper about the Titanic. Ever body is trying to blame somebody else for the big disaster. Father says that the lawyers in London and New York City will have a good time before this is all over. I do not think that by saying "Good time" he means anything like fun though.

Sunday, April 28, 1912

On yesterday we all went to see Mrs. Mayfield and Ledge. Mama and Father had been up there before Darling's funeral and of course we had Ledge to spend the night on that Wednesday of the April Fool's bear but we had not been to actually see them since Mr. Mayfield has been locked up for the killing. Father said all week that we must go and so yesterday we did.

Zeb did not go and Annie Laurie stayed home with him but Merry and the twins and I and Father and Mama all went in the wagon. It was hard to do.

When we got there we saw Ledge playing out in the yard. He disappeared inside when he saw us and I knew that he had gone to tell his Mama that we were there. By the time we got out of the wagon she was already out on the porch. She looked like she was glad to see us and even like she smiled through all of the frowning that covered her face.

She asked us to come in and since it was a pretty day we just all went up on the porch and set down there. For a little while we just set there and nobody didn't even say anything. We just rocked and set.

Finally Father said "Has Bull gone back to the Army."

Mrs. Mayfield said "Yes he went back last week."

I already knew that was true from Ledge telling me and I think that Father knew it too but it was like he just needed something to ask.

Then the strangest thing happened. Mrs. Mayfield looked at Father and Mama and said "I just know that he did it." She was now talking about Mr. Mayfield and not about Bull anymore. "I just know that he did it. Darling was so scared of him and he was so hateful to her." That is what she said.

Mama and Father just nodded and didn't say anything. There was not anything to properly say. We just set a little while more.

Mama then said "Is there anything you need."

Mrs. Mayfield shook her head. Then she said "You have given us a lot by just coming. Nobody else in the world has been here until you came today. That is what we need."

I understood that a whole lot. The best thing we could do was I guess to try to be friends and I was already trying with Ledge. Merry said then could Ledge and he and I just play for a while. We went off of the porch and climbed in the barn and swung on the hay pulley ropes for a while. Mama and Father and the twins just set up there and I guess talked some more.

After a while Father called us and we got in the wagon to go home. Mama asked Mrs. Mayfield if she and Ledge could come to eat Sunday dinner soon and she said maybe in a little while. We went home.

On the way home I got to thinking again about the Titanic. I guess that Darling must of felt like those people on the Titanic who realized they didn't have any lifeboats. Maybe Mrs. Mayfield felt the same way. The difference is that the Titanic people drownded in two hours and it must of taken months or even years for Darling to die. And Mrs. Mayfield is still dying it looks like. A lot of things are not over even when they seem to be over.

Sunday, May 5, 1912

We have been hearing all week that the jury has been getting picked for Mr. Mayfield's trial for the murder of Darling.

There is a big session of court starting up in Suncrest and Father has gone in there each day to see what is happening and to politick at the same time. When he comes home at night we get to hear all of the news.

Father explained to us that the law says that you have to get tried by what is called a Jury of Peers. He said that meant that the people on the jury had to be your equals and could not actually be better or worse than you were. I told him that I didn't think in that case that Mr.

Mayfield had any peers and he said that I may be right in that sense but that they had to make up a jury and have it as fair as possible.

It will be hard to make it fair since ever body around here knows Mr. Mayfield. Father says that is just the way it is. In big cities they may can have juries that don't know the criminal but in the country it is not so. Still the jury has to be fair.

It is a great relief to me that Father or Mama neither one is on the Jury. I guess that Champ or Lucee could of been or Harlan Junior or Sallie Jane but our family is not on the jury in any way shape or form. That is good because we are just too close to the Mayfields and besides that I do remember what happened with those who were on the Jury that sent Duck Mayfield to prison in the past.

Father says that he thinks they have a jury picked out now. It took all week because the lawyers can object so much to those who are getting picked that it may take fifty to get twelve. Then they have to have extras in case a real jury person gets sick or something.

The story from Father is that this coming week the trial will probably start. I would not like to go because it is Mr. Mayfield but in a regular trial I would sometime like to go.

Father will go and he will take Zeb with him for the watching of the trial. We all will wait to hear all about it and wonder about the uncovering of the story.

Sunday, May 12, 1912

Now it is official. Father is almost sure to get to go to Raleigh to be part of the Legislature.

This is because he has won what is called the Nomination of the Democrats.

How it works is that all of the people who wanted to run for the Legislature paid their filing fees and started making speeches. This last week there was voting by all of the Democrats to decide who would be running in November against the Republicans. This is about the same as a convention for the President but it is a lot easier and cheaper.

There are not any actual Republicans around here. Father says that there are several parties of Democrats though. He says that there are the Sheriff Black Democrats and the Yellow Dog Democrats and even the Prohibition Democrats. He is part of the Sheriff Black Democrats.

All of the Democrats though decided that Father is the one to run.

There is only one thing that I do not understand about all of this. Father came back from this Democrat meeting saying that he is now for Woodrow Wilson for the President. I asked him why he was not for Champ Clark anymore and what he said did not make a lot of sense to me. He said that in order to get to be the one to run for the House of Repersenatives he had to give up being for Champ Clark and join with the other Democrats who wanted Woodrow Wilson. He said "It was a trade." Those were his very words.

This is a new thing for me to learn about politicks. That no matter who you are for or even what you are for you have to do trading to get your own way. That is a hard thing and I hope that Father can do it OK. I am not sure about it.

Now in November he will be on the big ballot. There will probably be a Republican on the ballot but we do not know that now. There were not so many Republicans trying to get on the ticket.

So it looks like we are a family in politicks. This would be more exciting if it did not happen right during the very same week of the starting of Mr. Mayfield's trial. That seems to be the thing that makes ever thing else seem not as important as it would at most times.

Sunday, May 19, 1912

The trial is really going on full speed now.

I just do not understand what they could be talking about up there all day ever day in the Court House. It has gone on so long already now that Father has stopped taking Zeb and going into town ever day to listen.

He says that there are just a lot of witnesses and a lot of bad evidence. Mostly he says that ever body that was in the possie and searched has to tell their own version of the whole story and get questioned about it. They are eye witnesses to the evidence and besides they want to get to tell how they saw things. This part on its own could last for many days since there were two dozen or more in that possie.

One thing more is this. Zeb told us that the trial does not go on all day ever day. Father says that they take a lot of recesses to find out more things and to rest and to think things over. I guess it would not be so hard if you were trying a stranger for murder but when it is somebody that has lived here all of his life and the one killed is his daughter and besides all that given how it all happened then it just has to be something it takes a long time to talk about.

Yesterday we all went to town. The trial does not go on through Saturday so it was not busy in the Court House. But there were a lot of people there to talk about it.

I did not know that we were going to town for anything special until we got there. When we got there Father said "Now that we are in politicks we have to look nice. We are all going to get a haircut from a barber."

Father has had a haircut from a barber before but not a single one of the rest of us have. Mama always cuts our hair. I could not believe that this was going to happen.

We went to the barber shop. It has a red and white striped pole on the wall in front of it. That is the sign for barbers. I asked Father what that meant but before he answered Zeb said "They scare you white and bleed you red." Father said he didn't know but that it wasn't what Zeb said.

Anyway we went inside and there were three chairs but just two of them had barbers. It smelled so good in there just like some kind of herbs or something. Father said that it was something called "Bay Rum." I said that I hoped the barbers hadn't been drinking the Bay Rum and Father laughed and said it wasn't for drinking but for smelling. I have never heard of that.

We watched them cut two men's hair and then it was our turns. Merry was first.

That barber put Merry up in that chair and pumped a handle that made the chair rise right up until he was as tall sitting as the barber was standing. The barber put a sheet over him and tied it around his neck. Then he went to clipping. He could clip so fast that the hair just flew. You could almost hear those clippers going "Snip snip snip."

After the clipping was done that barber made a big mug of shaving lather and lathered up the back of Merry's neck and around his ears. He sharpened his razor and shaved around Merry's ears and neck. Then he rubbed something on Merry that he called "Witch Hazel" and let him loose. Merry looked wonderful and smelled real fine.

After that Zeb and I both got our hairs cut at the same time by both of those barbers. Their names were Mr. Caldwell and Mr. Hannah.

At the end we watched Father get his hair cut and his beard trimmed way back. We all smelled to high heaven.

Mr. Caldwell said "Well Cato you can go right on into proper politicking now. This whole bunch looks fit to go to Raleigh." It was just the finest thing you can imagine.

All the way home I could feel the air running cold where that barber had shaved around the tops of my ears and neck. It felt just like cold water was touching my skin. Besides that you could feel the back of your neck and it feels so funny. Mama always cuts our hair off even but that barber made it feel like a little crop of quills right on the back of your neck.

Today I did not want to wash my neck because I wanted the smell to stay with me but Mama said that we have to wash even if we have been to the barber shop.

Sunday, May 26, 1912

Father and Zeb went back to watch the trial this week. It is the longest trial for a murder ever held around here. We have done almost nothing ever day but wait for news of the trial. Even at school it is quiet and Mrs. Melville is letting us read silently a lot and not starting any new work. Ledge is still coming to school through all of this but his Mama walks him to school each day and then walks him home again. I guess she does not have anything else to do but to walk.

Part of the news is that there was a new piece of hard evidence presented at the trial. This evidence was the log chain that was rapped around Darling's body to weight it down when it was put in the side of the creek. I guess Mr. Mayfield thought that the chain and the rocks would keep everyone from ever finding her.

Anyway the log chain is one that had belonged to Mr. Tyndale at the blacksmith shop. It had his name on it and that might have sounded bad for Mr. Tyndale except that he had a record of loaning it to Mr. Mayfield over a year ago and it not being brought back.

It seems that Mr. Tyndale started writing down what Mr. Mayfield borrowed because most of the time he never brought any of it back. This log chain was actually written in Mr. Tyndale's shop record book as "loaned to Whitey Mayfield on March 12 1911."

Zeb told us all about this. He always goes to the trial if Father goes. The solicitor is Lawyer Stillwell from Asheville and Father is hoping to get to talk with him and see if there may be a chance that Zeb could come and read law with him after the trial. Zeb has been interested in the trial but is also talking like being a lawyer would have some faults in it after watching this trial.

Anyway we are all waiting for the outcome.

Sunday, June 2, 1912

Ever since Mama got that National Two Spool Sewing Machine for her birthday we have all been just as interested in it as could be. The way it works is just a mystery to ever one of us. Merry and Zeb have been wanting her to teach them to sew on it since she has been teaching the twins and even Annie Laurie but she has not given in to do it. Maybe that started the trouble.

When we got home after school on Wednesday Mama was not at

home. She had left a note to tell that she had gone by herself up to see Mrs. Mayfield and she would be back before supper time.

I guess that with her gone and all that Merry and Zeb just decided they would try sewing on their own.

They got into where that sewing Machine is and they actually sewed together two or three little pieces of cloth just by doing what they had seen her do. Then they started playing like they always do.

Zeb had got to watching the way that needle goes up and down ever time you pedal that pedal. He was pedaling the pedal and he started sticking his finger under where the needle is ever time it went up and jerking it out before the needle came down. Of course since he was pedaling the pedal he could tell exactly how fast that was happening.

Then he said "Merry I'll bet you can't do that." Of course Merry said that he could. He started doing it but the trouble was that Zeb was still the one who was pedaling the pedal of the sewing machine.

I don't really think that it was just pure meanness like Merry said that it was later on when he was telling about it. I think that it was just a game. Anyway Zeb started doing the pedal to see if he could catch Merry's finger and the long and short of it is that he did. On one of those times he pushed down real quick and hard on the pedal and that needle went right through the end of Merry's finger. Merry jerked back so hard that he broke the needle off and there it was sticking right clean through the end of his finger.

If you think that he was squalling when he got hit in the head that time they were building the swimming pond then you should have heard him this time. Of course he is bigger now and he can squall a lot harder. Besides this he was not hurt so bad that he couldn't hit at Zeb at the same time and with his crippled leg Zeb couldn't get away from him.

Right at that time Mama was coming home and what greeted her was the put together squalling of both of them. It was Merry just squalling and Zeb hollering "Quit it" at the same time.

She broke it up and then saw what had happened. I could see from her face that while Mama was mad that the needle got broke she was having to try not to laugh about what had happened.

Mama pulled that needle on out of Merry's finger and packed salt all around that finger to kill the germs. Then she said that she had some more needles for the sewing machine.

Zeb and Merry both got real mad when Mama said that it looked like boys were not quick enough to learn how to sew and that was why the sewing was to be done by the girls. But they couldn't either one argue about that.

After it was all over Merry said "I am really going to go off and join the Navy. Everything bad around here happens to me." Zeb didn't say a single thing. He just got up and you could see him limping worse than usual as he went on out of the room.

Besides all of this today was Merry's birthday. That finger stitching didnt make for much of a birthday if you ask me.

We are still waiting to hear about the trial.

Sunday, June 9, 1912

On last Tuesday the trial came to its end. During the last days Father and Zeb would not miss going a single day. I do not know if that has to do with politicks or just being curious. I would have missed school and gone too if I could have got to do it. There is only this week of school left in the year anyway. Also on these last days Ledge is not coming to school. Maybe he is just plain staying home.

Anyway Zeb said that on Tuesday they sent the jury of peers out just before dinnertime and when ever body got back from eating that jury had already made its mind up. The verdict was guilty.

After that verdict Zeb told us that the judge asked Mr. Mayfield if he had anything to say for hisself and that is when he confessed. Zeb told it. He said that Mr. Mayfield said "Now I might as well tell the truth. I did it. She was going to have a baby and she was going to tell about it and I just choked her to death." That is all that he said. He never did admit the part about it being him who was the daddy of that baby of his own daughter.

Now I never thought about what comes next. But the next part is so bad that I cannot even think about it. Zeb said for Father to tell about it and he did.

Father explained to us all that the Judge then sentenced Mr. Mayfield to hang to death. He said that the sentence is called "To hang by the neck until dead." That sounds just awful and especially since it is somebody that we have known. I just have to keep thinking about Darling being dead when I think about this.

The hanging by the neck until dead has to happen in the next sixty days Father says and the judge set the time as twelve noon on Wednesday the last day of July.

On yesterday we went up to see Mrs. Mayfield and Ledge again and had one of those silent visits where we just set on the porch and rocked and didn't hardly say anything. Ledge and I didn't play. We just set on the steps and listened to see if the grown ups were going to say anything.

Mrs. Mayfield only said "I don't know how I'm going to make it." And Mama said "You'll do it Mildred. We will all help you. You'll do it. You just have to keep on living."

This is the first year that we are not having a big celebration when school gets out. The end of the year just kind of ran out.

Sunday, June 16, 1912

Nobody can believe it but Merry is hurt again for the second time in two weeks and this time it really is Zeb's fault.

For two or three weeks now Merry has been fussing about one of his teeth hurting. Mama has looked at it and she said that it looks rotten to her and needs to be pulled. She put Oil of Cloves on it for several days and that helped the hurting for the time being but the hurting just came back over and over again. Finally Father said that Merry would just have to go to Doctor Gerald and get the tooth pulled out.

Merry fussed a lot about that but Father told him he was lucky to be living in the modern world because teeth were easier to get out than in the old days. Father told him that in the old days the same barber that had cut his hair the week before would pull that tooth right out with a pair of curved pliers. Now you get to have a real dentist pull it out.

So finally on yesterday Merry and Zeb and I got the wagon hitched up and started out to Suncrest to get the tooth pulled out from Merry by Doctor Gerald the real dentist.

All of the way to town Merry cried and moaned around and fussed and complained about the tooth. Zeb was driving the wagon and I was just riding along.

Finally we got to Suncrest and found Doctor Gerald's office. We went in there and it smelled like some kind of medicine that I have never smelled before. We waited there and heard a awful grinding noise which Zeb said was the driller that he drills out rotten teeth with. Merry like to have run off then until Zeb said that Merry's tooth was going to get pulled and not drilled out by that drill.

Finally a woman left that had her jaw swelled up. She was the one for certain that the dentist had been drilling out on.

That dentist called Merry back into another room where we could see that there was a chair a lot like the one at the barber shop when we got our hair cut before. Maybe that is why barbers used to pull out teeth since they already had the chair for it.

Anyway the pulling of that tooth did not take any time at all. That dentist just seemed like he got Merry's mouth open and the tooth popped right out. Merry came out crying a little and holding his cheek and Zeb paid the dentist two dollars and we got in the wagon to go home.

On the way back I thought that Merry would feel a lot better. But he kept right on wailing and hollering as much as he did on the way into town. Finally Zeb said "Maybe that dentist pulled the wrong tooth out Merry. Let me look and see."

Zeb looked in Merry's mouth and said "Lord Merry he pulled the wrong one. Father will kill you when we get home and he finds out that you paid two dollars to get the wrong tooth pulled out." He thought that this would take Merry's mind off of the hurting from where the tooth was pulled and get him thinking about something else. But the plan did not work.

Merry sulled up and got way in the back of the wagon as we went on toward home. Zeb was still driving and we just thought that Merry was pouting or something.

All of a sudden he turned around to Zeb and said "There smarty I got the right one out now." Merry was holding another tooth in his fingers. Zeb stopped that wagon right then and there and said "What have you done Merry."

What it turned out was that Merry had believed Zeb when he had told him he got the wrong tooth out and it scared him to death. What he had done was to put the tooth he thought was hurting right against the sideboard of the wagon and pushed until he pushed it toward the gap where the pulled tooth came from and he got it out too. There he was holding it in his hand.

Boy was Father mad when we got home. He was mad at Zeb for fooling Merry and he was mad at Merry for getting fooled and he was even mad at me just because I was there. He said "You boys won't grow another tooth once one is gone."

Now Merry had lost two teeth one good and one bad all in one day. I guess that that pulled tooth hurt so much he didn't feel any extra pain in pushing the second one out. I still cannot figger out exactly how he did it though. Maybe it really was rotten on the inside.

Now Merry is so mad at the world that he is really talking about running away to join the Navy.

Sunday, June 23, 1912

The news is bad for Mr. Roosevelt.

At the big Republican National Convention he tried his best to get nominated for the President again. The plan was to start out acting like he was for Mr. Taft. He was sure that people wouldn't want Taft and then they would pick him to run and he would not have made anybody mad for it at the same time.

The plan did not work and the Republicans have voted that Mr. Taft is the one that they want to run to be President again.

Father said that after that "The true colors came out." He read to us that the followers of Mr. Roosevelt got mad and they all walked out of the big convention. They have even threatened to make up a new political party just to get to run Mr. Roosevelt anyway.

Father says that this has happened before in the past but that it never works. He thinks that Mr. Roosevelt would just be wasting his time to do this.

Actually Father is very happy that Mr. Taft is running for the Republicans. This is because he says that Mr. Taft will be a lot easier to beat than Roosevelt would of been. I do understand this but I still think that it is too bad that Mr. Roosevelt has got put out. Maybe he will come up with something I'll bet.

We go up to see Ledge and Mrs. Mayfield about ever week now. They do not have much of a garden since all of this with Darling and Mr. Mayfield was happening right when you ought to be putting in your garden and they just didn't do it. So each week we go up there and take them a lot of produce to eat. Mama has even said to Mrs. Mayfield that maybe the both of them ought to get together and do some canning for the winter at our house.

Mrs. Mayfield doesn't answer but I think that Mama can convince her since they will surely starve otherwise.

Father says that they are talking in town already about the hanging. They say that it will be with a gallows instead of from a tree limb. Father says that hangings have just been back legal in North Carolina for two years and that many places they have not had a legal hanging since then. He expects that ever body in the county will be in town on that day. I will surely not be going.

Sunday, June 30, 1912

I am getting pretty discouraged with things around here. It seems that I have to work all of the time and there is no benefit to that.

All Father does is politick. He goes all week long all over what he calls the District and talks to groups of people about voting for him. A lot of the time Zeb goes with him and helps him.

I don't know what he helps him to do as there is nothing to politicking but talking. I guess that Zeb can do that and besides that maybe Zeb does help him with the horses and to drive the buggy. I think they ought to take the wagon since they could sleep in it but Father says that would not be fitting for a person who might be in the Legislature soon and besides that most places they go somebody puts them up for the night.

And then there is Merry. All Merry does is mope around and feel sorry for hisself. It is bad enough when Father and Zeb are here but when both of them are gone there is just no stopping him from that moping and whining. Mama can't seem to do much with him.

What is left over from all of this is all of the work for me to do. Annie Laurie helps me and so do the twins and Mama and Grandpa but I am really just the one who has to do what used to be done by Zeb and Merry both. I just wish that this election would get over with and Father would be out of politicks and that school would start back so I could get to talk with Mrs. Melville about things.

I do wish that I could talk with Mrs. Melville about the hanging of Mr. Mayfield. It is just exactly one month from today that the hanging is supposed to happen. I don't want to think about that but maybe I could talk to Father about hiring Ledge to do some of the work around here once that is all over. I wonder what it feels like to get hanged. Whatever it feels like it is probably not as bad as just waiting for it to happen.

Sunday, July 7, 1912

The fourth of July has come and gone.

We spent the entire fourth of July in Suncrest listening to politicians talk talk talk. We had to get up early in the morning and go to town. The good thing about it was that there was not any work to do after feeding and milking on a day like that. Father was all excited.

Except for the speeches it was quite fine. There was a little musical band that came from Asheville to play for the day. I don't know who hired them to come or paid them. There were six of them and they had horns and some drums and they were all dressed up and I have never heard anything like that in my life. They played all kinds of songs right there in the middle of town. I could of listened for a week.

There was a lot of eating and a horse race right through town and some gambling and a lot of speeches. It was pretty fine.

All of that is about forgot by Father by now though because of his reading about the Convention of the Democrats.

They have had their big convention this week and at the end it is Mr. Woodrow Wilson who will run for President for them.

It started out to look like it would be Champ Clark as the leader. We have heard the news ever day of this week. There was Champ Clark in the lead and then Mr. Wilson and at last William Jennings Bryan who has run for the President so many times he ought to be getting tired of it.

In the first of the voting there were not enough votes to get Champ Clark in and so they just kept voting over and over and over. Sometimes the votes changed just a little bit but after a while each time the votes were coming out just about the same. They were for Clark first Wilson second and William Jennings Bryan third.

They went on and voted forty five times and never did get anybody to agree on who was to be the one.

Then Mr. William Jennings Bryan took over. Father read to us that he stood up at the convention and said for all people who were for him to go over to Mr. Woodrow Wilson. That was the end of it for Champ Clark.

Father is happy because he thinks that the best chance the Democrats have is to put Mr. Wilson up against Mr. Taft. He says that if the Republicans had gone for Roosevelt that Clark would be better because Wilson and Roosevelt sound too much alike on a lot of things.

Anyway Wilson is the man but I cannot help but think of how Mr. Champ Clark must feel after all of this time of being out in front and now not being the one to go all the way. I guess the Big Missourian will just have to go back to Missouri.

The hanging is three weeks off.

Sunday, July 14, 1912

Death is in the air.

A while back Father read to us about a woman named Miss Harriette Quimby who was at that time the first woman in the U S A to get her license to fly a aeroplane. Today he has read to us in the news paper that this same Miss Quimby has been killed in the crash of her own aeroplane.

This aeroplane crash has brought on a great argument in our family. The argument got started so fast that I didn't really get to hear all of the details of the aeroplane crash or even where it happened. The argument is over what women ought and ought not to do.

Merry heard the news paper report and said all at once "See women shouldn't be doing things that were meant for men to do." Merry is always it seems the one to come out against things.

Then Zeb said "Now Merry what if somebody told you that something you wanted to do you couldn't do because you were a boy."

That made Merry mad and he said "I'm not a boy I am a man."

When that happened it was all over because the twins heard Merry say he was a man and they laughed out loud both of them.

A downright fight started and Father just stood back and watched it happen. It was Merry trying to kill both Mary Adeline and Margaret

Angeline. It wasn't any time until the two of them had him pinned down to the floor and had twisted his arm up behind his back and were saying to him "Holler calfrope. Holler calfrope."

Merry was as mad as a wet hen but it hurt him so much that he finally did holler "Calfrope." Then they let him loose.

Ever body was laughing at the fight. Finally Annie Laurie said "Well Merry I'm glad you don't have a aeroplane because if you did I'll bet the twins would be flying it." Merry just pouted and growled.

For those few minutes of that fight I actually forgot about Mr. Mayfield's hanging which is just over two weeks away. I think that may be why Father just let the little fight go on instead of putting a stop to it. He always seems to know when we need to be distracted and since all this family has talked about for days is that hanging we sure did need to be distracted from it on this day.

Sunday, July 21, 1912

A new baby has slipped up on us. Sallie Jane has had her new baby.

We have all spent so much of our time talking and thinking about the hanging of Mr. Mayfield that we have not been talking about how Sallie Jane has been getting a day at a time on toward having the new baby. She has got along so fine with this baby that I guess we have just not paid too much attention to it especially since it is not the first baby for her.

So this is it. On Tuesday the time came and when it came Sallie Jane had that baby before Doc Graham could even get there. It is a boy and it has been named Crymes Hawkins McGee which is after two of our Grandparents which we never did know. We have tried to have a happy time about all of this but it has been hard to be cheerful when the air seems so sad.

Sunday, July 28, 1912

The hanging day is Wednesday at Sunrise. Father told us that they have just finished building the gallows for the hanging. In the beginning people thought they would hang Mr. Mayfield from a big oak tree limb where the last hanging that was held here happened. But Father says that was not a legal hanging but what was called a lynching. For a legal hanging they have to build a gallows.

On this afternoon we all went into town to see that gallows. It is a little floor that is about ten feet off of the ground with a trap door in it. The hanging rope is above this and when the trap door opens the person drops through it. I hope there is a curtain or something so people can not see when the rope runs out.

I have thought about that gallows ever since we saw it this afternoon and I think that Father took us to see it so that we would all decide that we are glad we cannot go to the hanging instead of being curious about it.

What I have figgered out about Sallie Jane's new baby is that maybe about this same time Darling Mayfield would of been having her baby if her own Father had not killed her. Nobody has said this out loud but if I have been able to think it then I am sure that Father and Mama and even Sallie Jane and Champ have thought of it. It is a sad thing to know that ever time that new baby has a birthday we will have to think again about what was happening when it was born. Maybe what we should try to think of is that the new baby adds some happiness in the middle of a time of sadness.

Sunday, August 4, 1912

It is over. Mr. Mayfield is hanged dead.

On Wednesday morning I thought that I would surely be writing about this on that night without waiting until today which is Sunday. But ever time I started to write about it I started to thinking and imagining and I just couldn't get started to writing.

After we went into town last Sunday a week ago to see that gallows that was about all that I could think about. I kept remembering that there was a big crowd of people just looking and examining it.

I kept remembering how it was a scary thing just to look at that thing. It is one thing to just get mad and shoot somebody in a fit but it is another thing to build a machine that deliberately puts a person to death by a certain plan.

On Monday it started raining and it rained all day Monday and Tuesday both. Father said that this was the best thing that could happen since the rain would keep some of the crowds down and not turn the hanging into so much of a party. He said that a lot of people would act like this was just like a circus show.

The hanging was to be at high noon on Wednesday. Father said that it was his duty to go. That morning it was fairly pouring rain still and we told Father and Zeb who was going with him that we would be waiting when they got home.

This is so hard for me to tell about in a straight line because all of my thoughts keep going in circles about all of it. I really wished that we were already in school that day. On school days the time goes by faster than just sitting at home in the rain. Mama had asked Mrs. Mayfield if she wanted to come to our house and stay with her for the day. She did come and Ledge did come with her. Mrs. Melville was also invited and I was awful glad that she was there to be with us. Mama and Mrs. Mayfield spent most of the day together and it seemed like Mrs. Melville had come there just to be with me and Ledge. She had us read some aloud and she read to us. We read most of "Treasure Island" during the course of that day.

Mrs. Melville was very quiet. She read to us a lot and she just let us work quietly and not one single person got into any trouble at all during the entire course of the day. It rained all day.

With the hanging supposed to be at noon I thought that Father and Zeb would get home in the afternoon but they did not come home until nearly dark. By that time Mama had begged Mrs. Mayfield and Ledge to spend the night with us and finally they decided to do that.

Finally Father and Zeb came home. Mama met him on the porch

and told him that Mrs. Mayfield and Ledge were there. Father came in and didn't really say anything but just spoke quietly to both of the Mayfields.

Pretty soon he and Mrs. Mayfield went into the living room all by themselves and they talked in there for quite a long time. I guess that is when he told her what she wanted to know about what had happened that day. That must of been a awful time for both of them.

After that talking was over all of us had a real late supper together. Father told all of us that he had made the plan with Sheriff Black to take care of Mr. Mayfield's funeral. In all of this time I never did think at all about that. Father said that he would take care of a private burial on our farm. He said that there might be too much trouble about burying a hanged murderer in the church cemetery so he told the Sheriff that if Mrs. Mayfield wanted it so the body could be laid away on our land. I think this is probably the best since it does not seem right for him to be buried right in the same cemetery where Darling who he murdered is laid to rest. I never did know where they buried Duck after he got shot dead.

When we all went to bed Zeb told us boys about the hanging. Usually Ledge sleeps in our room if he is here but tonight he stayed in the room with his mother. So Zeb could tell us.

He said that there was a black cloth hung around the gallows from the floor down so nobody could see the body when it went down. He said that it was raining all day and that was a good thing because it did keep the crowd down and what crowd was there was quiet.

He told us that they brought Mr. Mayfield in a wagon from the jail. He had his hands tied behind him. Sheriff Black brought him and led him up on the gallows. The sheriff asked him if he had anything to say and Mr. Mayfield said "I am sorry. I have made peace with God."

Zeb said that all of this must of been quick but each thing seemed like it lasted forever. He said that there was a man there with a black hood over his head who Father called the Executioner. Nobody was supposed to know who this man is but Zeb said ever body really did know but they acted like they did not and that after this was over nobody would ever say anything to this man about the hanging ever again.

They put a hood over Mr. Mayfield's head and Zeb said that the executioner put the rope around the murderer's neck. The sheriff checked the rope and they said to proceed.

Zeb said that there was a rope fixed to hold the trap door shut and when the sheriff dropped his hand the executioner chopped that rope through with a ax. Zeb said that it happened so fast he did not even see Mr. Mayfield fall. One second he was there and the next he was just gone. Ever body just stood there and didn't make a sound.

In a few minutes Doc Graham came out of the curtains at the bottom of the gallows. Zeb said that he didn't even know the doctor was down there. He came up to the sheriff and told him that Mr. Mayfield was dead.

Then the sheriff told the crowd that the sentence was carried out and that they could all go home.

In the afternoon Zeb said that Father went around town and talked to a lot of people about what would happen to Mrs. Mayfield and Ledge now. He didn't want people to forget that they were what he called "The victims" of this whole business. Zeb said that Father also made the plans for the burying with the sheriff.

So this is all that I can tell about this now. Mrs. Mayfield and Ledge went on home the next day but I have a feeling that we will be seeing more of them on and on.

In church today Father said a prayer for Mrs. Mayfield and Ledge and even prayed for the souls of Darling and Mr. Mayfield.

Sunday, August 11, 1912

Mr. Roosevelt is going to get to run for the President.

On this week there has started a Convention of the Roosevelt Men. They have not actually done it yet but during the coming week they are well expected to make up what will be called the "Progressive Republican Party." Once that is done they will then nominate Mr.

Roosevelt to be their candidate for the President of the U S A.

In a more normal time this would be a exciting thing to hear about but after the hanging of Mr. Mayfield this week it is still hard to think of anything but this.

On last Tuesday Father and Sheriff Black did take care of the burying of Mr. Mayfield. Father told that they took his body up on our farm under the side of Cedar Cliff Mountain and they buried him there. They did not place a marker at the grave for fear that somebody would try to damage it out of hatred. Father said that they placed large rocks over the gravesite and that he and the Sheriff and Doc Graham were the only ones who knew where it was. I wondered if he would tell Mrs. Mayfield where it was. She may not want to know but I would think that some of these days Ledge would ought to know.

Father said they did the right thing. He had heard that many people really did not think that it was proper to bury Mr. Mayfield right in the church cemetery where his own daughter that he killed hisself was also buried. I believe it was a kind thing for Father to take care of Mr. Mayfield's body. Something had to be done with it.

Sunday, August 18, 1912

Roosevelt was officially nominated yesterday. There were a lot of big speeches and he accepted and vowed to fight Taft to the end. Nothing was said about Mr. Woodrow Wilson.

That makes it sound to me like Mr. Roosevelt is just interested in keeping Mr. Taft from getting re elected and not really interested in getting hisself elected. If he was he would have been talking bad about both of them. It is a sad thing for Mr. Taft that his old friend the very one who got him to be the President to start with is now so very turned against him.

Father has said to us that this election will be determined by the use of the train. When we asked him what he meant he said that he guessed that the man who traveled the most miles politicking would be the one to win the election and that the train was the fastest way for the covering of the most miles.

The plans in the news paper for the politicians say that they will be taking special reserved trains across the country so they can ride at night and stop many times each day to make speeches. That really does sound like great fun to me. I would love to go on one of those trains.

There is a train called the Pennsylvania Special that for a fact can go from New York City to Chicago Illinois in eighteen hours. This is so amazing to me that I cannot understand it.

If Mr. Mayfield had of got on one of those fast trains when the possie got after him he would have been gone for good I think. Those trains may help both the politicians and the criminals of the future.

What I wonder is if aeroplanes will ever be used in those political campaigns. Since the most that I have ever heard of a aeroplane carrying is two people there will have to be a long time before it would do any good. I think it would take at least a four person aeroplane to take enough people along with the President's candidate to run the speeches. It has got to take one or two helpers when the crowds get big and then there is the pilot.

Almost ever day Mrs. Mayfield and Mama visit. They seem like they talk for hours at a time. I have seen Ledge a lot but we just mostly play and he doesn't really talk about anything. He is a changed person since those old days of being the biggest bully in the school.

Sunday, August 25, 1912

The Mayfields are coming to live on our farm.

Right out above our big barn there is a little log house that we have always called the Pack House. It is the house where our Grandparents lived before Grandpa and Father built the house where we now live in the year of 1900. It is a good solid log house and we have used it through the years as a place to keep the things that we do not use but that are still too good to throw away.

Father told us that the house where the Mayfields live is not their house at all. I never did think about that but the story is out. The house and property where the Mayfields have always lived really belongs to Mr. Johnny Woody and Mr. Mayfield had worked shares for Mr. Woody to pay to get to live there.

With all that has happened this year Mr. Mayfield hadn't done any work at all in this crop season. Father told Mrs. Mayfield that she and Ledge could come and live in the Pack House as long as they wanted to and they wouldn't have to pay a thing because it was just sitting there empty.

On Monday we started to clean out the Pack House. Mama supervised the work and the rest of us did the labor. We carried things out the door one at a time and Mama told us to either put it on the porch of the house put it in the barn loft or throw it down the ditch where we throw our trash and garbage. Some of the things she told us to put back into the Pack House because she thought that Mrs. Mayfield might need them.

By the end of the day on Monday the Pack House was all cleaned out.

On Tuesday Champ came and so did Ledge. Champ came to supervise the repairing of the chinking between the logs of the house and since Ledge was going to live here he was supposed to help with any of the work we needed help with.

A lot of the mud chinking between the logs had already fallen out. Champ told us to push out all the rest that was loose but not to break it loose if it seemed tight. He said to push it out from the inside so it would fall on the ground and not in the house. The girls and I were left to do that part while Champ and Merry and Ledge took the mules and the sled down toward the river to get clay. They were looking for a certain red kind that would dry hard and turn water once it was hard.

We finished punching out the old chinking before they got back and when they was back we ate dinner and then started in to work again.

We used a tub to mix water into the red clay until it was a good thick mud. Then we started chinking in the cracks between the logs. Where the logs was wide apart Champ nailed in a piece of board to stop most of the hole before we put the mud in.

It was a lot easier to work in teams of one on the inside and one on the outside so you could push that mud in tight from each side. Margaret Angeline was my partner. It seemed like the girls could get the clay smoother than the boys could.

Something I hadn't thought of when we started was that the more chinking we did the darker it got inside the house. But finally we got all done and now that house is just as tight as Dick's hatband. We even touched up the mud in the chimbley rocks.

On Thursday Mama led us in scrubbing and mopping and sweeping until it started raining and we were tracking in more dirt than we were mopping out. It rained on into the weekend and so the house will just have to set there and dry out for a few days until the Mayfields can move in. We made a lot of mud.

Sunday, September 1, 1912

The Mayfields are here. It stopped raining last Sunday night and by Wednesday the Pack House was all dried out enough to move into chinking and all.

Father and Zeb took King and Outlaw to haul them around in the buggy for that fancy politicking that they are doing. That meant that the rest of us had to hitch the mules to the wagon for the moving part.

Merry and I did that part but he fussed so much about it that once we got to the Mayfield's house Ledge and I became work partners for the rest of the day.

There wasn't that much to move. Furniture and all we moved ever thing they had in two loads and we could of done it in one if we had packed tighter and took more things apart.

It seemed like the biggest problem was for Mrs. Mayfield to figger out what to do with Mr. Mayfield's clothes and other things that was his. Tools and all were just family property and they come on with the rest of the family. Besides there was not too much of that stuff anyhow. But with the clothes it was like she didn't really want Ledge to be wearing them even if he would grow into them later.

She kept one big old oil cloth coat that I guess she could wear to do chores in and then she built a fire in the yard and burned the rest. She took a stick and held out ever shirt and watched it burn one at a time like it was some kind of ceremony or something. But she was crying all the while that she done it. I do not think she was crying over Mr. Mayfield as much as just over the way things turned out.

Mrs. Mayfield kept all of Darling's clothes. She had them all folded nicely and she gave to Annie Laurie a little bonnet that had been Darling's. Annie Laurie did thank her but does not feel right to wear it.

So now the Mayfields are all here and yesterday Ledge and Merry and I mowed hay. It was to surprise Father when he comes home from politicking next week. Grandpa carried a straight chair to the field and watched us while we mowed. I think he is remembering what happened to Zeb's leg in that very same hayfield last year.

Sunday, September 8, 1912

School has started early this year and I am glad.

Once school starts there is not near as much time to think about things and with what and all that has happened this summer the less thinking about it the better.

Mrs. Melville is as good as ever but I do know that she is thinking also about the things of the summer. I know that because for the last two years she has had us to write on the first day about what we did in the summertime. But this year she has got us to write about one thing we have never done that we would like to do some day. I started to write that I would like to fly in a aeroplane but then I wrote that I would really like to meet the new President of the U S A whoever it turns out to be.

Mrs. Melville has started me right out in the eighth reader and that is one reader above Ledge even though he is still nearly two years older than I am. I guess with all that has happened to him he just needs to drop back a year or two and recover.

We have some new books this year and the one that I like the most is called the Elson's Reader. It is not such a big book but it feels very heavy for a book when you pick it up. It is just full of poems and stories and histories and such. I do surely like this book.

Inside the front cover it says that the book was made in New York City by a company called the Scott and Foresman. It sounds like a hardware store to me but they make fine books.

It was Mrs. Melville who got us to look inside that cover. But she did it so that we could see that the Elson's Reader costed fourty four cents. That one look told all of us that we would surely take very good care of those books.

So now school is back for another year. This is going to be the second year that Merry has been out of school since he got finished with ever thing. It is a good thing for him to be at home to take care of things since Zeb can't do heavy work and Champ is married and besides that Father and Zeb are gone off politicking anyway. But Merry fusses that he is having to do all of the work.

I personally think that Merry has gone sour. I do a lot of the work and now that Ledge is not only our neighbor but almost a part of the family he does a whole lot of work too. It is strange to me that Zeb is the one that got crippled but Merry has got to acting a whole lot more crippled than Zeb is.

Sunday, September 15, 1912

In the afternoon on Friday we saw Father's buggy coming down the road toward home. I and the girls had just got home from school and we ran to meet Father and Zeb but there was no Zeb.

Before we could even ask a question Father said "Zeb is going to be a lawyer." Then we heard the whole story.

During the politicking Father and Zeb had gone all over the whole district and one day they went on to Asheville and spent the night even though it is not in our district. It was for a big Democrat meeting and Father was to speak on behalf of the Democrats there.

Father told us that after the big meeting he and Zeb went home to spend the night with Lawyer Stillwell. Lawyer Stillwell is the one who was the solicitor in the Mayfield trial but after that trial he gave up his solicitor's job and has gone back to being a regular lawyer.

They got to know Lawyer Stillwell and Lawyer Stillwell got to know Father and Zeb. They talked late about Zeb and what had happened to him and how he couldn't handle horses with his cripple leg and brace and all.

Then they must of talked about Zeb maybe being a lawyer because Father told it that Lawyer Stillwell said "Zeb I am impressed with you. Why don't you just stay here with us and Read Law in my office. You can be my lawing helper while you learn."

Zeb must of said that he had to help Father win the election first because the next part made Father very proud as he told us it. Lawyer Stillwell told Zeb that ever body knew that our Father was going to win in this District without anybody's help.

I guess that did it. Zeb decided to stay and Read Law and Father let him. Now we will have a brother who is a real lawyer and a Father who is a politician and more work than there ever was before for me and Mama and the girls. I am glad that Ledge is here to be a worker.

Sunday, September 22, 1912

Ever since Zeb stayed in Asheville to Read Law Merry has been pouting. He says it is because he has to do all of the work. I think that Merry is just jealous because Zeb is off and learning about the modern world while we are here at home. I have tried to say to Merry that ever body's time comes and his will come also. But he does not listen.

On Thursday when school got out I came out the door of the schoolhouse and there was Merry waiting right on the steps. When I asked him what he was doing there he said that he had come to talk to Mrs. Melville. He said that he knew that since her dead husband had been a sailor then he thought that maybe she could tell him about how to join the Navy.

I said that I would wait til he was through the talking and then walk home with him and so the girls went on home and I messed around there while Merry talked with Mrs. Melville for what I thought was a pretty long time. I couldn't hear their words exactly but from the sounds of their voices it sounded like it was Merry who was doing a lot more talking than Mrs. Melville was. A lot of times when we ask Mrs. Melville things she wants to know what we think about them so I am not surprised about that.

Finally Merry came out and we walked home. He said that Mrs. Melville told him that ever man in her family had gone to sea and that almost all of them had died at sea. Mrs. Melville told Merry that he ought to read a lot about the Navy and talk with Father about it. This did not seem to make Merry happy but the overall talking I guess did because he has not been as pouting since then.

Sunday, September 29, 1912

Yesterday was a big work day for doing one of my favorite things. We started retting the flax. And now it seems like not just Ledge but also Mrs. Mayfield is one of our workers.

Father always says that this is a good country to raise flax because it is cooler and wetter here overall than out in the flatlands. So we grow a lot of it. We have learned in school that out in the flat part of North Carolina where it is real hot they grow cotton but here we grow flax.

We always save our own seed and we plant it real thick so it grows tall and spindley and then it will have longer stalks and less leaves. The longer stalks make longer fibers for linen later on.

Mrs. Melville never had seen flax growing so after I made a report on it at school she came yesterday to see what we were going to do with it.

I didn't know that Ledge's Mama could be such a worker but after we got going I saw she was strong and good at it. I bet it makes her feel good to just do some good hard work.

Anyway me and Ledge and Merry and Mrs. Mayfield cut the flax with flax knives. As soon as we got started cutting the girls and Mama started stripping the leaves off. They save a lot of that leafy part to dry separate because it has the seed in it for next year.

When those of us that was cutting got finished we went back to the piles of stalks that they already had the leaves stripped clean off of and we started tying them into bundles. We tie them using throw away white oak strips from chair bottoming.

Once they are bundled the actual retting starts. We have some troughs that we call our retting troughs that are really just long wooden boxes with the seams pitched up so they will hold water. We put the bundles of flax in the troughs weigh them down with some flat rocks and fill the troughs up with water.

Ever day from now on we will check the water in the troughs. The flax has got to stay covered up for it to work.

It will take four or five or six weeks for the flax to get retted. When the stalks are popping open and starting to fall apart it will be all done.

The real fun part is after that when we bust the stalks all to pieces against the corner of the barn and then hackle out the trash and the tow until we have nice linen fibers ready to spin into thread.

This year Mama has promised to teach me to spin flax. I think that it is just beautiful and I want to be able to learn to do that.

Today is the best that I have ever seen Mrs. Mayfield. Sometimes she smiled at me and she talked to all of us. Mrs. Melville tried to help just a little bit but mostly she was just a learner.

Sunday, October 6, 1912

Father has been at home from politicking ever since he got back from the trip of leaving Zeb in Asheville with Lawyer Stillwell. But from the reading we do in the news paper he is about the only politician that is taking much of a break. Father says he will make one more trip through the District before election day and then he is content to leave it up to the voters.

Mr. Roosevelt has just got back to his home in New York after making a train politicking trip for eleven thousand miles around the country. The paper tells that sometimes Mr. Roosevelt and his party just get off of the train make some speeches and then get back on the train and keep going without even spending the night.

I guess that when you have a train engineer to drive the train you could just curl up and sleep back in the train even if it just went all night. Father says that Mr. Roosevelt has a fancy car with even a real bed in it and that is likely just what they do. I cannot imagine going to sleep in one place and waking up in another without even seeing how you got there. It is a modern world.

As soon as Mr. Roosevelt rests just a little bit he is going to start right off on a new train trip into the midwest. Mr. Woodrow Wilson is just now starting on a four thousand and five hunderd mile trip to the west on a real fast train called The Federal.

Now this is the funny thing. Mr. Taft is the most behind of all and there is only one month to go but he is just staying home in Washington DC and not doing any politicking at all. I do not understand that but Father says that it is not considered good manners for the actual President to do politicking too much. "It is not dignified" is what Father says.

Well in one month from now the election will be over and there will be vote counting day and night until we know who all the new politicians are. We will all have to wait.

Sunday, October 13, 1912

Last Sunday night just about after the time that I got through with my writing I went to bed. Now that Zeb is off in Asheville Merry and I each have a bed of our own. Back before Champ ever got married we had four in our room and two to a bed. Now our room seems like it is half empty.

Anyway Merry and I were both in bed just starting to try to go to sleep when we heard this awful noise. It sounded like it was way far off and it sounded more than anything else like it was a girl or woman screaming.

I set right up in the bed and even in the dark I could see Merry already getting up. By the time we went downstairs Mama and Father and the girls were already there. I was scared but Father opened the door. We were in the dark because we had not lit any lights and we went out onto the porch and listened to see if we heard it again.

Then we heard it. It sounded like it was way up on Cedar Cliff and it did sound just like screaming in a high voice. The first thing that I thought was "No body lives up there. Who could be up there a screaming."

Then Father said "It's a Painter. We used to hear that there were some around here in the past but I've never seen one in my lifetime." Then we went back into the house.

Father told us all that he knew about Painters. He said that they were a kind of wild Mountain Lion or a Wildcat. Before many people lived around here there was Painters here and there is even a place on the far side of Suncrest that is called "Painter Creek." Father says that the Painters must of got short of food where they live and they must be trying to catch some livestock.

Even with what Father told to us I couldn't wait to get to school on Monday to ask Mrs. Melville about it.

On Monday morning when Ledge and I fell in together to walk to school I found out that he had heard it too. His Mama had called it a Bob Cat but it sounded like the same thing to me. At school it turned out that Mrs. Melville hadn't heard it where she lives but a lot of the children at school had heard it.

Mrs. Melville got a book out on wild animals and we looked it up and found it. Actually the Painter's real name is called the Panther. It is also called a Lynx or a Mountain Lion or a Bobcat because it has just a short little tail.

The Painter is a meat eater and it ranges all around. Mrs. Melville said that this may be a bad year for deer or whatever else the Painters eat and she guesses that they have come this close back to people just because they are hungry. I wonder if a Painter would eat a baby.

All through the week we have been hearing that Painter scream. We did not hear it on Monday but on Tuesday we heard it screaming way over toward the river. I realized that from where we heard it on Sunday to where we heard it Tuesday it could have come exactly straight through here. That scared me to death even though Father said he was sure it stuck to the woods. All the way to school and back I and Ledge were on the lookout all of the time. We have been jumping at ever sound in the woods.

By Thursday some of the men got together to make a plan to hunt the Painter. It only seemed to scream at night and so a night plan seemed to be the thing to come up with.

Since it had been heard in two such different places the men didn't know where to go to do the hunting. They were meeting up at Woody's store and it was our own brother Champ who came up with a good idea. Champ said "We ought to bring it to us. Let's find a way to bait for it."

Then Harlan Junior had a idea. He said "Let's all get together at night and cook some meatskins and guts and stuff. Hog killing is starting and if somebody will save the lights we can use them to cook up a smell that will draw that Painter. We'll get in a circle around the fire and we'll shoot that hungry Painter." That is what he said.

A lot of people thought it wouldn't work but there wasn't any other idea to try. Mr. Hawkes Taylor was planning to kill a hog if it was cold enough on Friday and so the plan was made for Friday night. Father went and he told us about it.

They went up on Cedar Cliff and built a fire. When it had burned most down they made a rack of green limbs over the fire and put the hog lights and skin on the rack and let it cook slow to make a big smell. In a little while they heard that Painter. It screamed and screamed and it came pretty close but not to where they ever saw it. It went all the way around the fire Father said way out in the woods and not close enough to see or shoot at. Still the men knew that the plan was working and so they planned to try it over again ever night they could until they drew that Painter close enough.

Champ and Harlan Junior did not go out with the men on Friday night but they did go on Saturday. They were awful disappointed on Saturday night though because all night long they cooked and that Painter did not scream even one time at all.

Tonight the men are not going out but tomorrow Father and Champ will kill a hog and there will be guts and skins to cook tomorrow night.

There are two things I think about. Father is going on his last politicking trip next week and I hope that the Painter is caught before he is away from us. Also if it is not caught before Halloween I am not going out of the house on that night.

Sunday, October 20, 1912

The news of the week is just about not to be believed. It seems like we just read about Mr. Roosevelt starting out on a new politicking trip to the Midwest and then this happens.

He got as far as Milwaukee Wisconsin with the big crowds and no trouble and then it happened. The whole Roosevelt Party was staying the night at a place called the Gilpatrick Hotel. It was on last Monday.

They were getting ready to leave the hotel to go to where Mr. Roosevelt was supposed to make a big speech. He had writ the speech all out and he had folded it and put it in the pocket of his suit coat along with his spectacle case.

When they all come out of that Gilpatrick Hotel there was a big crowd all around and there was a crazy man in that crowd. He had a gun and his name was either Mr. John Chrank or John Schrank. The news paper did not seem to know for certain how to spell it.

Anyway he hollered something about "Second Term" and then shot Mr. Roosevelt with that gun. The bullet hit the spectacle case and then went through that big folded up speech. The speech was so fat that it slowed the bullet down to almost nothing. That big speech saved the day. The bullet did go into the meat of Mr. Roosevelt's right breast but it did not seriously injure him.

The newspaper said that the crowd of people might have lynched that John Chrank right there on the spot if it had not been for Mr. Roosevelt hisself. Mr. Roosevelt told the crowd that he felt sorry for Mr. Chrank and that the crowd must let the authorities do their duty.

Later on in the week the news paper said it was likely that this Mr. Shrank would end up in what is called a Insane Asylum since that anybody who did what he did has just got to be a insane person. I guess that is right but I think there ought to be some kind of punishment for doing what he did. Father says that just being Insane is enough punishment for anybody.

After the shooting Mr. Roosevelt went right on and made that speech. It was the very speech that had the bullet hole right through it. Later on the news paper men asked him how he felt. Mr. Roosevelt said "It would take more than that to kill a Old Bull Moose like me."

Now the people are calling the Progressive Republican Party the "Bull Moose Party." I think it is a pretty good name.

After it was all over Mr. Roosevelt got the bullet took out.

Sunday, October 27, 1912

The jig is up. Champ and Harlan Junior got caught and Father says "The Jig is up." Here is the story.

On Friday night the men were all out cooking hog lights again and trying to lure that Painter in close. They had tried over a week by now and the Painter was getting to coming in near to the fire circle.

What I do not know is whether Father had noticed that whenever both Champ and Harlan Junior were in the Painter hunting party the Painter never screamed or if it was just his own good idea to do what he did. Anyway on this night the Painter was screaming and Harlan Junior and Champ were not there.

Father told the men his new idea. He told them that he thought he would go off into the woods and see if he could get on the outside of where the Painter was circling. He said he wasn't scared and that he had his gun. He would try to shoot the Painter as it came around and he would shoot the gun if he needed help.

Father went off into the woods on one side of the fire. In a little while the men heard that Painter circling back around toward where Father had gone off to hide. Ever body got real excited because they thought that at last there was a plan that would work.

The Painter let out a big scream and all of a sudden ever body heard both barrels of Father's twelve gauge go off "Blam Blam." In just a split second after that Champ and Harlan Junior both came jumping and hollering into the fire circle. "Don't shoot—it's just us. Don't shoot—don't shoot" is what they were hollering. They both had their hands up in the air.

About then Father came back in to the fire and ever body said that he was just a laughing his head off. Then the story all came out.

Harlan Junior and Champ had seem this advertisement in the news paper to order a thing that was called a Wild Animal Caller. They had got their money together and had ordered it. It was a thing that you blow in real hard while you work a little handle on it. That Wild Animal Caller makes a noise just like something screaming its head off.

After the Wild Animal Caller came Champ and Harlan Junior started their plan. They were going to keep up the plan until Halloween and then come out with it.

Anyway when Father hid out there in the woods and then saw them slipping around to blow that thing he shot the shotgun in the air over their heads. They thought they had just about both been shot and it like to of scared them to death.

And so as Father said "The Jig is Up." But it has already been a big trick and a treat for us for Halloween. I will not forget it. Still and all I am glad that the Painter was not real.

Sunday, November 3, 1912

This has been the last week of politicking before the election. In two days it will be all over but the vote counting and as Father says

"The shouting."

Father started out on one last little speaking trip this week. We thought he would be back on yesterday but by Thursday he was back. He said that it seemed to him like most people had already made up their minds on who to vote for so he didn't see any reason to waste time and food money doing any more politicking. So he came on home. It is good to have him here for us all to do the final talking before the election.

We had a election for play at school on Friday. Mrs. Melville wanted three boys to dress up and make speeches and play like Taft and Roosevelt and Wilson but she could not find either a boy or a girl who would like to play like a Republican. Besides that nobody in our school is big enough to even play like Mr. Taft.

Ever body in our school voted for Woodrow Wilson but that doesn't really mean anything as far as the nation goes because nobody in this township has ever even seen a Republican.

Anyway a lot has been happening. Mr. Roosevelt is back in New York after getting that bullet took out. He has doctor's orders to rest but the old Bull Moose as he now calls hisself is out making speeches and hand shaking.

Mr. Taft's Vice President Mr. James Sherman died this week and in respect of his dying Woodrow Wilson called off a big parade he was planing to have. Mr. Taft went up to Utica New York where the funeral was held and the news paper coverage of the funeral did give Taft a little publicity even if it was mostly what they called sympathy votes. Now Mr. Taft does not have even a Vice President on the ticket with him and if he did get re elected he would have to run the government all by hisself.

I do myself feel sorry for Mr. Taft. We even read in the news paper that he went to church last Sunday and the preacher preached a sermon in favor of Mr. Roosevelt.

There is one place that I would like to be on election night. It is called Times Square in New York City. The reason I would like to be there is that there is a tall building there that is called the Times Tower. It is a news paper building. The plan is that they will light up different colored electric lights on the top of that building to show who is ahead as the election returns come in. If the lights are white Wilson is ahead. If they are red Taft is ahead. If Roosevelt is ahead they will turn on green lights. There is another code of lights about the Governor of New York but I would not really be interested in that.

We do not have school on Tuesday because the schoolhouse is the voting place. Mostly I think ever body is just too excited to have school.

I can hardly wait. This is the first real election of a President where I have been old enough to know what it is about. And besides that our own Father is in this election too.

There was one funny little story in the news this week. There was a woman in Ohio by the name of Mrs. W.K. Ligette. She is what the news paper called a Society Woman. This Mrs. Ligette had been blind for four years and then all of a sudden she got her sight back.

When this happened people asked her how it was to be able to see again. She said that most in the world she was shocked to see what had happened to the fashions of dresses while she was blind. She did not say a word about being glad to see her husband or her children or even her own home. The first thing that she looked at was the fashion of dresses.

I am glad that our Mama is not what is called one of those Society Women.

Sunday, November 10, 1912

The Election is over and ever body got elected. What I mean is that ever body we were pulling for including our own Father got elected.

Mr. Woodrow Wilson is to be our new President. As Father said "Boy did he sweep the nation." Father went into town on election day and stayed all night long as the election returns kept coming in on the telegraph at the railroad station. The next morning he got home and told us all about it. I had not hardly been able to sleep any at all for wanting to know what was going on. I laid awake thinking about all of those people in New York City who got to see the code of lights on that building.

Father says that the results are not yet what is called official. But the votes in most cases were so wide that the outcome overall can't change.

On the next morning it looked like Mr. President Elect Woodrow Wilson had won forty of the forty eight states we now have. It looked then like Mr. Roosevelt won six states and poor old Mr. Taft won only Utah and Vermont. Later on in the week though it looks like Wilson may have won even more than that.

The news paper on yesterday said that this is the worst defeat of a candidate in history since U S Grant beat Mr. Horace Greeley. The news paper Editorials said "The Republicans are Destroyed." That is strong language to me.

Maybe it is true for now though since Mr. Wilson even beat Roosevelt in his home state of New York and he beat Mr. Taft in his own home state of Ohio.

On top of all that Mr. Locke Craig was elected the Governor of North Carolina. He will be the Governor when our Father goes to be in the new Legislature in the spring of the year. We have not even really started to think about that part yet but it will surely change all of our lives.

Father says that Mr. Wilson not only won as President but now in the U S House of Repersenatives the Democrats will outnumber the Republicans by a hunderd and fifty seven. When the final official count is over there looks to be even a Democrat majority in the Senate of the U S A.

It has been a good week for the Democrats.

I never thought before about what happens to the person that loses in the election but this week I started thinking about that.

If our Father would of lost he would just stay home and be a farmer like always. Since the state Legislature is just a part time responsibility he will still be a farmer for most of the time anyway.

If Mr. Wilson would of lost I guess that he still had his job as being the Governor of New Jersey. Since he won that opens up that job so that somebody else gets it I guess.

I also guess that with all the money that the Roosevelts have it will not much matter if Mr. Roosevelt gets a job or not. Maybe when he gets over being shot he can just travel around the world again.

Now as far as Mr. Taft goes I have read that he is just going to go on back to Ohio and be a lawyer again. I hope that he is a good one because he will need to make a lot of money to buy groceries. I wonder if he gets to take that cow named Pauline with him or if she now becomes Mr. Wilson's cow.

Maybe now Mr. Taft can figger out a way to get on the Supreme Court since I remember way back Father told us that is what he wanted to begin with. I somehow doubt it with Mr. Wilson who beat him in the White House.

So for now politicks is over. Maybe things can get back to normal around here.

Sunday, November 17, 1912

A real funny thing has happened this week that has got ever body to laughing.

On yesterday we finally got around to cooking apple butter and putting up apples and Lucee came to help Mama. We are a little late this year what with the politicking and all. So Mama and Lucee planned to put up the apples together and then split part of what they put up. Mrs. Mayfield was helping too.

On in the afternoon I and Ledge were playing with Lucee's baby Jeff. He is about a year and a half old now and can walk and talk a lot at the same time. That is actually not much of a baby anymore but more of a real young boy in some ways. We were making big piles of leaves under the maple trees where they have been all piling up. We are late with the leaf raking too with all of that politicking taking the spare time.

Anyway we were making piles of leaves and jumping in the piles.

Those leaves smell good when you jump around and play in them.

Sometimes we would make a big pile of leaves and then get little Jeff by the arms and legs and swing him back and forth and then toss him into the pile of leaves. He was laughing all over and ever time he landed he would come running right back and begging for us to do it again.

We all played until we were all worn out. Ever body ate supper together after that and then Lucee and Harlan Junior started home so they could get in before dark.

Just a little while after dark they came back. Even from in here in the house we could hear little Jeff crying like he was pitching a real mad baby fit.

"What in the world is the matter." Mama wanted to know. Harlan Junior had come to the door and left Lucee trying to manage that squalling baby Jeff in the buggy.

"We've lost Sweet Sue." Harlan Junior said.

Sweet Sue is Jeff's rag babydoll. He had been playing with the baby doll when we were jumping in the leaves. He must of forgot about that ragdoll while we were playing but on the way home he missed it and that baby would not go to sleep without finding Sweet Sue.

So Harlan Junior and Lucee came back to search for a lost ragdoll that was at this time in control not only of a baby boy but of a entire human family.

We all looked right quick in the house to be sure that the babydoll was not there but all of the time that we were looking we already knew the answer to that business. Ever body knew that the babydoll was in the yard and it was lost in those leaves in the dark.

Father got out some lanterns and we divided up into lantern holders and rakers. It is a big yard and there were leaves all over ever where. I was a raker.

Father did not do any of the work. He just stood on the porch and actually laughed out loud to watch while the rest of us raked leaves and searched for that babydoll. It was funny to hear. We could hear that baby crying and fussing out there in the buggy. We could hear

Father standing on the porch laughing. And we could hear "Scratch scratch scratch" as we raked those leaves that had already been raked up once in the daylight.

It was Mary Adeline who finally found Sweet Sue. That ragdoll was wet from the dew by now but Jeff didn't care at all. He grabbed that baby from Mary Adeline. After all that screaming I would bet that he was asleep in the buggy in less than five minutes of time.

Now all of this was not a very important thing over all to have happened. But in this modern world maybe it is a important thing to get to have a real good laugh about something.

Sunday, November 24, 1912

Zeb is home for Thanksgiving.

We did not even know that he was coming until he rode up on a strange horse on yesterday morning. I had not seen Zeb ride on a horse since he got crippled as he had always gone traveling with Father in the politicking. It was a surprise to me that he could ride that way.

Zeb explained that Lawyer Stillwell was going down to Greenwood to visit with his wife's people for Thanksgiving week and that they had closed up the law office. The horse belonged to Lawyer Stillwell who Zeb said has a Auburn automobile but still has some horses as well.

He went on to explain that this horse was real gentle and would let him get on from the wrong side without bucking around or anything. He told us that with his crippled foot in the brace he cannot get on from the left but if a horse will let him mount up from the right he can ride it just as good as anything. This is a fine thing to know because it makes Zeb a more capable person if he can get around on horseback.

We have all had a good time finding out all about the Law Reading. Zeb is liking it a lot and he likes being in Asheville North Carolina. He says that there is even one of the moving picture theaters there and he may save up and go to one of them. There are other things too and there are girls there that are happy to meet a unmarried man who is going to be a lawyer he says.

Nobody in our family has ever married somebody that they did not grow up with in all of our family history. Just about nobody ever married anybody who he was not already somehow related to. If Zeb gets a outsider girl it will be a new thing for us to get used to.

Anyway he said that Lawyer Stillwell has started him out reading all about the U S A Constitution in what is called Constitutional Law. Zeb says that he may not ever be called on to have a case involving that Constitutional Law but that Lawyer Stillwell says to start there because it is the starting place for all other laws. He and Father have talked a lot about it but it sounds very hard to me and also not very interesting.

I am glad that Zeb did get to come home and his being here plus his being able to ride saddleback on that horse are reason enough to have Thanksgiving.

Sunday, December 1, 1912

Father is as excited as he can be and Merry is just as excited as Father is. Mr. Woodrow Wilson has announced who is going to be in his Cabinet of Government and a man from North Carolina named Mr. Josephus Daniels is going to be the Secretary of the Navy.

Father says that he has met this Mr. Josephus Daniels at a big Democrat meeting once in Asheville where Mr. Daniels was giving the main speech. This Mr. Josephus Daniels is the editor of a news paper in Raleigh that is called the News and Observer. Father says that he had a government job when Grover Cleveland was the President as a worker in the Interior Land Department and it is the greatest honor that has come to our state since the War Between the States for him to be so high up in the government.

Of course this has Merry now in the determined mood to go off and join the Navy. He is just sure that he could go right up to Mr. Josephus Daniels and say "I am Cate McGee's boy. Don't you want me to take over a ship in your Navy."

I think that it is the silliest thing in the world for Merry to be thinking so on the Navy. He has never even seen the Ocean itself and more than that he has never even been in a boat as far as I know. How in the world does he actually think that he can be in the Navy.

Still and all Merry says that if Zeb could go to Asheville and learn to be a lawyer that he ought to be able to get to the ocean and get to be in the Navy. He says that if Josephus Daniels can go to Washington he can go to the Navy. I don't know about all of this. I am glad that a North Carolina man is got to be so important and I am glad that this has got Merry at least cheered up but I am not in favor of a mountain boy joining the ocean navy just because it is a idea that he has just got completely stuck in his head.

Sunday, December 8, 1912

Grandpa is really staying for the whole winter again this year.

Back when Father decided to run for the Legislature Grandpa decided to stay and help out last winter so Father could politick. Today he told us that for sure he was staying right on here as long as he is needed year after year. This is partly because Father will be gone more than ever to be in the Legislature.

All of us knew that he was staying longer than he used to because he usually goes back by train to Nashville Tennessee as soon as the first frost comes. But this year we thought that he was staying again just to find out how all the elections here were going to come out and so he would not miss out on any of the politicking.

But here he is set with us for the winter again. Nothing could make me happier than that.

It is funny how families change. You think one day that the way it is that day will be the way things stay for a right long time. Then before you know it it is changed. I can still remember clearly when even Champ was considered a boy. And it is so fresh in my mind when Lucee and Harlan Junior started that courting in the living room.

Now they have a doll losing baby.

So now Zeb is gone and Grandpa and the Mayfields are here. Father will be gone in the spring for a lot of politicking time when the Legislature meets so it is good. Things change.

The other news from Grandpa is that he has wrote to Aunt Louise about coming here to be with us at Christmas and Friday he got a letter saying to where she has agreed to do that. She will come to Erwin Tennessee on the twenty second of December and will spend the night in a hotel there. Then the next day she will ride the Narrow Gauge on up to Suncrest and we will pick her up there.

It has been years since I have seen Aunt Louise. I guess since Grandpa used to come to Nashville to be with her she just found out all about her family that she needed to know in that way. She was married but her husband whose name was Milton died before I can even remember and we do not have any cousins from her.

I will be glad for her to come and even if she does not bring nothing I will be glad to see her with us for Christmas. But the best part of it all is that we will keep having Grandpa with us all year long it looks like from now on.

Sunday, December 15, 1912

We have spent almost all of this entire year thinking about two things. One was all of what happened with the Mayfields. The other was our own U S A politicks. We have not paid much attention to the rest of the world.

Father has read to us today that there is a bad revolting taking place in the country of Mexico. There is a lot of fighting and violence down there and a lot of the people want the President killed and thrown out. There is even a army inside the country that is fighting against the real army.

Father says that Mr. Taft knew about this revolt but always said that it was a problem for Mexico to straighten out on its own. Mr. Taft was asked over and over again about helping one side or the other but he never did help either one.

Since the addition of New Mexico and Arizona as new states of the U S A we have our country closer to Mexico than it ever has been before. This probably means that whatever happens in Mexico will be of more concern to us than before.

Father says that he does not know whether Woodrow Wilson will take a different stand about Mexico or not. We will just have to wait and see. But Father says that this is something that we should all know and be thinking about.

While he was telling us this I think that Father gave away the real reason for doing the telling.

He said that if there is any fighting to be done either with or on behalf of Mexico it will be the Navy that does it. All of the important parts of Mexico are along the coast line and not along the border with the U S A.

He looked right at Merry when he told this just like he was trying to scare him. He told that with Mr. Josephus Daniels as head of the Navy we would likely hear more about this. If the navy goes to fight there he said some ships will get sunk and some sailers will get drownded.

Merry got to looking awful pale as he was telling this. I think that when he thinks about getting into the Navy he is thinking just of leaving home and getting out of work. He has just looked at a lot of pretty pictures of ships and not thought about getting shot up or drownded either one.

I have noticed that after this talk about Mexico Merry has not said much more about going off to the Navy.

Sunday, December 22, 1912

Christmas is Wednesday and our Aunt Louise is on her actual way here at this very time. I do not know if she has got to Erwin Tennessee yet or not but I think about traveling on that train and I imagine ever minute what it would be like.

I think that the most fun thing would be to go on a train in the snow. Grandpa says that they have big snow plows on them so that they can just keep going and push the snow right out of the way. We saw a picture of one of them in the news paper and the plow is like a laying off plow but it is as big as the entire front of the train. There is not snow now though so Aunt Louise will just have to be content looking at the normal scenery.

We have had a fine day today. We had a special Christmas Dinner just for our family and the Mayfields.

I guess that with Aunt Louise coming in just a day or two that Mama just has figgered that we won't see the Mayfields then and she just wanted to do something special for Ledge and his Mama. So after church today Champ and Sallie Jane and Lucee and Harlan Junior came home with us. Ledge and his Mama are also going to church at our church with us about ever Sunday and they were invited to come. Mrs. Melville was invited to come also and she did come with us.

We had a evermore big Christmas dinner to beat all time. There was a pork roast and sweet potatoes and fried cabbage and baked apples and ever thing to go with all of that. I know that we will have another big dinner on Christmas day but this one was just as good as any meal could ever be.

We did not talk at all about the sad things that have happened in the last year. We talked about good things and Grandpa told us stories about Nashville Tennessee and about time he spent long ago in the coal mines in New Philadelphia Ohio. Mrs. Melville told about growing up in Massachusetts. I believe that they were both trying to get us to think of other times and of far away. It worked for me and I think it did for Ledge too because both he and his Mama seemed to have just a fine time.

In the afternoon after Mrs. Melville went home Grandpa set and talked with Mrs. Mayfield for quite a long time in the parlor. I asked Mama if they was courting and she said "Of course not they are just grown up friends."

I believe that it is a good thing to have grown up friends and I do believe that after all that has gone by this year Ledge and I are ourselves about to get to be grown up friends.

This year's Christmas Roll Call was different from last year. It was the first time that I can remember that Aunt Louise has been here.

Aunt Louise got to Suncrest on the Narrow Gauge on Christmas Eve which was Tuesday. All the way home to our house she kept saying "It's just like old times It's just like old times." Then I realized that Aunt Louise grew up in the very house where the Mayfields now live with our own Father as her Brother and with Grandpa as her Father. It seemed a strange thing to realize that and to think that someday I may come back here to meet Merry and Zeb and all of the girls for Christmas and then be the one to say "It's just like old times."

School got out on the Friday before Christmas and so this last week there has been no school. On Monday Grandpa took me and Ledge out in the woods and the three of us got two Christmas trees which was one for our house and one for Ledge's house. We have now taken to calling the Pack House the Mayfield House and that is the way that it will be as long as they want to live there.

I and Grandpa nailed planks on that cedar tree bottom and stood it in the parlor and we decorated it with paper cut outs and strings of popcorn and some sparkle ropes that Aunt Louise had sent us last year from Nashville Tennessee. It made a beautiful house.

The smell of the house on Christmas day was wonderful. Aunt Louise and Mama got up early and kept on with the cooking that Mama had already started the day before. Oh it smelled like spices and meats and everything good that you can imagine.

I have to keep counting up to remember how many people were actually at our family house when the eating time came. There was Mama and Father and Grandpa and Aunt Louise as the old people. Then there was Champ and Sallie Jane and their Junior who is just now five years old and not a baby at all anymore and their new baby they call "Hawk" which is short for Hawkins his name. Then there is

Lucee and Harlan Junior and little Jeff who did bring his baby doll with him. Then there are the rest of us being Merry and the twins and I and Annie Laurie and Zeb who is home for a break from Lawyer Stillwell's in Asheville. That makes seventeen people in all who are what Father calls Our Immediate Family. It is almost hard for me to just keep up with all of us and I realize that as I write out my life I do gradually tell more about some than about the others. That is the way life is I guess.

Almost ever thing this Christmas has been happy except for one thing. At the table Merry wanted to tell his Christmas wish. When Father told him to go ahead he said "I wish I could leave this home and join the Navy." There was a long quiet moment after that and then Father told him that he just could not do that. He was needed on the farm especially with Father going to the Legislature and Zeb reading law. Merry pouted for the rest of the day about that and it kind of spoiled a nice day for all of us.

In the afternoon the Mayfields dropped by. Mrs. Mayfield had knitted wool caps for all of the boys and made aprons for ever one of the girls and even Mama. Father was not prepared for this but he did give them four oranges that came out of a sack that Aunt Louise had brought to us from Nashville Tennessee.

1913

I am now thirteen years old and Father is sixty three. We both had our birthdays on Wednesday and Mama fixed us a supper of fried chicken and made my favorite Spice Cake. Then I got the best present of all brought by Aunt Louise from Nashville Tennessee for Grandpa to give to me and saved for my birthday.

This present was a new book. It is named The Three Musketeers and it is by a French Man named Alexander Dumas. I have stayed up late ever night since then reading in it and I have already read more than half of it.

What I see is that this book is just exactly like our family. The Three Musketeers are just like Me and Merry and Ledge. They always stick close together but one is always kind of on the fussy side and that is like Merry.

Also there were once four of the musketeers but one is gone now and that is just like our Brother Zeb. Anyway I do so like that book and I will read it over and over again I know.

On yesterday Father asked me to go for a walk with just the two of us. We talked as we walked for a long time.

Father wanted to know if I was still doing this writing out of my life. I do not show this writing to anybody and he had not asked me about it for a long time. I told him that I am still writing and he said that he guessed that I was just going to write myself grown up. I didn't understand that and he told me to later read what I had been writing and I would likely see myself grow up in a way that I never seen as it was happening. I don't know about that. I don't care about going back and reading my own writing. It is the writing of it that is fun. Anyway he told me that if I was to keep writing it should be for my own reasons and not anymore at all because I thought he was making me. I will for now keep on writing for my own good.

Father told me that with Zeb gone to read hisself into a lawyer that he guessed I was the actual man of the family now. I said "What about Merry." All he said was "Oh you know how Merry is. You are the one that I can depend on when I am gone off to Raleigh to be the best help to your Mama." That was a nice thing for him to say about me but it was scary about Merry. I mean I have been thinking that Merry is sour but I never thought that Father might see him the same way.

"You are thirteen years old now Medford McGee" Father said. "That is old enough to be a man." I think this is the scariest thing that my Father has ever said to me especially since I know that he will be gone to the Legislature in the spring and I just may have to be a man where I like it or not.

So it is 1913 and I am who I am. I hope that this year goes slower than the last one so I can keep up with it.

Sunday, January 12, 1913

Aunt Louise left on yesterday to go back home to Nashville Tennessee but just like he promised Grandpa has stayed here to be with us.

Early yesterday morning we got up and loaded ever body up into the wagon along with Aunt Louise and her things. She brought ever body so many Christmas presents that she didn't have as much to take back as she did come with.

We all went into Suncrest to take her to catch the Narrow Gauge to Erwin. After the train came and took her off we went around town a little while before heading for home. I couldn't keep from noticing how much things have changed since I was a young boy.

I can remember that just two or three years ago we saw our first automobile which was Doc Graham's Ford. Now there are automobiles just all up and down the street. And the horses do not seem to be scared of them even one bit in this world. Most of them are Fords but there are also Hupmobiles and Marmons and once in a while a Chevrolet or a big Studebaker.

There is now electricity in Suncrest and all of the stores have electrical lights. I have heard that there are even electrical stoves that you can cook food on without even building a fire in them first. I have also heard that talking telegraphs are coming which are called telephones.

The reason that I am thinking of these things is that I am thinking of what it will be like for our own Father to go down to Raleigh to be in the Legislature. He will be coming out of one world and going into another one. I mean that our home world is a world where things still happen the way they always have and we live in the old ways but he will be going into the Modern World of the state capital and it will be different in ever way. I hope that our Father can deal with all of that. It will be hard to make laws for ordinary people while sitting in the middle of a big and modern city which is not where most ordinary people live. We will miss him and will be thinking of him day and night.

In the afternoon Father bought me and Merry a little bucket of peanut butter. It was so good that we took the top off of that little tin bucket and we ate it all up with our fingers on the way home. I like to of got a belly ache from that.

Anyway finally we went home.

Sunday, January 19, 1913

The twins have started courting.

I guess that since time just goes on one day at a time I never did actually notice that my sisters Mary Adeline and Margaret Angeline were getting about grown up. When I stop to think about it I realize that they are now eighteen years old each and this is their last year in school. They will have to do something after that and so it is about time for the courting to start.

Today was the day. About three o'clock in the afternoon a buggy pulled up in the yard in front of the house. When Father looked out he said that the horses were Mr. Johnny Woody's horses. He is the one that has the store and that owns the land where the Mayfields used to live. We figgered that Mr. Woody was coming to see Father about some kind of business or some politicks. But no it was both of Mr.

Woody's big old boys.

They are both finished with school and so I don't know them very much. Their names are Robert and Jackson and that is what they are both called without any nicknames at all. They were all slicked up to beat the band and still had on their Sunday clothes. I didn't know why they were coming.

Later on it looked like it was all a plan all the time. I think that because when they came at three o'clock in the afternoon Mary Adeline and Margaret Angeline were still both dressed up in their church clothes where they usually get out of them just as soon as they can when we come home from church. Those Woody boys are always at church and I think that the girls heard that they were coming.

Anyway they came to the door and asked if "Miss Mary and Miss Margaret" were available to be visited. Those girls were back in the kitchen and they were both just giggling to beat all. It was Father who had gone to the door and he told the Woody boys to come into the parlor and he would see if the girls were at home.

Both of them went up to their room and brushed and primped for what seemed like a hour before they went into the living room to see those boys.

I and Ledge were in the kitchen whittling on some walking sticks. We both went upstairs into me and Merry's bedroom because it is right over the parlor. We put our ears to the floor and tried to see if we could hear what was going on down there. We couldn't hear a thing.

After that we went outside to play around because it isn't very cold today. Ever chance we had we would sort of walk past the parlor windows and see if we could just sort of glance inside. All we saw was that the girls were sitting side by side on the settee and the Woody boys were sitting side by side in two chairs across the room. If that is courting then I don't get it.

After the courting was all over Mama asked the girls which boy came to see which girl. The girls said that they didn't even know. Both of the boys had just talked the same with both of the girls.

Mama told Father that it sounded safe to her. It sounds to me like those girls will never have a chance in this world of getting married when they can't even tell which boy is courting after them.

After supper tonight me and Grandpa and Ledge had a long talk about courting. He may be eighty three years old but he still remembers a lot of things about being a boy and he is good to talk to.

He talked about how when he was a boy he got scared one day that he was going to die. The thing that scared him was that he noticed that black hair was starting to grow out under his arms and between his legs and he thought that he had some kind of disease.

I and Ledge both laughed out loud about that but both of us had already talked about that happening to us and we had each been scared until we figgered out that it happens to ever body. There are also other things that are starting to happen to my body now that makes me know that Father is right when he says that "I am the man of the family." I will not write about them but anyone who has ever got to be thirteen years old surely knows what this is all about.

I may even decide that it is time to start courting girls myself one of these days. There are one or two at school that I just might have in mind.

Sunday, January 26, 1913

There was big courting here this afternoon again. Those Woody boys came back to see if "Miss Mary and Miss Margaret" were available for visiting. This time when me and Ledge looked in the parlor window Mary Adeline was sitting on the settee with Jackson and Margaret Angeline was sitting in the chair next to Robert. I don't know if that is the way it is going to be or if they are just trying that out like you would try on new shoes to see if they fit.

Anyway those Woody boys stayed until Father had to call the girls to eat supper and by then the boys had to go home in the dark.

Besides that Grandpa and Mrs. Mayfield set in the kitchen and talked for the same time. I don't think that what they are doing is courting though because they do not care when Ledge and I come in the kitchen and the twins about die if we go anywhere near that parlor. I think that Mrs. Mayfield and Grandpa are just fine grown up friends. Besides he is old enough to be her father. Maybe that is what grown up friends are like.

Me and Ledge have been picking out girls at school that we might be interested in after a year or two. But for now we will just enjoy the courting of the twins and not have to get into that trouble on our own.

Groundhog Day, February 2, 1913

If the old Groundhog is right it looks like winter is over. Today was about as cloudy and bad a looking day as it could of been and that is a good sign if you believe in groundhogs. I don't know whether to believe in groundhogs or not. Grandpa says that the signs know more about the weather than the groundhogs do and that the signs say that the bad winter is not over yet.

Maybe I am not all the way grown up yet because I do not know how to read the signs yet. Grandpa has a almanac with the signs in it but still and all I do not understand that. He says that in the later spring he will show me how to plant by the signs and then I will learn all about it. I do not think that Father plants by the signs as much as Grandpa does. Maybe in the modern world we will not know about such things.

Almost ever week Father gets some mail from Raleigh about going down there to start into the Legislature in the spring. That time is coming. It will be after the inauguration of both President Wilson and Governor Craig. We had all just better get used to it.

Sometimes I get to thinking that all of the news in the world is bad news. Then something happens or we read something that gets me to feeling better again. This week it was our reading in the paper about a wedding that did it. It was not quite a year ago when that ship the Titanic hit that iceberg and went down and all those rich and poor people both drownded. This week we have read that two of the survivors of the tragedy have got themselves married for good. Their names are Mr. Karl Behr and Miss Helen Newsom. I cannot think of a finer thing as a sign for good in the world than the story of this wedding. How a tragedy can end up starting up a wedding is a sign that there is good in the world.

It did say in the paper that Miss Newsom was gave away at the wedding by her stepfather. That got me to knowing that her real father must be dead. So I realize that even in the middle of this time of their happiness it is not as happy as it would be if her real daddy was there to be a part of it.

What I guess is that all in all the good and the bad in the world balances out. When bad things happen I hope that the good will come back and balance it out. But when things are going good it is scary to think that you may have to put up with some bad things that are sure to come later.

Sunday, February 9, 1913

One of the things that I have noticed about getting grown up is that I do not pay as much worry to the weather as I did when I was a boy. When I was younger I did worry a lot about whether it was going to be cold in the winter and even about things like whether or not it would rain on me.

I think that I did that worrying because as a boy you do not give any thought to being prepared for anything. And I guessed that if it got cold that I would just be out there without any coat on at all just a freezing to death. Now I do not worry about weather much because I give more attention ahead of time to how to dress and I think in preparation for the time to come. Now that this is the way it is I do hardly ever get cold even when the winter is as cold as it is now. I just start out with one layer of clothes over another and if you put on enough you will finally stay warm.

I have been doing a lot of reading of the news paper on my own these days. Even though all of us can read very well now we have always deferred to Father to read the news to us on Sunday. But I have got to thinking that if he is gone to the Legislature maybe I will be the one who is the news reader. I don't think that Merry would want to do it and the twins have their minds on those Woody boys. Annie Laurie is a good reader but not good enough for something as important as the news.

This week I especially noted two stories of interest to me. One was about a man named Mr. Robert Smith who lives down south of here a good ways in a place called Hominy.

It seems that this Mr. Smith was a old man who was known to be incurably ill by all of his neighbors. On Tuesday of last week the word went out that Mr. Smith had died and since ever body knew that he was incurable they were not surprised. They all set out to bathe him and I guess they dressed him and laid him out to be a corpse.

People from all around came by to pay their respects.

About seven o'clock in the evening one of the men who had helped to lay him out noticed that his arms looked like they were sort of out of place. He went over to the corpse and the corpse opened one of his eyes and said "It is raining ain't it." It said that ever body in that room remembered something they were supposed to be doing somewhere else.

A little later some of them came on back and they set up most of the night while the corpse once in a while said something or another. About eight o'clock the next morning they pronounced him dead again.

After that it said that they held the body for three days to be real sure he was dead before they buried him. I do think that was a good idea.

I thought this was a funny story but I decided not to tell it or read it to Ledge because it might get him to thinking about his own dead sister or his hanged daddy not to mention his brother Duck. It may be a good idea to read over the news ahead of time if I am going to be the one to read it out loud so I can check out what may or may not be the best things to read out to ever body. I wonder if Father ever did that.

There was a little story beside that one that I thought was very sad.

A man way down below Canton named Mr. C.B. Phillips died a while back. It doesn't seem like he either had any children or if he does they do not care anything about the land where they come from because the paper said that his entire homeplace is going to be divided up into thirty little farms and be sold off to just anybody around who had the money to buy one. The paper said that even some people who have been renters can now buy a farm of their own.

It is good for people to get land of their own. But I do think it is sad for land to pass completely out of a family line with either nobody interested or maybe just nobody at all to take it over.

This got me to wondering what will become of our homeplace in the years to come. I mean Champ has already gone off and got his own place with his wife's daddy. Lucee has gone off and lives where they heired that land from Mrs. Elisabeth Chambers. Zeb has left home to become a lawyer and I just know that he will never come back and live here with us. Merry is just busting to run off and join the Navy. The twins are both courting those Woody boys and their daddy has more land than anybody else around here. That leaves just me and Annie Laurie. The Mayfields don't really count since they are not kin to us at all. I just wonder how much longer Father will be able to be in politicks and we still can work the farm. But we have to eat somehow. I guess that I will probably be the one to live here for the rest of my life. I better learn how to make soap and ever thing else as well.

We did kill another hog this week and made most of it into sausage. But I have helped Mama do that so much that Grandpa didn't have to tell me a thing. He did argue to put more pepper in the sausage than we usually do though.

Sunday, February 16, 1913

Today I asked to be the one to read the news paper out loud to the family. Father said that he would love for me to do the reading and I would also get to pick out what to read as that is part of the reader's job.

I picked two things one of which Father had never picked out to have us hear about. Actually it is not something that you could just hear about. You have to see it. It is called The Weather Map of the newspaper.

I have been looking at this Weather Map for some time now and it is just very interesting to me. It shows the entire U S A and has lines and figures to show the temperature and the areas where there are storms and such. I do not know how in this world they can put that weather map together. I would think that you would have to fly way up in the heavens until you could see the entire of the U S A before you could make such a map. Father says that weather reporters from all over the country send in reports on the Wire Service and that then somebody smart in Washington or New York City puts all of the reports together and that makes the weather map. My guess is that a lot of these weather men rely on the flyers of aeroplanes to tell them what is going on all in all.

Grandpa keeps a little diary where he writes down the temperature and the weather conditions ever day. He has been doing it all of his life. He says that from this he can just about predict the weather from year to year but not from week to week. He predicts what at school we call The Averages.

Grandpa is not very interested in the weather map. He says that the weather has more to do with the signs than it does with any old map. I do look forward to learning about the signs.

We also got a package this week from Aunt Louise. It came so we could try out a new thing called Parcel Post that the Post Office started on January the first. It is a way to send boxes and such in the mail.

She sent Mama some sewing patterns for her birthday and some pencils to each of us. Mostly she sent it just to see how the Parcel Post works. It is real fine.

There has now been fighting on the border between United States troops and Mexican troops. A patrol of fifteen American troops in Arizona was walking the border and some Mexican soldiers fired at them. They fired back and then they got help and the news paper says that more than two thousand shots were fired. Now I really do not know who counted them but that is what it said.

Both sides claim that the other side fired first and there is really no way to finally settle that. Besides there is great fear in Mexico City of a big uprising there.

In spite of what Woodrow Wilson says I do not see how the United States can stay out of it when there is actual shooting right across the border into our country. I am sure that Mr. Taft is glad that in one week he will be out of office and not responsible for anything more at all.

Just as all of this is happening ever body in Washington DC is getting ready for Mr. Wilson to get inaugurated. Half of the news paper is about trouble in Mexico and the other half is about all of the parties and such that are going on in Washington over the inauguration.

If I could have any wish in the world right now it would be to go to Washington and see that inauguration.

We have read that down in Greensboro North Carolina a person can catch a special train for paying just $9.40 and that train will take you overnight to Washington DC and arrive in time to get to see all of that inauguration and such. Then when it is all over with you get back on that special train and ride back to Greensboro.

If I lived close to Greensboro and had about ten dollars to include some food then I would take whatever time out it took to get on that train and go to Washington. Merry can have the Navy. This is what I would like to do.

After I read the news paper out loud to the family today Father said that there was one little story that I missed. I asked him what it was that was as important as war in Mexico and the inauguration of a new President.

He then read that a new Amendment called Number Eighteen has been added to the Constitution. This new amendment says that Congress can put tax on the money that people make each year. It is to be called The Income Tax. We did not notice this in the news because it just has quietly happened after the right number of states passed on it and because there is so much big and loud news about Washington and Mexico.

But Father says the people of the United States will be worrying over this new "Income Tax" long after anyone even remembers the war in Mexico and long after Woodrow Wilson's name has even been forgot. I can hardly believe that. I think that Father is just practicing up for making political speeches in the Legislature. I wish that he wouldn't exaggerate so much when he gets to making political speeches.

Sunday, March 9, 1913

President Wilson is sworn in.

Not only on Tuesday which was the inauguration day but on ever day since then the news paper has been positively filled with articles about the new President and the day of his swearing in. It has been hard to wait to get home each day in order to get the new paper in the mail and read of the latest happenings.

Tuesday sounded like a wonderful day. It was cloudy in Washington DC but during the ceremony it said that the sun broke through the clouds and when Mr. Wilson raised his hand to shade his eyes from the sun it looked like he was saluting the sun as his partner. It said that Mr. Taft stood by and wished the new President well.

The new Vice President is Mr. Thomas R. Marshall of Indiana.

We do not pay enough attention to the Vice President I think. After all it was by being Vice President at the time that Teddy Roosevelt became one of the most famous Presidents we ever had and the youngest one of all time.

Anyway there were a lot of parties in Washington and a lot of speeches. When I heard that Mr. William Jennings Bryan was going to be the Secretary of State then I knew that there would be plenty of speeches. We have even had to read some of his long speeches in school for Mrs. Melville.

As a part of the ceremonies of being President Mr. Wilson was given a pet lamb from the Central Park Zoo in New York City. It did not tell if the lamb had a name or not or if Mr. Wilson gave it a name. The importance of this lamb is that it's grandfather was born on the very day on which Grover Cleveland was inaugurated President for the second time in the year 1893. Father says that the lamb is given as he tells it "To show that everything that goes around comes around." That we do now have a Democrat President again is actually what all of that means.

There have even been some articles about what the women wore to some of the parties. I think it is silly to write about such in the news papers of the world but perhaps some are interested in such things.

The interesting article about women was that a whole raft of women in what they call the Suffrage Movement marched into Washington for the inauguration to do a plea for women getting to vote. It said that this was the biggest show of this kind ever put on in the world and that sooner or later maybe the women that own land will get to vote.

What I think is this. Some women have jobs and already work for pay just like men do. Now with that new Amendment which makes it to where you may have to pay tax on the money you get paid I believe that there will not be a chance in this world of collecting such tax from working women if those same women do not get to vote.

This is what is meant by "A matter of time." In time more and more women will work. Then men will want them to vote so that these women will pay tax just like men will have to do. What most politicks boils down to is a balancing out of ever body's selfishness I do believe.

Our news paper said that our new Governor Locke Craig rode a fine horse in the inauguration parade and looked like a good horseman for the entire country to see. The new Governor said that he had not ridden a horse for years but it was fun to do it at this time.

I am glad that our Father is a good horseman because that will be helpful to him as he has to go to and from Raleigh to get to the Legislature though he says that from Asheville he will ride the rest of the way on the train.

One other thing. There has not been hardly one thing said about the trouble in Mexico all during this week of parties in Washington DC. I'll bet the new secretary of the Navy is surely scared about that.

Sunday, March 16, 1913

Father has spent this entire week getting ready to leave for the Legislature. He will depart home tomorrow morning and get to Raleigh on Wednesday night.

Though we have been in school all week Father met with me and Ledge ever afternoon to go over things. We have gone over how to do ever thing that we have already known how to do for years. Father says that he just wants to make sure.

He has been spending a lot of the days with Champ and Merry. Even though Champ is married and has his own home he will be here looking out for things more than ever while Father is gone. Of course Grandpa will be the real boss of things except for Mama.

Father bought a new horse this week from Mr. Woody. It is a young mare which he has named Artemus. The mare is so that he will have a way to get to Asheville to catch the train without having to take either King or Outlaw from us and our work on the farm. That is a good idea since this is just the time of the year when the most work is just starting out. We plowed most of the day yesterday.

The new mare is just old enough to really ride. She is a little too wild for me to try her out but since Father is a experienced horseman for sure he can handle her just fine.

This is the plan. He will ride the mare to Asheville to begin with on tomorrow. There he will leave the mare with Zeb at Lawyer Stillwell's house to be taken care of while he is gone.

In Asheville he will catch the train and ride to a place called Salisbury. He says that is where all of the train lines meet and you change from one train to another to go on longer trips.

In Salisbury he will catch another train and this one will take him all of the way to Raleigh. He has taken a room in Raleigh in a hotel. The room is being shared with a Mr. Carter from Rowan County. He is another Democrat that Father knows who is also to be in the Legislature. Mr. Carter has been there before and that is why Father wanted to bunk with him so as to learn his way around.

The Legislature session will last forty days. After that Father will be back home. He may have to make some other trips to Raleigh but mostly he will be here after that. I think that he is about ready to go now.

Tonight we had long prayers for the President and the Governor and for all of the families that will have to get along on their own while their fathers are in the country's service. I am proud of Father and even Mrs. Melville has told the class that our entire school should be proud of him.

Sunday, March 23, 1913

We have got our first family telegram.

It came on Thursday after Father got to Raleigh on Wednesday late. It was from Father to tell us that he was there and was safe. He sent it early in the morning on Thursday and it got to the station at Suncrest before the mailman left to bring the mail. He brought it to us and we heard from our Father a message that he had just sent the very same day that we got it. I know the telegram by heart. Mama had already read it but she read it to us again and again as soon as we got home. Then we each got to handle it and read it for ourselves.

It said "ARRIVED LAST PM STOP MOVED IN WITH CARTER STOP WEATHER FINE STOP ALL IS WELL STOP LETTER TO FOLLOW SOON STOP."

I did not understand what all of the stopping was about but Grandpa said that they can't send a period over the telegraph and that the word stop means the same as a period. He says that if you want to ask a question in a telegram the sentence then ends with the word "QUESTION." It seems strange at first but it is the way it is with telegrams and other modern inventions. We have to adjust.

Every day since then I have almost run home hoping for another telegram or at least to get that letter that was promised. Nothing has come yet. Mama says that there will likely not be another telegram because those are expensive. We will wait for the letter.

We are doing pretty well. But with school and springtime together it is hard to get a good start made in any real plowing and planting. Grandpa cannot really work the horses or the mules but he has borrowed a team of oxen from Mr. W.L. Landers and he plows a good deal each day with the oxen. They are more predictable than the mules and slower than the horses.

So here we are while Father is in Raleigh. Mrs. Melville asks about him each day and we are studying more this year about government I think because Father is in the center of it and that is a new thing for where we live.

Sunday, March 30, 1913

What a hard week this has been.

On Tuesday after school we went out to the barn to feed. When Ledge and I got there we found that King had got down on the ground of the stall where he was put up. Ledge and I tried and tried to get him up but we couldn't.

We went back to the house to tell Grandpa and Mama. The only other time this has ever happened Father was here and he knew just what to do. But I did not.

Grandpa went out to the barn with us and also Mama and Merry and the girls went along. By the time that we got back King was flat out on his side on the ground and not moving much at all.

Grandpa tried coaxing and pushing and he got all of us to help to try to lift and push but nothing worked. Grandpa said that sometimes a horse just gets down in a small place and can't get back up on its own but this was different. He wondered if King had ate something that had poisoned him. He asked us if we had seen anything funny at all but we had not.

There is not a doctor of horses around here and we couldn't bother Doc Graham with animal business. Grandpa said that the horse wasn't bloated that he was just sick someway.

Before bedtime King just stopped breathing and died.

On the next afternoon we got home to find that Grandpa had pulled the dead horse with the oxen team way down from the barn into the edge of what is usually a cornfield. He had tried to start digging a hole to bury it in but with not much success. Merry had dug the most and then after school me and Ledge dug some.

Before dark we had the hole deep enough and we helped Grandpa roll the dead horse into the hole. Then we said goodbye to our good old horse King and we buried him deep in the ground.

King and Outlaw are the only horses I can remember us having in my life and I think that maybe he just died of old age all of a sudden. It does happen even with people and so I think that it could with animals.

Now we will have to work with the borrowed ox team and with the mules except for single tree work with Outlaw on his own. I don't know what else to do.

We did get the letter finally from Father on Friday but after the horse business I didn't have as much interest in politicks.

He said that they were meeting day and night to get business over with. In the opening session the new Governor Locke Craig begged the Legislature to give a lot of money for the North Carolina exhibit at a big worldwide fair called the Panama Pacific Exposition.

The reason for this is that the main United States exhibitions will be of the Navy ships presented by Mr. Josephus Daniels and the Governor thinks that while ever body is knowing that Mr. Daniels comes from North Carolina the world would want to know more about our state. Father says that they voted for it hoping our state will gain in prominence.

He also said that they voted to continue a state school for the feeble minded and to prohibit selling or giving away the salts of cocaine. There are also resolutions about convicts working on the highways and a lot of other things that don't really sound interesting at all.

What they need to do is start a state school for horse doctors so that what we had to face this week wouldn't have to be faced so often. Especially by a family whose Father is not here to lead the decisions or the action either one.

Today is Easter Sunday but I have hardly had time to give any thought to that. It is the first Easter when Father is not here at home. In his letter Father told us that the Legislature was out for Easter and that he will be going to the Methodist church down there in Raleigh with some others from the Legislature who are from too far away to go home for the weekend.

Sunday, April 6, 1913

On the day after the horse died Mama wrote a letter to Father to tell him what happened. She also wrote to Zeb in Asheville at the same time so he would know about King dying since he will see Father on the way back through Asheville before he comes home and is here with us. I guess when Father gets the news he will decide what we are to do next.

One idea I have is that Father could bring the new mare home and leave her here for us to work with. Then he could buy a automobile and learn to drive the automobile. That way he would have a way to get all the way to Raleigh hisself and not have to go by horse and then train down there and back.

I think that this is a good idea. If we are going to live in the modern world and if our Father is going to be a leader in the modern world then he needs a automobile. This may be just the occasion to get one after all.

I have told Ledge about this and we have looked at advertisements in the news paper for several kinds of automobiles. However when I told Mama about what I thought she said "You won't get me in one of those machines. What we need is another horse."

We are doing pretty well all in all with Father gone and our horse dead. On Sundays ever body comes for dinner. This includes Champ's family and Lucee's family and the Mayfield family. We also have Mrs. Melville here for Sunday dinner about half of the time. It is like with Father not here we all draw together for one another. Mostly we talk about what we think he might be doing down in Raleigh.

I look in the news paper each day for what they call the Legislative News. I have read about some of the same topics that Father's letters tell that they are talking about and I see that some of the Legislator's names are mentioned. I am hoping that Father will say something to get his name in the newspaper but it has not happened. Maybe the beginners don't get to say much.

Well it has been over two weeks now that we have been on our own. I do not much feel like the man of the family what with having to go to school and all. I will not yet start counting the days until our Father comes home. When the forty days is half over then I will be able to let myself count the days. I sure am glad that Grandpa is here.

Sunday, April 13, 1913

Things have settled some this week largely due to a hard talk Mama and Grandpa had with all of the family at suppertime on Tuesday. Mama started it but Grandpa did most of the later talking.

We were sitting all at the table as usual and it was one night when the Mayfields were not eating with us. As we always do I brought up wondering what Father was having for his supper that same night.

Mama seemed like she was close to tears when she said "Now I love your Father just as much as any of the rest of you do but we have got to get on with our own living. We can't run this farm and run that Legislature down in Raleigh at the same time." By now she was just about crying and Grandpa took over.

What he explained was that ever body has to tend to what he called "The business at hand." Father's business at hand is the Legislature and so he cannot do the farming right now because he is in Raleigh. Our business at hand is to tend to our own farm and our own school work just as well as we can.

He said that if all we do is wonder and dream and think about what Father is doing and counting the days until he comes back that is not taking care of our business at hand. He said that it is fine to miss Father but that we have to get on with our lives like we are grown up and capable and not like we are just as he said it "Stirring the pot until he gets back to the stove."

It was a hard talk but it did make sense. I have not been thinking very forward about this at all. After all Father ran for the Legislature because he had faith that we are old enough to take care of things on our own not just hold things together until he gets back.

After that talk school has gone better and without so much daydreaming. On yesterday I and Ledge and Merry and Grandpa made us a work team and we planted corn all the live long day. Grandpa had already plowed and harrowed the long flat field we call the black bottom and we planted the entire thing in that one long day.

It is our main corn field and now it is all in. Grandpa said that we might have planted it a little earlier going by the calendar but going by the signs now is just right. He said that if we will notice our corn planted later by the signs will come up and grow faster and bigger than some of the neighbor's corn that was planted earlier just by the calendar. I believe this will be true.

A letter did come from Father yesterday saying that he would buy a new horse in Asheville on his way home and lead it with that new mare Artemus. There goes my plan for a automobile.

Grandpa has really been teaching me and Ledge all about the signs. We have been planting nearly ever day in the afternoon after school and each day we get out the almanac and see what the signs say is the right thing to plant.

We are also learning from Grandpa about what parts of the body are weaker at certain times because of the signs. For example if the signs are in the head you don't want to go get a tooth pulled because it would hurt terrible and cause you a lot of trouble afterwards. If you have to get a tooth pulled you want the signs to be way down in the feet or at least in the bowels.

I wish that I had known more about the signs in the past. It would be interesting to know where the signs were for example when Merry got hit in the head that time they were digging that swimming hole. It would also be interesting to know where the signs were when Zeb got crippled. Not that it would have helped to change what happened any but it would be interesting to know. After all if the signs had been worse Zeb might of lost his whole foot.

Thinking about our dead horse I wonder if the signs affect animals as well as people. Grandpa says that they surely do and that animals are more sensitive to some things than people are except for the Indians who live by the signs without even knowing it.

I asked Grandpa if the signs had any power over the Legislature. He said that is one place where the signs take a vacation. Grandpa said "Nothing has any power over that bunch of old men." Then he laughed. I didn't much like that but I guess I know what he means even if our Father is one of them.

So time goes on and the spring planting is almost done. And I am secretly counting the days until Father is home even if we are not supposed to do that. It is just a little bit more than two weeks.

Sunday, April 27, 1913

Father writes that he has met Josephus Daniels but the occasion was not a happy one. It seems that the Raleigh "News and Observer" news paper building which is owned by Mr. Daniels and was personally run by him until he went to Washington to be the Secretary of the Navy caught fire and burned to the ground one night this week.

Mr. Daniels was in New York City speaking at a banquet at the time but he caught the train and came to Raleigh early the next day. When that train got into Raleigh Governor Craig hisself met Mr. Daniels at the station along with a delegation from the Legislature. Father represented the beginning legislators in that delegation.

This entire group went with Mr. Daniels and the fire chief to look at the remains of the building. Nothing was left but one big printing press.

The chief told them that if there was a way to of got a stream of water on to the top of the building they might of got the fire out. But there was not. Maybe they should not build buildings taller than they can spray water to the top of.

When Mr. Daniels asked the chief if he knew the cause of the fire the chief said that they believed the fire started on its own in a pile of rubbish in the basement. The Governor seemed relieved to hear that Father wrote. He said that the reason the Governor and the Legislators were interested was out of fear that the fire might of been set by somebody not liking Mr. Daniels. If that had been true they wanted to show quick support of Mr. Daniels and make a reward to find the firestarter. It seems though to of been a accident.

We read about this fire in our Asheville news paper and it said that the damage was $75000. Another news paper in Raleigh called the Raleigh Times is going to loan equipment to keep the News and Observer going until a new building is built. It said that their list of subscribers did not burn up.

So Father now knows the Secretary of the Navy who in turn knows President Wilson. He said that Mr. Daniels was a fine man who seemed to be a assertive leader in all ways.

After all of this from both Father's letter and the news papers we have read all that Merry wants to know is whether Father asked Mr. Daniels if he didn't need Merry in the Navy. I can't believe he would think of that at a time like this. Merry even went on to say that he had been doing research. He has found out that a new sailor in the Navy gets paid $300 a year plus their clothes and their food. And if you stay in the Navy a long time he says you can get on up to $438 dollars a year.

Merry thinks that would make him rich. I wanted to ask him how many years like that he thought it would take to make up the $75000 Mr. Josephus Daniels lost in one night in that fire. I didn't waste my breath though because he wouldn't answer even if I asked.

So Father is getting well known and Merry is getting well on out of his senses. Both have been coming for a long time.

Sunday, May 4, 1913

Father is coming home this week but there is news even bigger than that. Mrs. Melville is getting married.

During Easter there was so much going on around here that we hardly had time to notice that Mrs. Melville had a guest. It was a old friend of hers from Boston Massachusetts who is actually her second or third cousin.

The friend is a man named Dr. Phillips and now it turns out that the two of them are going to get married. He is also the benefactor who long ago paid for our globe of the world.

This is the story. Mrs. Melville and her husband who is dead were friends with Dr. Phillips and his wife in Boston for many years. This was not just because Mrs. Melville and Dr. Phillips were distant relations but because they actually just were friends that liked one another.

Of course Mrs. Melville's husband drowned on the ocean long before she came here to teach us in school so she has been without a husband for a while. It seems that about a year ago this Dr. Phillips's wife died with the new monia or something like that. He has been writing to Mrs. Melville and just by writing they decided to get married.

They had not told anybody I think because until he actually came to visit I think that the two of them were still not sure that they were going to do it.

When I first heard of this I was just sure that Mrs. Melville would be going back to Boston and that we would have to start over with a new teacher. That worried me because Mrs. Melville has given me most of my growing up education.

But there is no cause to worry. This is the plan. Dr. Phillips is going to move here and marry Mrs. Melville and the two of them will stay here. His full name is Dr. Samuel Phillips MD and he is going to go to working with Doc Graham as a second doctor. Doc Graham says that he is getting old and needing some help and that besides that there are getting to be more people around here than he can take care of. I am sure that Dr. Phillips will have a automobile.

Now this is the other news. This Dr. Phillips has a daughter who is just exactly the same age that I am. Her name is Susannah and I have seen a picture of her shown to me by Mrs. Melville when she came to dinner today and sprung all of this big news on us. She will move here also and will go to school with us. Mrs. Melville says that she has red hair.

So that is the big event of the week.

I expect that Mrs. Melville is about the same age as our Mama and I cannot imagine a woman of that age getting married and starting all over again with her life. But Mama says it is not like starting over. She says it is more like finishing what never got finished to start with and it is a very fine thing to do she says. I think that Mama loves being married to Father very much.

It is a funny thing how I have spent over a month counting the days until Father comes home and now this new news has sort of taken my mind off of that. I wonder if that new girl is nice and if she will think that we talk funny.

Sunday, May 11, 1913

Along in the middle of the afternoon of yesterday we heard a horse come galloping down the road and we looked out of the window. It was a strange horse that we had not seen before and on it was a dressed up man none of us had ever seen. He even had on a fine looking hat while he rode the horse.

The strange man came to the door and knocked on it. Mama was not sure whether to go to the door or not. Ledge was over here and he and all of us went behind Mama as she went to the door.

We opened the door and the strange Man grabbed Mama. Just as she screamed she realized that it was Father. He had his beard shaved off and she had never seen him in her life without his beard. We had been looking for him to come home since Friday.

The whole trick was that he had got Zeb to stay back in the woods with Artemus and Father had ridden the new horse up to the house by hisself just to see if he could trick us. Is was a trick all right.

I have never seen my Father without his beard. None of us have. When I got over the shock I could not get over how very much like Champ he looks when you can see his face. He explained to Mama that the style of wearing beards is going out and that the men in the Legislature do mostly not have beards. He shaved off his beard to show that he is not a "Backwoodsman" is what he said.

Later on Father told us that in Raleigh you can go to the barber shop and get shaved for fifteen cents. He does not do this ever day because it would cost too much but he said that he does get a barbershop shave about once ever week.

We stayed up most of the night hearing about Raleigh and the Legislature. Father has made many friends there from all over the state. His best friend is a man named Mr. Furnifold Simmons who is from Newbern down near the ocean. Mr. Simmons is one of those in charge of things and he has helped Father find his way around.

Father told us about the hotel room of Fayetteville Street. It is four stories tall. When I heard of that I got scared about a fire like the one that burned that news paper building. But Father said that the hotel had water hoses rolled up in a rack on ever floor. The hotel even has bathtubs where you can get a hot water bath whenever you want one.

Father told us about a lot of the eating places and about how is it so much warmer down in Raleigh that it is just like summertime is already there. He told us about the room where the Legislature meets and tried to help us to see how the Capital building looks. There is a big statue of George Washington right in the downstairs hall.

Father told us about his work on some committees about the Rural Land Bank and about roads. He told about a lot of new laws. One makes employers let their employees off for up to two hours to go and vote on election day.

Anyway I do know that it will take as long for Father to tell us all about the Legislature as it did for him to be there. We will be talking for days.

We filled him in on the news about Mrs. Melville and we told him again all about King dying. That is when we met the new horse.

It is a big Belgian and its name is Prince Albert. That is a good name for a horse that is taking the place of one named King. Zeb rode Artemus home since now he is so good at riding that he can even get on with his braced left foot and so he can ride about any horse.

Tomorrow we will take Father all over the farm and show him what we have got started. The corn is up and so is a lot of the garden. I will be proud to be able to show him how well we have carried on things while he has been gone. It seems now like he was never away.

Sunday, May 18, 1913

What no one in this world could have foreseen has happened. Our Father may be dying. I have to think carefully to recall just the way it all happened.

On Monday we took Father all over the farm and showed him all that we had done. He seemed so very proud of me and Ledge and Merry and the girls and Mama too. He told us again and again of how well we had done everything while he was gone.

On Tuesday and Wednesday he and Champ and Merry and Grandpa worked all day while I was at school and they got everything else on the whole place caught up to where it ought to be at this time of the year. It was Wednesday afternoon when it happened.

When I got home from school Father had cleaned up and even shaved after all the work they had been doing for the day. He said that he was going to saddle up the new riding horse Artemus and ride up to Mr. Woody's store before closing time to get a new bridle for the new horse Prince Albert. He is a much bigger horse than King was.

I had known all along that Artemus was high spirited. I had seen him dance around when Father had gotten on him several times before. We don't know exactly how it happened. Father saddled up the horse and led her to the back door to tell Mama he was going. Then we heard the horse whinny and Father hollered. When we all got out the back door that horse was running out toward the road and was dragging Father who was hanging there by his left foot caught in the stirrup.

It was Ledge who took off like a flash while all the rest of us just stood there staring. He ran after that horse and called to her and caught up with her at just about the same time that she stopped on her own anyway. Then the rest of us went running. Father was unconscious still hanging by his foot and there was a big gash across the top of his head where that horse's hind foot had kicked his head in the running. We all thought he was dead on the spot.

Me and Ledge and Merry lifted him up while Mama got his foot loose from the stirrup. Then we laid him down on the ground and by then Grandpa was there. Grandpa put his ear to Father's chest just like he knew that Mama didn't want to and then he said "He's not dead yet. I can hear his heart beating."

We got him into the house as easy as we could and put him on the bed. Mama washed his face and started cleaning the gash in his head and Grandpa said to me did I think I could ride that horse and get Doc Graham.

I was scared to death of that horse but this was a time that you couldn't say no any easier than you could just die and so I said "Yes Sir I can do it."

After all the wildness I had seen in Artemus before that horse now was just as gentle as could be. I shortened the stirrups and got on and I rode as hard as I ever had in toward town to Doc Graham's. We rode like the wind Artemus and me and I never had one bit of trouble. It was like the horse wanted to get help as bad as I did.

When Doc Graham heard of it he said "I wish Phillips was here." Then he went out and cranked the Ford and took off leaving me and Artemus to ride on back home on our own.

When I got back he was still listening to Father's chest like he had been listening for hours.

I watched Doc Graham lift Father's eye lids and look into his eyes one at a time. I watched him not sew up Father's head but just bandage that gash like he didn't want to disturb his head any more that it already was. I watched him listen to Father's chest some more.

Finally he stood up and talked to all of us. He said "His heart beat is strong but it is not regular. He is breathing good sometimes but sometimes not so good." He said to Mama "I just don't know Martha. I just don't know."

Doc Graham ended up staying with us all night long. He kept checking over and over again. When he left after breakfast he told Mama to turn Father back and forth from one side to another ever once in a while and to send one of us to get him if he started feeling hot. He said if there was a fever then there might be swelling and bleeding in his brain and the pressure would have to be relieved.

It has been four days now and Father is still unconscious. Mama can prop him up and pour water into his mouth and he sort of chokes and swallows it but he has had no food.

Doc Graham comes ever day. He says that if Father would come to soon that he might live but that ever day he stays unconscious the hope dims. We can do nothing day and night but simply wait.

Sunday, May 25, 1913

Tonight is the last time that I shall ever write about my life. Father is dead and my writing is over. I could never believe any of this if it had not just happened.

It was not more than two hours after I finished my writing last Sunday night that Father died. He just simply stopped breathing and did not start again. He had been unconscious for four and a half days.

We simply set with him dead in his bed for the rest of the night talking about memories and all of the fine things about our lives together. By daylight Mama sent me and Merry into town to tell people and send messages.

First we were to stop by Mr. Woody's store or his house if the store was not opened yet and tell him. Then we were to stop by Mrs. Melville's house on the way to Suncrest and tell her. Then we were to stop by Doc Graham's house and tell him. Then we were to go to the Suncrest telegraph office and send a telegram to Lawyer Stillwell in Asheville so he could be the one to tell Zeb and send him home.

We did not know how to do this but Mama said that we would take five dollars with us and the man at the telegram office would help us to do it. After that we had a list of places in town to tell and then to come on back home.

It was a hard thing to do but once we got started all of the people that we met had such kind things to say and were so helpful to us that it was not as hard as I had at first thought.

By the time we got back home in the afternoon the whole house was full of people. There were Woodys and Taylors and Hannahs and even Sheriff Black and his wife. Ever body we knew looked like they were there.

Mama and Mrs. Mayfield had bathed Father's body dressed him in his finest suit and made a corpse. Mama had even shaved him. Mr. Wainwright who is the finest furniture maker around here brought a beautiful cherry coffin and gave it to Mama. He said that he had originally made it for hisself but that he would be honored if she would consider laying our Father away in it. He just looks like he is sleeping but those last four days of being unconscious have made his face look thin. Mama even combed his hair to cover up the gash where the horse kicked him.

It is a strange thing to think that none of us had ever seen him without a beard until a week before he died and now he will spend all eternity clean shaven.

Reverend Sharpe was there and Mrs. Mayfield and Mrs. Melville seemed to be running things. Mama was all nicely dressed like she was going to church. She was sitting beside Father's coffin in the parlor right where the twins have been courting those Woody boys. She was having a roomfull of visitors one after another.

By the evening there was food all over the house and about nine o'clock a man came to the door who Merry and I saw was the man from the telegraph station. He had ridden all the way out from town to bring Mama a telegram.

The telegram was from Governor Locke Craig. Lawyer Stillwell had sent the Governor a telegram once he had got the message about Father's death.

The Governor's telegram sent us all sympathy and said that he was sending a repersenative right then to start out for the funeral and if the funeral was not until Wednesday then the Governor's repersenative would be there.

Usually a Funeral comes the day after somebody dies but Mama decided then and there to have it on Wednesday even if it meant a awful long time of waiting. It is good that the weather is not too hot yet or the corpse would not be fit.

It seemed like that ever body that I have ever known came to our house over the coming day. I do not think that any of us slept any at all and I especially felt for Grandpa as he seemed to be suffering more than anybody. After all Father was Grandpa's child.

We had not sent a telegram to Aunt Louise but then we thought of it. Mama paid that telegraph man right while he was here and he sent it. We had a telegram back from her the morning of the funeral but the mailman just brought it with the normal mail. She is sad but not coming. She is also glad she came for Christmas.

The Governor's representative arrived Wednesday morning also. Mr. Carter Father's bunkmate in Raleigh came with him. I think they had traveled all night. They came in a big automobile of some kind.

The funeral was at the church on Wednesday afternoon. There was a lot of music and the Governor's man whose name I never did catch had to make a speech from the Governor. It was not much of a speech but the idea was kind.

Father was buried at the top of the hill above the church next to where my dead brother and sister are also buried. I guess they were waiting for him when he got there.

The hard part started then. For after the funeral we have been forced to think about the future. Grandpa has been in charge of most of this thinking since our Mama is not yet in shape to think after Father's death. None of us are. Grandpa is surely the strongest one of us all even if he is the oldest.

Grandpa has figgered that we are as a family what he calls "Land poor." What that means is that we have over six hunderd acres of land but when we put all of our cash money in this world together we have less than five hunderd dollars.

Grandpa says that this would not be any problem in the old days when we were truly homesteaders and all that we needed to do was to clothe and shelter and feed ourselves. But in the modern world where there are things like doctors and telegrams and parcel post it is just essential that a family have some way of having a cash income besides just food and clothing that they make for themselves.

What Grandpa is doing is trying to figger out some way to get some income started into the family. He believes that we can start trying to grow more things than we really need and regularly sell them. We have done this on occasion before but never according to a plan.

Our life is going to be very hard and I am in fact forced to be grown up. I do have to go to school for three or four more years but I shall stop being a child and shall work as a adult in ever way.

Maybe the way it is is that while your Father is still alive you are not really grown up no matter how old you get. Then once your

Father dies you are then grown up no matter how young you are. That is something I have been thinking about a lot.

Anyway there will be no more writing out of my life. After all Father said just this last year that he guessed I was "Writing myself grown up." Now I believe that is exactly what I have done. I have in fact written myself grown up and so I can say to my Sunday writing what Mrs. Melville says on the last day of ever school year "Finis and farewell."

Epilogue

January 2, 1993

I have wept and I have laughed as I have once again lived those childhood years. I do not want to go back except in memory, but memory is the dearest thing an old man has.

Grandpa stayed on with us for the rest of his life. He lived six more years and died in 1919, just shy of his eighty-ninth birthday. Grandpa plowed the garden with the ox team the week before he died. He and Mrs. Mayfield were, as I remember, best friends to the end.

Champ and Sallie Jane had five more children. I have seen none of them for years. They all left Close Creek and "went North to seek their fortunes." That is the way Champ always answered when people asked about them. Except for an occasional Christmas card, I would not even know where they all live. Champ died in 1959 and Sallie Jane lived until 1964.

Lucee and Harlan Junior had no more children after little Jeff. The two of them died in 1967 and 1968 but little Jeff, the one who lost his rag doll, died in 1988. His widow still lives in a new house built on the same spot where the old Elisabeth Chambers house stood.

The twins did, in fact, marry the Woody boys. That could be another story all in itself.

Margaret Angeline married Jackson and Mary Adeline married Robert. In 1922 Jackson was killed in a sawmill accident and two years later Mary Adeline died in childbirth. Less than a year after that Margaret Angeline and Robert got married. They each had two children and later had two more children themselves. I remember that many people enjoyed talking about this turn of events, especially trying to figure out how all of these children were related to one another.

Zeb became not only a lawyer but ended up serving for many

years in the same Legislative seat that Father so briefly held. He did marry a "stranger" from Asheville, but she turned out to be a Palmer who was, in fact, distantly related. Zeb later developed diabetes, and before he died in 1958 he lost that crippled leg.

Less than a year after Father's death, both Merry and Ledge left home to join the Navy together. It was in part Grandpa's plan. There was such a need for cash money that the two of them joined up and started sending home twenty dollars each every month. It was likely this very thing that saved the whole family.

Ledge came home after his term was up, but Merry decided to stay in the Navy. Merry was killed in 1917 in the Mediterranean when an observation plane accidentally crashed into the island encampment his unit had set up.

Mama lived until 1943.

Ledge? Well as it turned out Ledge married my sister Annie Laurie. In fact my niece, Laurie Anne, the one who preserved this journal and just gave it back to me, is the daughter of Ledge Mayfield and my sister, Annie Laurie. Laurie Anne had never heard the story of her own grandfather, Ledge's daddy. Her mother, Annie Laurie, had kept this journal shut up in a cedar chest and Laurie Anne only found it when her mother died last summer. Now the story is out.

What about me? Well dear Mrs. Melville did get married to the doctor with the red-haired daughter. I married Susannah Phillips in 1922 and she lived until just last year. We were married for seventy years and lived right on that same farm where I was born and grew up. I still live there, but it is much closer to Suncrest than it was in 1913.

Susannah and I had no children. The two of us both ended up being high school teachers. She taught English and I taught History, each for forty years right in the same county where we both finished growing up.

Yes, all of my dear relatives came on yesterday to my birthday party, and there were in all two of us left. Laurie Anne and I are the end of the line, but at least now we can both remember.